Praise for
The Impossible Texan

He backed her into the corner out of view. He allowed himself the luxury of staring deeply into those captivating green eyes.

"How dare you!"

"Exactly." With the sense of urgency that was pounding in his veins, he took her face in his hands. She put her hands on his chest to push him away.

He pulled her closer. "How dare I!" he whispered into her cheek, and felt her shiver. He brushed his lips against hers as softly as he could until the power of her nearness drove his kiss deeper. For a second or two, she lowered her guard and softened. Tyler felt as if he were nearly drowning in desire.

Marlena found her strength and shoved Tyler away. "Don't!" she hissed, jabbing a finger at him. "I swear, Tyler Hamilton, if you ever touch me again, I'll . . ."

Tyler smiled. He picked up a pebble from the path and held it up to her like a poker chip. "My wager is that you'll yield. . . ."

THE
IMPOSSIBLE
TEXAN

Allie Shaw

IVY BOOKS • NEW YORK

A Ballantine Book
Published by The Ballantine Publishing Group
Copyright © 2001 by Alyse Pleiter

www.randomhouse.com/BB/

Library of Congress Catalog Card Number: 2001116167

ISBN 0-8041-1964-3

Manufactured in the United States of America

First Edition: May 2001

10 9 8 7 6 5 4 3 2 1

For Jeff
For everything

❧ Acknowledgments ❧

Like most debut novels, to call this a one-person feat would truly be fiction. I owe debts of gratitude, large and small, to many people. First of all to my own personal hero, my husband, Jeff, who put up with being married to not just one woman, but a whole novelful of characters; and who knew when to say "just stop it and go write." To my daughter, Amanda, who is chairman of my personal fan club and humility committee. To my son, Christopher, who cochairs that committee. To Gail, who said, "I think you can," even before I thought I could. To Karen Solem, my agent and guiding hand, who knew when to encourage and when to kick. To my friends and family, who have endured endless conversations, petty details, moaning, readings, and rereadings as this book came into being. To my editor, Charlotte, who pushed, then pushed again in all the right places. And last, to the folks who kept me from putting my historical foot in my mouth (or tried to—if I did it's hardly their fault), mainly James Rost and others at the Austin History Center. God's richest blessings on you all, and look out—I'm pretty sure there's more where this came from.

⊰ Chapter One ⊱

Marlena Maxwell wasn't sure she could stand one more minute of tea. The stays in her corset were surely growing longer, poking her with agonizing little fingers. Mrs. Dorlan poured her typical stream of gossip into Marlena's uninterested ear. Enormous gaps in the old woman's teeth made her whistle when she spoke, and she smelled like old wool and wet talcum powder. The combination made her presence almost intolerable in the July afternoon heat. Marlena took another sip and nodded in feigned attention, but the tea's flimsy taste only reminded her how much she disliked tea—and tea parties. She mentally created a list of half a dozen things she'd prefer to be doing.

Without thinking, she returned the cup to its saucer with such a clink that even Mrs. Dorlan paused in surprise. Marlena sucked in her breath. She knew a particular pair of eyes would now be scowling at her from the settee by the window.

Claudia Maxwell, the undisputed matriarch of the Maxwell household and a consummate tea party hostess, glared at her daughter from across the room. Her palpable disapproval had a way of halting time for its intended victims while the rest of the world glided by unaware. "Lena, my dear," Marlena heard her mother's

1

silent voice inside her head, "it's hardly what a lady would do."

The schedule Claudia Maxwell had maintained the last month might have had even the most dignified lady banging her teacup. The endless teas drove Marlena crazier than her corset stays. To make matters worse, she somehow always ended up mercilessly cornered by Mrs. Dorlan. She would have gladly traded places with her youngest sister, Andrea, who was too young to be expected to sit through the party. Marlena was certainly having trouble, even if she was twenty-four. Yet her mother and her younger sister Diana seemed to thrive on all the formality. Perhaps the endless string of teas was her mother's idea of what a senator's wife should do during campaign season. The closer the race, the more Claudia Maxwell broke out the cucumber sandwiches. It was getting to be a very close race.

"Oh, dearheart," chirped Mrs. Dorlan around a mouthful of pastry, "it was such a dreadful shame when Ogden Mathers died right in the middle of your daddy's campaign. Imagine that. I gather it was the strain that did him in—after all, he was getting on in years. Don't you worry though, dearie, word is out that the new campaign manager Senator Maxwell hired is a right smart fellow. Not that I think your daddy has anything to worry about, though. 'Course, you know he'll always have my vote as long as I live. He's a good man—"

"*Hired*, Mrs. Dorlan?" Marlena stopped her short, placing her hand on Mrs. Dorlan's shoulder. "Did you say you heard Daddy *hired someone* to replace Mr. Mathers?" she asked, just a little too loudly.

Marlena caught her mother's near-imperceptible cringe as she was pouring more tea for a guest. She had suspected her mother was keeping something from her. Now she knew. The cat was out of the bag, thanks to

Mrs. Dorlan's uncanny ability to sniff out even the best-kept secrets—and her insatiable appetite for revealing them. Marlena bet her mother was instantly sorry she had confided in even her closest friends. But why hide it? Something bigger was certainly afoot.

If anyone knew, it would be Mrs. Dorlan. She interpreted Marlena's widened eyes as deep pools of interest and coconspiracy, and lapped it up like cream.

"Oh, yes. My goodness, I'm surprised you didn't know," she whispered, patting Marlena's hand and moving her powdery face closer. "Within four short weeks of that dreadful tragedy, your smart daddy has hired himself a most extraordinary campaign manager. A young fellow. Bit of a mystery though, regarding his schooling and such, but I am sure he comes from only the best of families. Not that I ever doubt your father, mind you; you know I'll vote for him till the day I die." The excitement of revealing such a juicy secret had her heavy body almost bouncing in her chair.

Marlena was miles ahead of her, furiously plotting a way out of the room. Her mother shot her a "don't you dare make a scene" look from over the top of her teacup.

That did it. "Don't you dare" never worked with Marlena Maxwell. She took an enormous gulp of tea and launched into an alarming yet ladylike coughing fit that had even Mrs. Dorlan worried.

"Oh, my," Marlena sputtered between coughs. "Oh, good heavens. My goodness. Would you excuse me?" Swooning just enough to keep anyone from stopping her, she glided out of the room, hiding her face behind a lace hankie. She was through the parlor door and halfway to the kitchen before her mother could rise from the settee.

Muttering about mothers and tea, Marlena burst through the kitchen door and nearly knocked over a housemaid. "He hired someone! And just when did he think he was going to tell me about this? Sarah, for God's sake, please tell me there's coffee in here." Marlena grabbed a cup and made for the pot on the stove before the girl even had the chance to answer. "Did he think I wouldn't know? Did he think I wouldn't *care*?" she asked no one in particular, pouring coffee into her cup, then dumping three spoonfuls of sugar into it and stirring so hard the saucer filled from the overflow. "I suppose I shouldn't bother my pretty little head about such things," she mocked, banging the coffeepot back down onto the stove. She snatched the cup and left the saucer rocking on the table. Mumbling something scathing but unintelligible from inside an enormous gulp of coffee, Marlena shot from the room.

Cook clicked her tongue and picked up the wet saucer. "*El Señor* has trouble coming now. No man that smart deserves a child with such a hot tongue. *Madre de Dios,* he has enough on his mind these days."

Sarah chuckled and put down the bowl of potatoes she'd been holding. "I'd sure like to be a fly on the wall in Senator Maxwell's office right about now."

The July heat made Senator Jason Maxwell's leather chair creak. His cigar smoke hung thick in the air despite a faint breeze. He was a large man, big and solid enough to fill the role of Texas senator but with a laugh hearty enough to make him protective rather than intimidating. His once black hair, now peppered with the gray of twelve years in office, seemed reluctant to stay neatly combed back and broke intermittently into curls on his forehead. His shirt opened atop a loosened lariat tie even though his vest stayed properly buttoned. The senator's jacket and a hero-size Stetson hat hung on an antler coatrack in the corner of the room. He gestured with the cigar in hand, tapping a thick finger on the top of a large pile of papers.

"These numbers do not make a man easy, son. I've got trouble comin' on all sides with Mathers gone, and I need you to hit the ground runnin'." The sound of a distant door slamming pierced the momentary silence. "Now, I took a king-size chance on you, Hamilton. You've got fire and I need it to win this race. Kenton's mad as hell at my beating him last time and he's running full out to bring me down. I don't trust him to keep it a clean race, either. I need to know you're up to the challenge." He stopped as a cautious figure appeared in his office doorway while a second door slammed, this time much nearer. "Yes, Miss Edgerton, what is the crisis this hour?" he asked wearily.

"Senator," began Deborah Edgerton, half looking behind her. "It's Lena. I can hear her voice coming down the hall."

Another nearby door slammed and the senator took his hand off the pile of papers and laid it on his forehead with a defeated sigh.

"I would guess at this point that she has heard of Mr. Hamilton's . . . um . . . arrival," continued Deborah. Maxwell opened his mouth to continue when the outer door to his office flew open, sending a few papers on Deborah's desk scattering to the ground.

"Daddy!"

Deborah cocked her head to the side helplessly and stepped back with the air of one who knew when to get out of harm's way.

"Daddy, I hope you're not busy, because I must talk with you this minute. Good afternoon, Deb," Marlena said without stopping or even looking at Deborah, but plunking her coffee cup down on the desk. "My father has no appointments in the next few minutes, I hope?" Without waiting for an answer she strode straight into the office and stood, with her hands on her hips, squarely in front of his desk. "Senator Maxwell," she said sweetly through gritted teeth, "you'll never, ever guess what Mrs. Dorlan just told me at tea. Just when were you thinking you might tell me about this? Daddy, how could you? Without even talking to me! I could just—"

"You could just say hello to Mr. Tyler Hamilton the third, Lena dear. I think that would be an excellent start," interrupted the senator before Marlena could launch any further into her tirade. She spun on her heels.

Her mouth opened and shut again.

There, leaning casually against the credenza, was the most stunning man Marlena had ever seen. Despite her racket, Tyler Hamilton had only just now looked up from his stack of papers to view the intrusion. He wasn't classically handsome, in an artistic sense, but he was stunning. Stunning. It was the only word that came to mind. A pair of tortoiseshell spectacles framed searing, ice-blue eyes. Large black pupils flashed in disarming contrast. A broad, brilliant grin stole across his face. He hadn't flinched. He hadn't even moved. And yet he filled the room.

"Good afternoon, Mr. Hamilton," she blurted out after a moment or two, wrenching back her composure. The senator leaned back in his seat, grinning at having pinned his daughter with a single sentence. "I am Marlena Maxwell, Senator Maxwell's oldest daughter and a *frequent aide* to him in his campaigns. I'm pleased to make your acquaintance." She presented a hand, palm down, in a gesture that practically demanded he kiss it. It had no effect. He simply eased up from the credenza and accepted her hand. He was dressed impeccably despite the July heat, right down to onyx cuff links and a perfectly looped watch fob. He bowed slightly but never lowered his eyes. They were extraordinary in color, but it was the edge in them, the dashing glint, that dug into her stomach.

"The pleasure is all mine, miss, I assure you. I am most delighted to meet the senator's family."

The power and indisputable origin of his accent dropped Marlena's jaw.

She stood staring for a moment and then turned back to her father as if Hamilton weren't even in the room. "You hired a *Yankee* to run this campaign?" She spit the word out as if it were the lowest of insults.

"Now, wait just a minute, young lady. Mr. Hamilton is a political-science expert and a damn fine man from Harvard University, and I'll not have—"

"I don't care if angels brought him from heaven. He's from *Boston*! Are you out of your mind, Daddy?"

"We will discuss this later, when you can speak about it calmly."

"But you've—"

"That's enough! I will not have my judgment questioned."

"But—"

"*Have I made myself clear, Marlena?*" Her father only called her by her full name when he was truly angry with her.

She backpedaled, started to reply, thought better of it, and moved toward the door. But Marlena couldn't quite hold her tongue all the way out of the office. Quietly, but loud enough for her father to hear, she said, "Miss Edgerton, it seems my father has taken leave of his senses. Please inform the proper authorities that he is no longer fit to govern in the state of Texas. Thank you." She reclaimed her cup with a wink and a flourish.

"Marlena Winbourne Maxwell—"

"Good afternoon, Father." The outer door slammed

again. Senator Maxwell's hand returned to his forehead.

Marlena stopped just outside the office door, unsure
of where to go. Returning to the tea party was out of
the question, although it would serve powdery old Mrs.
Dorlan right to find out that Senator Maxwell's snappy
young campaign manager was a *Yankee*. At times like
these Marlena would normally tear into the office and
plop down at a desk, working the problem out in the
hum of the office. Now with *him* in there, it was the last
place she wanted to be. By default, she headed for her
room.

It was inconceivable. Ogden Mathers had been
Senator Maxwell's campaign manager for over twelve
years. He was family. He was creative and loyal and
supportive. More important, he let Marlena have her
way. Through Mathers' spinelessness, Marlena virtually
ran her father's campaign. She was good at it.

This replacement was ridiculous. After all, wasn't the
senator's now famous summer barbecue her idea? It
certainly wasn't Mathers who wrote the glorious acceptance speech in the last race. Now some textbook-
laden Bostonian would be writing this acceptance
speech? That was, Marlena reminded herself, if her father won the opportunity to give it at all. Marlena
lurched onto the satin lounger beside her bedroom window and threw her head back to stare at the ceiling.
What if Daddy doesn't win?

The thought had never occurred to her before.
Naturally, Mathers' death presented some obstacles,
but it never occurred to Marlena that her father
wouldn't win, or that he would hire someone else to
finish the campaign. November was four short months
away. This was a heated race. Surely he would lean on
her to pull him through. She sank lower into the plush

chaise, tucking her chin down and wrapping her arms around herself.

Surely not, it seemed.

Marlena moped in her room, listening to the chatter of the ladies as they dispersed from tea. She frowned at her room's ornate furnishings. She picked at the moiré bedspread and poked her fingers through the lace in the curtains. She ran her fingers through the gold fringe trimming her chaise. Everything here seemed so dark, thick, and fussy. These things were opulent, but they were not terribly useful.

Now, with Hamilton in the office, she would probably be banished into the not terribly useful role of ornamental daughter. Her head rocked side to side as if reciting a nursery rhyme as she ticked down a list of airy adjectives: pretty, conversational, charming—and useless. Her hand wandered to her pocket, pulling out a gentleman's pocket watch. She fingered the lumpy freshwater pearl fob that fastened the timepiece to her skirt waistband. Marlena traced the barely visible "SWM" monogram on the lid. The watch had been her grandfather's. She opened it, soothed by the familiar ticking heartbeat. Grandpa might have talked her father into letting Marlena run the campaign. He'd at least have asked her opinion before hiring that invader downstairs. And he'd never, ever have hired a Yankee to do a Texan's job. She snapped the watch shut in defeat, feeling cooped up in the Austin town house. Thank God they'd be going out to the ranch tomorrow.

"It's a fine idea, but there's more studying to do before we map strategies, Hamilton," came her father's voice distantly through the open window. He and Hamilton were walking through the courtyard.

"I understand, Senator, but we do have to act quickly if we're to gain the upper hand," replied the jarring voice. The pair strolled off down the street, probably to the corner tavern to toast the new appointment.

Marlena couldn't just sit by and let this man take over. She did the only thing that came to mind: jumped up and ran down to the office, where Deborah was leaning against the desk as if timing her appearance.

"I cannot believe it, Deb."

"Rather handsome, and suave, don't you think? Even if he is a Yankee."

"He won't last a minute here. The second he opens his mouth they'll eat him alive. He's not a Texan. He's stuffy. He's . . . he's"—Marlena's eyes rolled upward as she searched for the most dreadful adjective—"cavalier."

"I know some folks who'd consider that a Texan trait. Your father says he's brilliant. Besides, just because a man fails to kiss your hand when you offer it doesn't mean he's self-possessed." Deborah sat at her desk and stacked a pile of filing cards. "I'm not sure which man got the best of you."

Marlena shot her a look and began riffling through the afternoon's mail, sorting envelopes like playing cards. "I will ignore that last remark. I need information, not insults. What does Daddy have him doing first?"

"Coming out to the ranch for the weekend."

Marlena dropped the envelopes in her hand and stared at Deborah in disbelief.

Deborah spread her arms in an all-too-accurate impersonation of the senator. "That's right, Lena honey, your father wants Mr. Hamilton to get to know the whole family."

"Dear Lord!" cursed Marlena. She narrowed her eyes at Deborah. "How long have you known?"

"Only just this morning. Your mother's furious. They were in here arguing about it this morning. No sir, Mrs. Maxwell is far from thrilled with our new campaign manager. No matter how blue his blood is."

"Cut me, and I'll bleed red all over your carpet just like everyone else," came a distinctly Northern voice from the door. Tyler Hamilton walked in, clearly amused at his timing. "Why, hello again, Miss Maxwell. Two reporters cornered your father on the street. He's in the library giving an interview. If you hurry, you can still declare his unfit state of mind to the press."

"As his campaign manager, Mr. Hamilton, I believe my father's public image is now your concern. That is, after all, why my father has seen fit to *import* you."

Hamilton cocked an eyebrow at the jab.

Marlena went further. "Oh, my, but if he is speaking to the press, shouldn't you be there with him? Or is he not quite ready to debut his Yankee associate? Tell me, did my father give you a reason why it appears no one in the state of Texas seemed qualified enough to fill this job?" She was sorry the wounded edge in her voice left no question as to who she meant by "no one."

The question hung in the air like Maxwell's cigar smoke.

Tyler Hamilton gave a long, slow exhale. He lowered his eyes, ran a hand through his thick blond hair, and sat down on a desk corner. "Miss Maxwell"—he took off his glasses and looked up—"I cannot succeed and fight you at the same time."

The simplicity of his statement left Marlena with no reply. She'd expected an immediate defense. She leaned slowly onto the desk behind her. The edge in his eyes was gone, replaced by a penetrating, astounding warmth. Trained full force on Marlena. With considerable results. Results that made breathing rather difficult all of a sudden.

"Look, Miss Maxwell," he continued, "I'm no fool. I know what you've meant to your father's success. Miss Edgerton has been rather . . . complete . . . in her explanations of how this campaign has operated. Besides, I've read Mathers' own paperwork, and it would take a slow-witted man not to recognize what . . . shall we say 'influence' . . . you have had on this campaign. As I see it, you, most of all, know what is at stake here."

He picked up the stack of papers next to him on the desk and held them up to Marlena. "Your father is a great man. He has the ability to help Texas reclaim its role in the Union. Not just the statehood on paper—that's already done—but the spirit of a union, and the chance to get on with the business of life and prosperity. It's not a popular stance with some people, and you know it. You've helped him get as far as he has. Your father has the courage to take a stand, even though it may cost him dearly. I don't have to tell you Dickson Kenton will do all he can to destroy that chance.

"I have the science, Miss Maxwell; I have the strategy, the ideas, and the numbers." He shook the papers. "But politics has to have a face. A soul, if you will. Now, you, you have the style, the personality, this campaign needs. Men vote with their loyalties as much as their wallets or their minds." He lowered the papers and stared directly at her. "I just can't afford to fight you and Dickson Kenton at the same time. I am going to need your help."

Marlena just stood there. No reply came. A small sparkle of hope flashed through her chest. Here, perhaps, was a man who understood what was important to her. He'd already recognized her role in the campaign. Could it be? He had just asked her for help. Even Mathers had not understood her view. She locked eyes with Hamilton. There was a reaching in them, an invitation for their mutual ideas to meet. *It could be.* Her thoughts and his eyes spun sparks inside her head. Maybe, just maybe, Tyler Hamilton wasn't so inappropriate after all. He could certainly communicate. In fact, he'd disarmed her in two paragraphs.

Paragraphs.

Persuasion.

A speech.

A sale. Her hand tightened on the desk behind her. *No, you don't.*

This was too quick, too perfect to be genuine. Hamilton's little plea wasn't for his benefit; it was for hers. She wasn't being respected; she was being patronized. Make Daddy's little girl feel appreciated so we can get on with business. The sparks in her head leapt into flames. No silver-tongued Yankee was going to get the best of her. Certainly not this way. How could she have even thought he would understand what all this meant to her? It was just the way a man would handle a woman who couldn't seem to fit—who wouldn't fit—the standard mold. Charm her back into place.

In seconds she shifted from fascinated to fuming. Marlena moved slowly, leveling her eyes like a cat. He'd almost succeeded, and that made her angriest of all. "You're very good at what you do, Mr. Hamilton. I can see why Daddy hired you. You seem to know just what to say, and you sound *ever* so genuine. I'm sure lots of folks will be just *charmed* by you." She overemphasized the word. "Save the propaganda for the campaign trail, Mr. Hamilton. I'm immune." She turned and left the room, slamming the door.

Hamilton stared at the door for a minute, the sound still vibrating through the room. "She likes to slam doors, doesn't she?"

Miss Edgerton offered no reply.

Not ten minutes later, the office door opened in a more genteel fashion to reveal the woman Tyler could only assume was Mrs. Maxwell. She had the look of someone who'd rather be elsewhere.

"Jason?" she called in a melodic voice. She hadn't

seen Tyler in the corner behind her, but walked to Miss Edgerton's desk. "Is Senator Maxwell here, Deborah? I thought he was going out with that . . . that young man . . . but I thought I heard his voice in the house somewhere."

Tyler wasn't sure her hesitation in referring to him boded well. He put his glasses back on quietly and watched.

"No, ma'am, Mr. Hamilton is right behind you. The senator is with some reporters in the library."

Rather than whirl around as her daughter did upon their surprise introduction, Mrs. Maxwell drew herself straighter—if that was possible—and turned slowly around.

"Mrs. Maxwell, may I present Mr. Tyler Hamilton the third." Miss Edgerton seemed a bit uneasy at having to make the introductions in her employer's absence. "Mr. Hamilton, this is Claudia Maxwell, the senator's wife."

Tyler could see the source of her daughter's beauty. She was a graceful woman with fragile, crisp features. It was easy to see the chemistry that created Marlena; her mother's doll-like figure wrapped around her father's heroic personality. Where Marlena was fire, Claudia Maxwell was cream and china. Her meticulously crafted appearance was marred only by the intrusion of a savage-looking scar that ran across her left cheek and over her jawline. She noticed that he noticed it.

"How do you do, Mr. Hamilton?" She extended a wisp of a hand.

Tyler took the tiny hand in his own and inclined his head slightly. "Quite well, Mrs. Maxwell. I am so very pleased to meet you."

He felt her hand flinch the tiniest bit in his palm.

"Thank you." She slid her hand from his grasp. "Welcome to Texas." She smiled graciously and walked over to her husband's office door. "My husband tells me you are unstoppable."

Tyler grinned. It was a perfectly extreme, Maxwell-esque adjective. "A kind thought, but surely it is the senator who is unstoppable. I merely assist."

"Of course. You are from Boston?" She nearly succeeded in hiding her revulsion at the fact. Had Tyler not been gauging her responses so carefully, he might have missed it. But it was there, lurking underneath the cream and china.

"Born, raised, and educated there."

"Harvard, yes, so I've been told. Well, I'd best go see to the house before one of those reporters shows up in here." She moved to Miss Edgerton's desk. "Deborah honey, tell Jason I'll be in the parlor when he's done."

"Certainly, Mrs. Maxwell."

Claudia turned to Tyler. "Good afternoon, Mr. Hamilton. I'm sure I'll be seeing you again."

"It will be my pleasure, Mrs. Maxwell." Tyler opened the office door for her and she glided into the hallway.

He shut the door slowly, exhaled, and turned to Miss Edgerton. "Exactly how angry is she that I am here?"

She arched an eyebrow. "You're rather astute."

"She's rather good at hiding it."

"Mrs. Maxwell's talent for hiding her true feelings is the stuff of legend. The house staff lives in fear of her."

"Surely I have no reason to fear?"

She simply peered up at him from over the top of her spectacles.

"Thank you, I'll keep that in mind. I do bleed red, remember. I don't mean to pry, but tell me, do you know . . . ?" He touched his own left cheek, indicating where Mrs. Maxwell's scar had been.

Miss Edgerton set down her papers. "There was an

incident with some soldiers during the war, when they
lived in Galveston. No one discusses the matter, really."

"I see." Tyler moved toward his desk.

"No one knows much, but there is one thing I do
know that you should consider carefully about that
scar, Mr. Hamilton."

Tyler stopped. "And that is?"

"A Yankee bayonet made it. She bleeds too, remember."

Tyler sat down very slowly.

⊰ Chapter Two ⊱

Late that night, as the full moon lavished light through Tyler's apartment window, he sat sipping brandy and mulling over his first day as a professional campaign manager. Much of it met his expectations. He'd daydreamed in political-science classes of hectic campaign offices, brimming with newspapers and poll statistics, smelling of poster ink, strong coffee, and cigars. He'd seen himself mapping strategy with a larger-than-life senator or governor, shaping and molding his public persona around the issues of the day. Giving ideas and philosophies human legs, arms, and voice. All these dreamlike elements were there in his day today. But in so many ways they were totally different from how he'd imagined them. His dreams had stone walls, New England accents, and dignified passions. Here, ideas didn't just take human form; they took hero form. Texas was big, loud, hot, and overly friendly. But here, Tyler Hamilton III was not preceded by Tyler Hamilton II. Not even by Tyler Hamilton I.

Tyler was smart enough to recognize that even if his father and grandfather hadn't preceded him into Texas, their reputations had. Talent aside, he knew the name was what had opened doors for him. He'd gotten used to that. What rubbed him the wrong way all through Harvard was the instant, thoughtless acceptance of his credibility. He had never really had the chance to prove

himself. All he'd had to do was competently fill the
legacy. It wasn't hard to be good when no one would
think of you in any other terms.

Tyler was tired of a thirdhand name.

He smiled as he remembered his mother's shock
when he told her he was going to Texas. She obviously
had other plans for her son. Tyler Hamilton II just
gave his son a "boys will be boys" look and told him
to remember the pride of the Hamilton name. Funny,
that's just what Tyler sought to escape. Taking on
the Maxwell campaign was one-third running away,
one-third shock value, and one-third pure impulse.
The combination would either be brilliant or disas-
trous.

Tyler took a healthy swig from the snifter. Today had
been squarely on the brilliant side. Knowing he'd have
to be as big as Texas in his "Bostonianism" to get
the maximum shock, he had poured every ounce of
charm he had into the entire day. Every time he said
"Harvard," the *ah*s in his regional pronunciation grew
longer. He'd accomplished a great deal in one day only
because everyone was too overwhelmed to put up any
objections. Employing the element of surprise, he'd
quickly and easily established his turf and his terms.

Not that Maxwell was a pushover. Nothing happened in that office unless Maxwell wished it to, despite
his easygoing personality. Tyler knew he was getting his
way because Maxwell agreed with him, and for no
other reason. In eight short hours he and Tyler had
forged a strong, challenging relationship. Despite the
quick rapport, even Tyler was surprised when the senator invited him out to the family ranch for the weekend.
Especially for the big barbecue. He'd hoped Maxwell
would be subtler in his announcement of Tyler's appointment. But then, this was Texas. And this was

Jason Maxwell. Tyler guessed subtlety wasn't often part of the picture.

He lurched out of his chair to flip open a trunk latch and dig for his riding gear. Behind six or seven hefty textbooks lay a framed Harvard diploma. The ornate frame had been a gift from his father. It was adorned with the Hamilton family crest and credo: "Foremost with Honor." *And Duty, Dignity, Formality, Propriety,* added Tyler silently. His family was seeping with honor, duty, and dignity. So much so that it became more than a little stifling to a young man eager to prove his worth in this world. Sometimes Tyler felt his family was so busy doing what was *correct* that he wondered if they were doing what was *right*.

Finally Tyler's hands found the velvet of his riding jacket and held it up. The English tack seemed over-dressed for the Texas countryside. He took another long drink as he surveyed the clothes. He didn't know whether to expect riding tack or cowboy chaps tomorrow. This state was new and wonderfully, deliciously foreign.

His mind wandered to the day's largest surprise: Marlena Maxwell. Their first meeting was an incendiary introduction. She was a sight. She was a tiny thing, like a doll. Astoundingly beautiful. Her eyes could draw a man in from across a room. The combination of their cool mossy green with the fire behind them had more power over Tyler than he liked. He'd known before she'd opened her mouth that she was dangerous.

She didn't enter the room; she burst upon it. Meeting her was like being handed a lit firecracker. He'd never seen a woman act like that. It was both annoying and utterly fascinating.

There was much more to this family than met the eye. She'd never have been so upset if something big weren't at stake. There wouldn't be any stakes unless Maxwell had allowed her a sizable role in the campaign . . . until now. It was easy to put two and two together and understand where Miss Maxwell's fury was coming from. All the more reason to present a flawless, unflinching first impression.

She had to be held at bay. What amazed Tyler was Marlena's brashness in speaking her mind. Even in anger, no proper Boston lady would have spoken to her father—or any man—like that. Especially not in front of company. Door slamming, mocking, name-calling; my God, she even drank coffee. He'd never met a female who didn't confine herself to tea gussied with cream and sugar. He chuckled at the thought, running his hand through his hair again and then finishing his brandy.

Then there was the day's second meeting with Miss Maxwell. He had sized her up accurately, learned all he could, and taken a stand. The best surprise attack with her, however, was to drop the flawless front. Pretend not to keep her at bay. He had actually meant two-thirds of his speech. He really did feel he couldn't fight her and Kenton at the same time. He startled himself with the realization that this was the first time he had encountered a woman he considered a worthy adversary. Someone who might just be beyond his ability to control. She could be distracting—in any number of ways. Whatever fed that passion for life also fed a hot temper that could spell danger for all he had to accomplish. The stakes were too great.

He was convinced he'd played her right. At that moment when their eyes locked in the office, something clicked and he felt the alliance was forged. But that click felt just the slightest bit unstable. Damn it if she hadn't seen through the rhetoric. She sensed the truth in what he was saying, but somehow she'd recognized the performance. Tyler put the snifter down and paced over to the window. *Distracting, to be certain.* He pulled his glasses off and kneaded his forehead in fatigue. In an instant he withdrew his hand, realizing that it was exactly the pose Senator Maxwell had taken when Marlena left the room. Shaking off the unnerving sensation, he shut the window and went to bed.

Claudia Maxwell smoldered in the early afternoon shade of the porch. She sat drinking iced tea with her sister, Julia Martin. The air hung damp and quiet, broken occasionally by the sound of the ranch staff setting up for the evening's barbecue. The ranch house's massive porch jutted out over an enormous lawn, dotted with weathered old oak trees and a long wooden fence. The Maxwells' Double X ranch spread as far as either woman could see. In the far pastures longhorns meandered about in the hot sun. The hustle of settling in at the ranch had quieted. Most of the weekend's guests were napping in their rooms, sparing themselves the stifling afternoon heat in preparation for the evening's excitement.

Julia punctuated her criticism with a jab of her sandalwood fan. "I'd have thought you could have spoken to Jason about this."

Claudia furrowed her brow. "Good heavens, Julia, don't you think I am beside myself? Yesterday's tea was close to unbearable." Her hand strayed to the whitish blue gash across her jaw. There were days when she could forget about that scar, but those days hadn't been lately. Lately she felt as if the entire world gaped at her flawed face.

Julia clucked and shook her head. "Your own husband, of all people. I mean, for gracious sakes, Claudia, haven't you been through enough?"

They rocked in silence for a moment.

"Tell me, Julia, how am I supposed to explain such

public inconsideration? That Texas' finest senator—
that my husband—is soliciting advice from a *Yankee*?"

"I don't mind telling you, I don't envy you one bit."

Claudia's hands flailed in frustration. "Union, unity,
I've had all I can stomach in speeches and such, but I
don't believe I can stand to see a Bostonian at my dining
room table."

Julia leaned in to her sister. "Have you even tried to
reason with Jason? Talk to him? You would think he
could understand the terrible position he's placed you in."

Claudia shook her head. "Jason simply doesn't see it
that way. 'The war is long over, Claudia,' he says. 'As
members of the legislature, we must set an example in
our efforts to remove judgment.' I tell you, it's straight
out of some campaign speech." She turned to her sister
with a tight throat. "I am wounded. Deeply wounded.
My feelings aside, I fear he's gone too far. This could
cost him dearly in November, ideals or no ideals." For a
moment she felt the hurt would overpower her composure. Taking a deep breath, she applied the gracious
campaign face that was her best weapon against the
pain. She sighed and leaned back in her chair. "My
goodness, but it's hot. I really should lie down before
this evening."

Julia said nothing. She simply reached out and patted
her sister's hand in righteous sympathy.

"I'm sure the senator will be happy to speak with you
on Monday, Mr. . . . ."

"Hasten, ma'am, Samuel Hasten, with the *Austin
City News*. How rude of me not to introduce myself
first." The young man tipped his hat and gave her an
appealing smile despite his salesmanlike demeanor.
"Actually, we've met before, at the senator's press con-
ferences. You are Miss Edgerton."

He stepped into the office and handed her a packet of papers. "You've always been most cordial to me, Miss Edgerton."

"Thank you, Mr. Hasten, it's kind of you to say so, but I'm still afraid I cannot help you. Senator Maxwell is away for the weekend and will not return until Monday. I'll be happy to tell him you called." She continued locking up the office.

"Gone to the ranch and left you to do the filing. Hardly sounds fair, if I may take the liberty of saying so."

Hasten's frank implication turned Deborah cold and formal. "Mr. Hasten, is there something you require?"

Hasten became flustered, as he seemed to realize he'd touched a nerve. He pulled his hat off in a nervous gesture, exposing the head of thick red hair that gave him such a boyish appearance. "I'm sorry, Miss Edgerton, I never meant to be impolite." He let out a strong sigh and gazed out the window. "I guess I'm just angry I'm working on such a fine Saturday, too. I meant no harm." He paused and picked at imaginary lint on his hat brim.

"I won't count the day as a total loss, however, Miss Edgerton. I'm pleased to have had the chance to truly meet you. You . . . well, you are always nice, even when you have to tell me to go away. It's a pleasure, miss, it truly is. And I just . . ." He looked at her with warm eyes. "Well, I just have always been rather fond of your voice."

Deborah was drawing the breath to say good-bye when he broke in to interrupt her. "I've kept you, and you're trying to get finished up here and be on your way. Well, I'll just come back for my quote on Monday. Well, then." He turned and looked directly at her, mouth open, framing the words in slow motion before he finally spoke them. "Miss Edgerton . . . may I . . . may I walk you to your coach?"

Deborah halted, surprised. It was a moment before she replied to his rather forward proposal. "It is a gracious offer, Mr. Hasten." He instantly warmed, opening his mouth to say more. "But the senator's driver is taking me to the ranch in an hour or so."

He shut his mouth. "Of course." He seemed dejected, but not defeated. He pointed at her with his hat, grinning. "You'll be attending the barbecue, won't you? Of course."

Deb stood for a moment, deciding. It was a charming smile.

"Perhaps Monday?" She found herself smiling in return. "After all, you'll need to come back for your quote, won't you?"

"Why, yes, Miss Edgerton, I certainly will."

Dusk seeped across the wide green lawn of the Double X ranch house. High torches festooned with red and white ribbons threw their speckled glow across a sea of red-and-white-checkered tablecloths. Mounds of yellow roses spilled out of glass bowls adorning each table. An enormous barbecue stood off to the side, sending spectacular smells circulating amongst the guests. Three pigs rotated over the slow coals, spitting and hissing under a saucy coat. Sweet corn boiled in an enormous vat off to the other side, while a breathtaking display of breads, rolls, and other treats promised a delectable complement. The scents had wafted through the house for several hours, encouraging appetites and building anticipation for the evening's events.

On the porch's front steps, Claudia and Jason Maxwell extended a grand hospitality to their guests. Maxwell was a host at his best, dazzling in a white suit and hat, clasping hands and arms in boisterous hellos. He was bigger than life and a born leader. She looked born to the part as well, radiant in her peach gown and with two peach roses tucked elegantly in her silvering hair. She kissed cheeks, blushed at compliments, and clasped hands with the air of a queen beside her king. Together on the steps they made a glorious picture.

Tyler stood under a tree on the far side of the lawn and watched the spectacle in admiration. Jason Maxwell didn't just legislate Texas—for God's sake, he *was* Texas. Right down to the Stetson and the yellow rose in his lapel. His genuine nature was the only thing that kept him from being a cartoon. Yet he wasn't contrived in the slightest. He was what he was, and perhaps that was the secret to his success.

Tyler and Jason had discussed at length Tyler's introduction for the evening. He would lie low for the first part of the party, attracting little attention while the guests warmed up to the event. Just before the meal, Maxwell would give a short speech, during which he would introduce Tyler and invite him to sit at his table. Tyler would say a few sentences in greeting and thanks. Both knew that his accent, not his words, would convey the real message. The guests would then have the entire meal to gossip, gawk, and get the initial shock out of their systems. As the evening progressed toward dancing, Tyler would have the chance to mingle and charm the now well-plied guests.

He had taken extra care to dress impeccably in a light gray summer suit, vest, and coat. Away from the office, his glasses were tucked into his breast pocket. Even doing his best to be unnoticeable, he was noticed. Several of the crowd's young ladies had managed to pick him out of the fringes and send warm glances his way. It felt intoxicating to be the surprise element for once, instead of the requisite Hamilton family representative. He leaned back against the massive oak tree and sipped his drink, smiling.

One by one, Tyler watched each of Maxwell's three daughters come out of the house to join their parents on the porch steps. Andrea, the youngest—had Maxwell said she was eight or nine?—bounded down the stairs in a pale yellow dress shortly after the party began. She kept her place by her parents for half an hour or so, saying hello and impatiently knocking her foot against the step behind her. At last the excitement of the evening surely got the best of her, for she tugged her mother's sleeve until Tyler saw Mrs. Maxwell lean down and whisper something that sent the girl racing off across the lawn. Diana, Maxwell's middle daughter, joined the entourage shortly before Andrea left. She had all the graciousness of her mother, but she hadn't acquired the casual elegance of years in the spotlight. Her cream gown gave her an adult appearance, but her mannerisms still revealed her seventeen short years.

Tyler straightened up when Marlena came down the steps. Her black hair gleamed next to the auburn coloring of her sisters and mother, the dark hair clearly a gift from her father's side. She stood out in the crowd— nearly as much as her father. Presence, his law school professor had called it. "Intensity of character. Presence is what makes men great." Presence in a woman was . . . was what? He knew the answer even before he finished the thought: incredibly attractive. The mint color of her gown set off her green eyes like emeralds against the black velvet of her lashes.

Her hair was caught up in a weaving of curls and sweeps, with two cream roses peeking from the onyx curves to match the cream lace trim on her dress. Tyler felt an unsettling, instinctual urge to see that hair unleashed. His fingers twitched, and he realized he wanted to let them wander through it. He shook his head, brushing off the spell that her hair seemed to cast over him.

Even dressed for a special occasion, she was still wearing the odd watch he'd noticed earlier. She took something as unconventional as a man's pocket watch and gave it her own style, so that it suited her. He had to admit he liked her. Of course, the fact that she was breathtaking made it easy to like her. Too easy, perhaps. Her confidence was extraordinary. She was clearly in her element. Unlike her younger sister, she accepted the spotlight with grace, kissing her father on the cheek. He watched her as she flirted with the older statesmen and complimented their wives. There was no mistaking the asset she was to this campaign.

Such amazing intelligence and daring in such a delicate form. She was beautiful, sharp, unpredictable, and unlike any woman he could remember. She was also, Tyler reminded himself with a slight sigh, an unaffordable distraction. The boss' daughter—what could be more impractical right now? From the safety of this distance, however, she was a pleasure to behold, which he wasn't about to deny himself.

Gradually the guests found their tables and sat down. As Maxwell made his way again to the front steps, the crowd's hum died down to silence. Tyler's breath began to race, but with practiced determination he forced calm back into his body. Maxwell was speaking, but Tyler didn't hear what he said. The thudding of blood through his veins was drowning out any other noise.

In the instant his ears registered Maxwell saying his name, Tyler's composure snapped back into place. Not the slightest outward hint of nerves showed as he strolled the distance to Maxwell's right hand. He even smiled at one or two ladies as he crossed the lawn. Men clapped politely. Women stared. Young ladies' heads turned toward each other in favorable whispers.

Claudia Maxwell bit her lip. Jason Maxwell enveloped
Tyler in a broad smile and an enormous arm before
stepping aside to let Tyler say a few words. Those few
words that would cause such a commotion . . .

Tyler took a deep breath and began clearly, calmly,
and undeniably Boston-born: "Good evening, ladies
and gentlemen. It is with tremendous honor that I come
to the service of Texas' greatest contemporary statesman." He'd crafted his first sentence to contain several
words with distinctly Bostonian pronunciations. He
paused a few seconds to let the shock sink in. "Jason
Maxwell embodies Texas' future. He gives this great
state the chance to fulfill its destiny as part of the greatest nation on earth. I pledge my efforts to keep the senator in service to Texas, where he belongs." Tyler took
his glass from the table and raised it in a toast. "To
Jason Maxwell's reelection!"

The glass seemed to hang in the air for an unbearable
eternity.

In the split second before some man shouted "To
Maxwell!" in reply, Marlena stopped breathing. She
hadn't realized she was holding her breath until she
heard her mother's and sisters' breath letting out in the
same instant of relief. As long as the crowd was talking,
the evening was salvageable. Appalled silence would
have meant disaster.

The buzz of shock and gossip, however, indicated that
once again, Jason Maxwell had successfully played the
moment. This would be all over every paper by morning. The senator would be granting nonstop interviews
for the next week on his shocking choice of manager. It
would give him the perfect platform to promote the
unity and full restoration he wanted so badly for his
home state. Her father was clearly thrilled. He and Tyler
clasped hands and laughed as they sat down to eat, despite the near-roar of gossip at every table on the lawn.

Marlena had known by the empty place setting that she was going to have to face that strutting rooster all through dinner. At least it was less disconcerting than having him at her side, but certainly not by much. He slid into his chair with a satisfied smirk. She watched his blue eyes dance around the table, observing, calculating, and measuring responses. Marlena nearly rolled her eyes in disbelief at his cockiness. As if sensing her disapproval, he focused squarely on her with a blinding smile. This was going to be the longest evening of her life. Her hand squeezed around the watch at her waist as if the pressure could make time flow faster.

Finally Tyler couldn't seem to contain himself. "Quite a commotion, don't you think, Miss Maxwell?" he said after devouring a thick square of corn bread. His question was polite enough, but his eyes brandished a hidden translation: *Admit it, Miss Maxwell, it worked.*

"Quite. I should only hope it stays in your favor. Butter?"

You're not out of the woods yet, Yankee. Just because they're not instantly lynching you doesn't mean this will work.

"This promises to be a truly wonderful evening. Mmm. This corn bread is outstanding. Your mother outshines her reputation as the state's most gracious hostess." *This will work because I can make it work.*

"Hospitality, Mr. Hamilton, is at the very nature of the Texan spirit. Would you like some ham?" *You're a novelty. Don't mistake civility for acceptance.* Marlena had never seen anyone eat so much in the first minutes of a meal.

"Thank you, Miss Maxwell. It smells delicious. It seems Texans know how to eat." Tyler directed the comment at Andrea, who giggled that the evening's important guest was paying attention to her. Claudia smiled slightly, the senator beamed, and Marlena fumed.

Tyler glared at her. *You'd best get used to me.*

Marlena ground her heel into the grass beneath the checkered tablecloth and stabbed her ham. If Texans knew how to eat, it seemed Bostonians had written the manual. Her corset stays began poking her again.

As full dark descended on the Double X lawn, well-fed and slightly tipsy guests mingled about on the grass. Marlena had left the table as soon as etiquette would permit. To her horror, not only had Hamilton managed to make a gracious and impeccably mannered glutton of himself by eating everything in sight, he'd succeeded in charming Andrea and Diana before dessert was even served.

She strode across the lawn for a glass of peach wine, silently cursing her demure little sisters, who concerned themselves with little more than embroidery. If they would use their minds a little more, they would be able to see through the charm Tyler was pouring their way. She wished Deborah had been seated at her table, for she would have seen through it, as well.

"Lena, my dear, you look as if you've got a bone stuck in your throat. Smile, dear; this is an election year," her father teased, wrapping a thick arm around her shoulders while he waved at a distant supporter with the other hand.

"Daddy. Honestly. He's shameless. He had Andrea and Di eating out of his hand before the ice cream melted."

"Exactly, sweetheart. Silver-tongued. Half the guests will be charmed within the hour. He's certainly a shock, but you and I both know what kind of press this is going to buy the campaign. You know me better, darlin', than to think I planned it any other way. Monday, you come down to the office and talk a while. Hamilton's got ideas. Good ones. I think even you'll like them, no matter how hard you try not to." He turned her to face him, placing his hands on her shoulders. "Now, Lena, I have a job for you tonight. You're not going to like it, but I'm asking you as your father to obey me in this. Do you understand?"

Marlena was already getting her back up. She didn't like what she had seen so far, and that didn't bode well for whatever was to come. She crossed her arms in front of her and waited. "Good Lord, Daddy, I endured dinner with him. What more could you possibly ask of me?"

She knew the answer before she even finished the question, for the band started to play from the porch. Her father just stood there, looking at her.

She tried to pull away, disgusted. "No. Absolutely not. Daddy, you can't be serious. I won't. Get Diana. For God's sake, I don't care if you get Andrea to do it. I will not dance with him. He probably doesn't even know how."

"He does, and you will. You will because I ask you to. Now." His voice assumed that indisputable tone again.

"Daddy . . ."

"Now, Marlena. You *will* do this. And no one will guess how you feel about it. Do I make myself clear?" He smiled, but his grip on Marlena's shoulders let her know he would bodily take her to the dance floor if required. She yanked out of his grasp and headed for the dancers. If there was no stopping this circus, she might as well retain some grace in the process.

Out of the corner of her eye, Marlena caught sight of Tyler as he stood with the other guests along the rim of the dance floor. He was chatting amiably with some of the senator's supporters. He looked up for a fraction

of a second and caught Marlena's eye. There was that
glint again. And an exasperating grin that showed he
knew exactly how events would flow from here.
Marlena strained to keep her annoyance from showing,
making small talk with guests while her father and
mother took the floor.

As the lilting waltz filled the warm night air, she
could see her parents discussing something. While they
smiled for the audience, Marlena could tell a serious
conversation was taking place between them. She didn't
have to guess the topic. Her mother and father both had
the uncanny talent for being privately furious with each
other—or her, or anyone, for that matter—and yet ap-
pearing charming and happy to the public.

Her back stiffened as the second verse began. She
said a quick prayer for some of that public charm to be
hereditary, watched Tyler lift a hand to the couple he
was speaking to, mouth the words "Excuse me," and
cross the dance floor as if he owned it. Marlena continued her conversation, refusing to acknowledge that she
was expecting his request. She wouldn't give him the
satisfaction of even thinking she was waiting for him.

"Miss Maxwell, may I have the pleasure of this
dance?" Marlena feigned surprise to the couple next to
her and whirled around with her hand to her breast in
textbook belle fashion.

"Why, Mr. Hamilton, I should be honored." She ex-
aggerated the Southern accent and batted her eyelashes.
Hamilton didn't flinch, but graciously held out a hand.
Marlena placed her hand in his. The spark in his touch
was surely her imagination. Perhaps the second glass of
peach wine had been a mistake. He pulled her out onto
the floor. His free hand clasped around her waist and
guided her strongly to the center, where her parents
danced.

Well, if Daddy wanted a show, he'd get one. "I trust

they waltz in Boston?" She tried to paste a sugary smile on her face, but the look in his eyes made it impossible.

"Why, Miss Maxwell, I was indeed relieved to learn they waltzed in Texas," he returned, spinning her impeccably around a corner. He pulled her an inch closer.

Marlena should have known he would be an excellent dancer. It fit the persona. She loved dancing, but always seemed to let her enthusiasm overwhelm her partner, which made her hard to lead. Hamilton met her enthusiasm with equal authority, however, leading more strongly to channel her energy rather than fight it. The effect was mildly intoxicating despite Marlena's best efforts to remain annoyed. He lifted his arm and pulled her under it for a turn, slowing the movements down so that they came close together. He stopped her from backing away. Marlena tried to ignore the way his hand slid around her waist as she turned.

Relenting, she let herself enjoy it just a bit. Hamilton's knowing expression told her that he was enjoying the moment, as well. Too much. He was looking right at her, but she could return the gaze of those steely blue eyes for only a second or two. He was too close. The allure of his eyes was too intense.

Most men danced with Marlena as if she would break. Tyler held her and looked at her as if he knew damn well she could hold her own. He pulled her close to him again in another turn. There was something about him, the way he regarded her, that she found captivating. His hand, locked below her shoulder blade, seeped heat through her dress. It pressed against her breathing. It forced her close. He looked at her as if he knew something, some secret about her. It was annoying. And disarming. And several other things. They danced the next two waltzes without speaking.

When the band began a livelier tune, Tyler's awkwardness with the country-style music broke the spell.

"My apologies, Miss Maxwell, but I'm afraid we truly don't do this one in Boston." Whoever it was Marlena had seen during the waltz vanished instantly behind the dashing facade.

"Unwilling to try, Mr. Hamilton? I thought you braver than that."

"Unwilling to risk my dignity on the night of my introduction. Please go right ahead with another partner. I wouldn't dream of stopping the"—he looked around at the now crowded dance floor and gestured condescendingly—"gaiety."

"Undignified? Gaiety?" Marlena frowned at him. "Indeed, what would come between a proper Boston gentleman and a little Southern amusement?" At that moment, a rowdy couple bumped into her, sending her off her balance, into Tyler. Her cheek fell against his chest. For a split second she felt him breathe. Then he wrapped both hands fully around her waist to hold her upright. It was entirely too close to an embrace. His eyes went wide for a moment, and she saw something in them, but then he broke into a teasing grin. "It seems there isn't much to come between us at all."

Marlena flushed, more with anger than embarrassment, at his suggestive remark. "What's to come between us, Mr. Hamilton, is nothing but trouble." She huffed off the dance floor with all the visible grace she could muster, trying to think of some way to escape to the kitchen for a decent cup of coffee.

A few minutes later, Tyler stopped his conversation just momentarily when he heard the porch door of the ranch house slam shut.

⊰ Chapter Three ⊱

The shutters sliced moonlight into silver ribbons and scattered them throughout Marlena's room as she lay awake, rebuking herself for the three cups of coffee she'd sneaked in the kitchen after the scene with Tyler Hamilton. She had reappeared outside after regaining her composure, and they had ignored each other for the rest of the evening. Or tried to. Her gaze would stray to him, picking the set of his shoulders out of the crowd. She stayed with Deborah or went about her business charming supporters and their families. Tyler had done the same. There were the old war wives and widows who clucked their tongues about the impropriety of it all, but for the most part Hamilton's charm won out and the gossip had begun to slant just slightly in his favor by the end of the evening. It must be nearly three o'clock in the morning now, by Marlena's guess, and the party had ended only about two hours ago.

Hamilton and her father grew nearly intolerable as the evening wore on, wrapped up in their own success. Marlena fumed. She hated to admit that Hamilton had, in fact, charmed an impressive portion of the guests to the point where they would converse with the Yankee. What people said in polite situations, however, and what they said inside ballot boxes, was quite a different story.

How dare he show such confidence when his battle

had only just begun? How dare he look at her that way in front of everyone or pull her so close on the dance floor?

How dare he get under her skin so quickly?

No matter how she tried to argue with herself otherwise, Tyler Hamilton *was* under her skin, and she couldn't stand it. Where Marlena's sharp tongue and opinionated nature offended most young Southern gentlemen, it seemed to captivate him. Those who had courted her were either weak fellows without enough backbone to stand up to her or military types who seemed to view her as something to conquer. She didn't want to be conquered or kowtowed to. Marlena wanted to be matched. So why was it so disturbing when she finally got it? *Because it has come in the wrong package,* she thought to herself.

She hated the way his face kept creeping into her thoughts as she tried to sleep. Those moments when he held her, his hands nearly encircling her waist to keep her from falling. The sharp scent of starch when her cheek fell against his shirt and she felt his breathing. The strength with which he danced seemed to somehow communicate a—she searched for the word—*respect* for her and her capabilities, even though his words said quite the contrary. She sat up and hugged her knees, wriggling her toes up under her night shift in the creamy blue light. If respect was indeed what she was sensing, she couldn't help wondering: What was he feeling? Was she just imagining what seemed to be going on between them? She got up and walked around the room as if to leave the feeling behind in her wake. Resolutely, she opened the shutters and breathed in the velvety night air. *It's just a sensation. An emotional response. You don't have to act on it. Real attraction is about the mind and heart loving the same things, not hands on your back during a waltz. Or blue eyes. Or . . .*

She made a sound and shook herself. *This is ridiculous.* She took a deep breath and pressed her hands into her forehead, dragging them back through her thick black hair as she inhaled again. *Time to give this brain something else to think about than Tyler Hamilton.* She reached for her wrap and padded barefoot down the hall to head for the study.

Tyler inspected the way his brandy snifter distorted the image of the full, round moon. He was near the end of his third glass, having downed the first pair and three sandwiches with Senator Maxwell before the statesman retired. The spirits were shaving the edge off his concentration, and now, alone in the study and offstage, he indulged the sensation.

He thought of dancing with Marlena. It was no crime, he told himself, to admit how much he enjoyed being close to her. Her body came just barely to his shoulders. She seemed so light and petite, and yet still so sharp and forceful. Her scent—a mixture of lilac and soap and powder and something all her own—mingled with that of the roses nestled in her hair, to waft across him as they moved. It seemed so much more airy and natural than the perfume of Boston's ladies.

They were only dancing, and clearly she hadn't agreed to it willingly, but he'd enjoyed the control over her. She fought him turn for turn, push for pull. Somehow that added to the potency of it all. He had poured every ounce of charm he had on her for the sheer pleasure of it. When she gave in just a bit, the effect was dazzling. She was beginning to undo him. And Tyler Hamilton III did not come undone.

The milky glow through the windows gave the study a heavenly quality, pouring thickly over the walls of books. He polished off the glass and turned on his heels toward the largest of the leather chairs in the far corner.

Misjudging the distance, he veered off balance and slumped down awkwardly into the seat. He'd started to laugh at himself when the door creaked open.

A nightgowned, onyx-haired figure padded into the room. Tyler held his breath. It was her. Dear God, as if fate knew the sight of her would send him over the edge, she walked into the shaft of moonlight. The light glowed ever so slightly through her shift—just enough to outline the inviting curves of an impossibly tiny waist. Her hair, that black mass of curls that invaded his thoughts by day, was falling unleashed and shimmering around her shoulders. It was longer than he'd expected, and moonlight turned it to spun silver. His response to the sight was instantaneous and primal. The urge to touch her shot through him. To wrap his hands around that waist and pull her close.

She headed directly over to the far wall, searching for a specific volume, with her fingers wiggling as she scanned an upper shelf. Tyler found himself clutching the chair arms. Finding what she wanted, she stepped up on a little stool and stuck her other foot out behind her as her small body strained for the book. The pose made her appear to Tyler as a tiny, floating fairy. His composure edged out of his grasp.

"Honor obligates me to inform you, Miss Maxwell, that you are not alone." His voice was thick and husky despite the formal wording.

Marlena gasped and nearly leapt off the stool to flatten herself against the desk, hugging the book to her chest. "Dear God! What are you doing in my father's study?" Her voice changed from fear to anger as soon as she recognized his accent. "Mr. Hamilton, exactly how long did it take for your 'honor' to find its voice? You don't seem to have leapt at the chance."

"Sometimes a unique opportunity presents itself and a man needs a moment to take stock of the situation."

The keen sensations—not to mention the brandy—running through his body undermined his sense of propriety.

"Tyler Hamilton, you are drunk." She pulled the wrap around her, but it only draped itself more alluringly around her figure.

"Your father and I have celebrated this evening, that's correct, but I'd hardly call it what you are implying."

"What I am implying, Mr. Hamilton, is that you ought not to be lurking around the house at this hour. I think you should leave now."

He had no intention of leaving. "Miss Maxwell, I do believe we are in the same room at the same hour. Ought you not to be in bed, as well?"

She grasped the book rigidly and her voice rose slightly as she said precisely, slowly, "I live here."

Tyler became grandiose. "Ah, indeed, Miss Maxwell, you do. This is your home, your palace, and you play your role with consummate skill. You are a credit to every image of the Southern gentlewoman." He pointed at her with a slightly wavering finger. "I may have been the stunt, but you were the center of attention." He rose carefully from the chair. "Damn it, you're better at this than I am. Surprised? I noticed. I watched you. But now that the party is over, now that the guests are gone or to bed, where is that legendary Texas hospitality to one's houseguest?"

Marlena's temper ignited. Even in the darkened room, Tyler could see the green in her eyes. "You *are* a stunt, Mr. Hamilton. You may be a very clever stunt, but you're still no more than a ploy. I'm glad you realize it, because when November comes it will be all you have left for your résumé." She made straight for the door.

Tyler sprang from his chair and beat her to the door,

grabbing it from behind her with both arms. It brought him right up to her back, to where he could smell the scent of roses still clinging to her hair. She froze. He could hear her gulp in a breath. She took a step closer toward the door, and he followed her. He slowly closed the door from behind her.

With another gasp, Marlena turned and flattened herself against the door. It brought them face-to-face and recklessly close. The book dropped from her hand and she stood there, breathing. The gaze of her wide, green eyes held such a mesmerizing intensity it was impossible to look away.

They were closer than when they'd danced. Only inches were between them. Tyler ran his eyes over her face and neck, dizzy from her nearness and breathing hard from the burst of energy. She would be so pleasing to touch. In those seconds, he imagined he could pick her up effortlessly with one arm. How light her body would feel draped against his shoulder. How her hair would spill silkily down his chest. How her cheek would fit into the curve of his neck. He could just reach out and . . . his muscles strained against the yearning. His jaw clenched. He could not tear his gaze away. It was there, that lightning between them, no matter how hard they tried to mask it. He could not, would not restore the distance between them. Within six inches he could press her up against the door and bury his face in that creamy neck and kohl hair. It was only inches . . . mere inches. . . .

Tyler fought for breath and pressed his eyes shut. Marlena had stopped breathing altogether. *This can't happen. Not now. Don't let it. If you let yourself touch her now you won't be able to control this.*

Tyler tightened his breathing and said slowly, distinctly, "Don't . . . slam . . . another . . . door."

And then, against his better judgment, he added, "Marlena."

It was worse than touching her. He felt rather than saw her hands rise toward his shoulders and then fall away again. He remembered what her touch had felt like on the dance floor. *Don't let this happen. Stop. Now.* Her breaths were fast and shallow.

Tyler forced himself to cross the room. He planted his hands across the tall window and let his head fall down. He heard nothing for a moment, then closed his eyes as he heard Marlena fumble clumsily with the doorknob and throw the door open. Only when he heard her footsteps race up the stairs did he allow himself to exhale.

In the chalky dawn of four o'clock, a heavy brown package thumped into the dust at the back entrance of the Austin Mercantile. It was late; the paper usually arrived near three o'clock. An hour later, the clerk spilled coffee on the parcel as he ripped open the covering to reveal the *Austin City News* Sunday edition. Behind the wet stain, roaring out from inside the brown casing, came the headline: MAXWELL TURNS YANKEE. "Hey, Mike, send Matt over to the *City News* and let them know we'll probably need an extra run. Looks like this morning's paper's gonna be a big seller," called the clerk as he smeared away the coffee. He shook open the paper and took another long drink, humming inside his cup as he scanned the incendiary article. This wasn't a complimentary piece. Just the kind of thing that sold quickly. He'd better see about getting that extra run here before the store opened at eight.

The sun was just coming in through the front windows of the *Austin City News* office when Arthur Stock kicked his boots up on his massive oak desk to look over the morning edition. He rubbed his face with fatigue, having worked through the night to get the paper out with the front page he now surveyed. This was the opportunity he'd been waiting for, and he wasn't about to let a single issue get sold without the story. Returning from Maxwell's barbecue, he'd had the driver drop Mrs. Stock off at home and take him straight to the office. There had been only two or three times he'd stopped the presses to rerun the first page, but this one was worth the extra effort.

The managing editor, looking jaded, knocked on the door with a pile of papers. "Mr. Stock, here's the pay schedule for the extra run. I hope you got what you wanted. It's going to cost you a pretty penny."

"Damn it, Jacobs, don't you think I know that? You're a good businessman, but you make a lousy journalist. News, Jacobs, this," he said, holding up the front page and slapping the headline with his hand, "is news. We'll have covered our expenses by ten o'clock. Make sure the next shift has extra men—I reckon we'll do a second run before nine and maybe even a third. What is the *Star Journal* running this morning?"

"They're coming out late this morning too, sir. I'd venture that means they're covering the Maxwell appointment as well. I'll have the first edition brought to your office as soon as it hits. Anything else, Mr. Stock?"

"No, Jacobs, go home and wash up. Or get some coffee. But do something so you don't look like that at nine o'clock, understand?" Jacobs nodded and left the papers on the desk.

Arthur Stock scanned the list of expenditures and added his flamboyant signature to the bottom of the page. This was getting to be an expensive business. What was the world coming to when it cost him four hundred dollars to get a late-breaking story out? Well, it was worth it.

He'd put up with Maxwell's idealistic unity-happy politics long enough. He'd been pleasant and cordial all through the campaign, knowing that Maxwell had a decent chance of retaining his seat. These days it didn't pay to make enemies in the Senate—they were mucking around in too many economic and trade issues that could cause trouble for an enterprising businessman like himself. But Maxwell's sideshow last night had been the last straw. Maxwell had made his Yankee an issue, not him. Maxwell was the one who had made a public spectacle of his new Northern associate. This story was certainly juicy enough to risk the ramifications. He had enough readers who still didn't care much for the North. There were plenty of well-qualified, good Texas boys who could have filled the job. There were plenty of well-qualified, good Texas boys who had never lived to get the chance. He tossed the paper down onto his desk and went for more coffee, stretching as he disappeared through the door frame. The paper nearly knocked down a small silver frame containing the published obituary of Captain Arthur Stock, Jr., "fallen in battle, November 2, 1864."

By nine o'clock four papers had been delivered to the doorstep of the Double X ranch house. The *Star Journal* had covered the story evenly, simply stating facts, and had left the matter completely out of the editorial pages. Two other small local papers covered the party in the social pages, one simply giving Hamilton's biographical information without comment and the other leaving it out altogether.

The *Austin City News*, however, left no one in doubt of its position on the subject. It was scathing. Stock had done a brilliant piece of negative journalism, staying safely within a condemnation not of Hamilton personally, but of Maxwell's making such an issue of the appointment. The subtextual position against a Yankee running Maxwell's campaign, however, came through loud and clear between the lines. Stock's editorial page drove the point home even further.

Diana and Andrea were, as usual, the first downstairs to breakfast. Jason and Claudia Maxwell came down together, speaking softly. When the senator saw the stack of newspapers, he simply took a cup of coffee from the sideboard and disappeared with them into his study. Hewitt, the family butler, had discreetly hidden the *Austin City News* on the bottom of the pile.

Halfway through breakfast Marlena came down, looking bright but quiet. She scanned the dining room for the morning papers until her mother said, "Your father has them in his study, dear. I'm sure he'll share them with you when he's ready. You look a bit tired, Lena. Did something keep you up last night?"

Marlena jumped a bit but hoped she hid it well. "Hmm? Oh, well . . . yes, you know me at Daddy's parties. I had too much coffee and it kept me up." She wanted to pretend last night never happened. Maybe Tyler wouldn't remember after all that brandy. Maybe she had dreamed it all. But she knew better than that. "I'm fine, really, Mother. It was a lovely barbecue; even the crusty old Dobsons seemed to enjoy themselves." She poured herself a cup of coffee, hoping Cook had made it strong. She would have preferred a newspaper to hide behind for whenever Hamilton showed up, but she hid in her coffee cup instead.

In a few minutes Tyler Hamilton did enter the room, looking like he'd had the best night's sleep of his life. The glasses were back on his energetic face and he was dressed only slightly more casually than he had been at the office.

"Good morning, Mr. Hamilton." Claudia Maxwell was cordial but cool. Thankfully, the place she motioned for him to sit at was next to Diana, far away from Marlena. Diana warmed up to him immediately, clearly still taken with him from last night's attention.

"Do you like eggs Benedict, Mr. Hamilton?" she said, sounding as adult as possible. "It's one of Cook's specialties."

"It's one of my favorites, Miss Maxwell. The senator is not exaggerating when he brags about your mother's reputation as a hostess."

Marlena sank farther inside her coffee cup. *Good Lord, doesn't he ever stop?* She was grateful when he turned his full attention to his breakfast plate. He devoured the eggs Benedict enthusiastically and accepted seconds. She believed he would have eaten thirds if her father had not returned from the study with a pile of papers and a serious look on his face.

"Well, sir, what are the reviews?" asked Tyler brightly, reaching for more toast. Her mother placed her napkin curtly on the table, for she was never pleased to have business discussed at breakfast. Marlena stopped stirring her coffee. Andrea fidgeted with her butter knife. Tyler quickly picked up on the uneasiness and turned to his hostess. "Forgive me, Mrs. Maxwell. Would you prefer the senator and I talk about this elsewhere?"

"Well, I—" she started.

"Normally, Mrs. Maxwell prefers that I not discuss politics at the table, Mr. Hamilton," the senator broke in, "but I believe today should be an exception, Claudia." Marlena could see that the look on her father's face troubled her mother as much as it troubled her. It wasn't a look either of them saw often. One by one he tossed the papers, folded open to the coverage of the barbecue, onto the table. Marlena beat Tyler to the *Star Journal,* while he took the two local papers, offering one to her mother. She held up her hand in silent refusal, her eyes fixed on the copy of the *Austin City News* her husband still held in his hand. The senator was holding out.

"What does it say, Jason?" she asked tightly.

"Andrea, Diana, why don't you go sit outside on the porch," he said calmly, his eyes fixed on his wife.

Diana whined at being excluded. "Oh, please, Daddy, I'm old enough to hear this. Make Andrea go."

"Outside please, girls. Now." They filed out, defeated. Marlena watched her father slowly place the newspaper on the table. Even from the far end, Marlena knew her mother could read the headline. Claudia Maxwell put her elbow on the arm of her chair, turned her head to the side, and rested her chin on her clenched fist. She folded up like a book, into a sharp, tight posture.

Tyler stopped eating. Marlena plunked down her spoon and grabbed the paper, standing up. She read the article and editorial aloud, circling the breakfast table as she read. She paused every now and then before a particularly nasty phrase, watching her mother draw up tighter and tighter until Marlena thought she would cave in on herself. When Marlena finished she returned the paper to the table. Tyler picked it up as if to personally confirm the harsh words.

Marlena wanted to scream out, "I told you so!" but the concerned look on her father's face silenced her. This was not his plan at all. Marlena knew he had expected a good deal of controversy and some criticism—as a matter of fact, he was counting on some shocking front-page headlines—but not on the level of Stock's vindictive editorial. Nothing in Stock's actions at the party last night had given any indication of this. She couldn't remember the last time she'd seen her father so surprised.

Senator Jason Maxwell never miscalculated. Even Hamilton seemed to have been wounded through a chink in his armor. "This is malicious," said Marlena. "The edition is probably selling quickly all over town with a headline like that." She looked right at Hamilton. "It's going to do a lot of damage. Daddy, what are you going to do?"

"We're going to hold a press conference, that's what we're going to do."

"Sir?" Hamilton looked justifiably taken aback.

"We're going to hold a press conference, and invite every reporter for a hundred miles. If I'm going to have to convince Art Stock of my position, then I might as well do it in front of all of Texas. If they're going to read his thoughts, I'm going to make damn sure they're going to read mine, as well. He can't deny me rebuttal—not in a campaign year. He's got to print something of my response, and I'm banking the other papers will print more. This is not exactly the coverage I had in mind, but I still believe it can serve our purpose."

Mrs. Maxwell stood up. She glared at her husband for a long moment through eyes that were brimming with tears, yet frighteningly cold. Her tiny hands were clenched into delicate, white-knuckled fists. Without saying a word, she turned and left the room.

"Daddy, I think . . ." began Marlena, looking worriedly at her mother's exit.

"Just leave her alone for today." He planted both massive hands on the table. "Now, ladies and gentlemen, we have work to do. Lena, please have Hewitt ready a driver, then take Deborah and go bring back the office press files. Make sure you go in through the house—I want to keep the office locked up until Monday. Hamilton, in my study."

Tyler scooped up the papers and grabbed another cup of coffee before heading to the study. It took a moment before Marlena realized she'd been left out, dispatched with Deborah to "fetch" files while those two planned a solution to the strategic challenge of a lifetime. She stood there livid, hand on her hip, foot tapping in anger, biting furiously into a piece of toast.

"Hewitt!" she finally called in a sharp voice. He appeared at the kitchen door.

"Yes, Miss Marlena."

"Get me a carriage, a driver, and Deborah. We've got to go *'fetch'* the office files."

⊰ Chapter Four ⊱

Deborah was waiting in the parlor when Marlena burst in, a coffee cup in one hand and a teacup in the other. "Deb, things are in a mess—oh, well, I guess I don't have to tell you." Marlena extended the teacup.

"It's rather dreadful press. I can't believe anyone would write such a thing about your father."

"I know. Mother is furious. Daddy and the Yankee"—she cocked her head toward the study—"are locked in there, trying to plan what to do next." Marlena drained her coffee cup and plunked it down. "We've been dispatched to bring the press files out from the office. The driver's waiting outside."

"All I'll need is a bit of breakfast—" Before she could finish, Hewitt magically appeared at the parlor doors with a basket. Deborah smirked. Marlena snatched the basket, blew a kiss at Hewitt, and whooshed for the door.

They sat in silence for a few minutes as the carriage pulled out of the long ranch drive.

"I didn't see an argument last night," Deborah remarked, adjusting her glasses. "Did Stock have words with Mr. Hamilton or the senator at some point?"

"That's just it, Deb. There was nothing. Stock has hardly been one to keep his views to himself, especially where Daddy's concerned. Both Hamilton and I spoke with him, and I know Daddy did too, for that matter. No one expected this. Not even Daddy. I know he was

49

planning for press coverage, but I don't think anyone foresaw this."

"And your mother?"

"Good Lord, Deb, it was worse than an argument. She didn't say anything. She just stood up and walked out of the dining room after we saw the papers. I'd have rather she railed at Daddy. It was awful. Eerie. No one's seen her since then."

"Hamilton?"

"That's the worst of it. He and Daddy are locked up in the study, plotting and planning. Where I"—she corrected herself—"where *we* should be. He's in there with Daddy, calling a press conference." Marlena's growing agitation at being out of the thick of things was obvious.

"A what?"

"You heard me; we are holding a press conference Tuesday morning for every paper within shouting distance. Batten down the hatches, Deb, my dear; it's going to be a long day." Marlena smiled for the first time and unwrapped a muffin and handed it to Deborah.

"Why a press conference?" Deborah bit thoughtfully into the muffin.

"It gives Daddy the chance to tell his side. I didn't like the idea much at first, but I have to admit it is growing on me."

"I'm sure it isn't what the *Austin City News* is expecting."

"Certainly. What I am still unclear on is where our dear Mr. Hamilton fits into all of this."

"Mmm," said Deborah, taking another bite of muffin. "That is something to consider. Your father is still committed to his appointment?"

"Even more so. I'd wager Daddy feels that now he has an even stronger point to make. It's as if Stock's reaction fortified Daddy's argument. This isn't even about Tyler Hamilton anymore."

"So it would seem. Tell me, Lena, how do *you* think he fared at the barbecue?"

"Hamilton? Oh, really, Deborah, you were right there. You saw how unbelievable he was. All pomp and charm and poppycock. There wasn't a clear head at our table by the time he had finished. Diana and Andrea were practically swooning. It was all I could do to get through dinner."

"What I saw was you dancing with him after dinner. For three whole waltzes."

Marlena's glare spoke loudly that she wasn't eager to talk about that part of the evening.

"Daddy made me. It couldn't be helped. I could have strangled him for making me. He gave me no choice."

"I see." Deborah finished her muffin without saying another word.

"Deborah, Daddy gave one of his ultimatums. You know how he gets. Everyone was watching."

"And . . ."

"And he was cocky and callous and God knows what else."

Deborah planted her chin in one hand. "What else was he, Lena?"

"Nothing. Absolutely nothing. There's nothing more to say. I danced with him and he was a rogue. Swashbuckling. Self-possessed. I would have stomped on his feet if I'd thought of it."

"Of course." Deborah wasn't buying any of it. She'd seen the two of them. Marlena was so busy convincing herself of what didn't happen, that what did happen was all too obvious. This certainly was going to be an interesting day.

It was nearly lunchtime when they returned to the ranch house with the files. The men were still holed up in the study. Marlena and Deborah stopped off in the

kitchen, only to learn that Claudia had yet to emerge
from the bedroom, where she had hidden herself since
breakfast. Marlena doubted they would see her until
supper, at this rate. Grabbing a cup of mercifully strong
coffee, she and Deborah went to the study.

The massive white doors rolled open to reveal what
looked more like a war council than an orderly study.
Books had been pulled from the shelves and lay open,
strewn about the room. Stacks of papers and collections
of scribbled scraps were everywhere. A large board had
been propped up between two of the leather chairs. On
it were tacked clippings of Stock's article and editorial.
They had literally cut up his argument and begun to
fashion attacks and counterpoints piece by piece. A battlefield of lines, circles, and arrows connected sections
of Stock's words with handwritten outlines of her father's position. He was sitting at his desk, behind an
ashtray bearing the remains of at least three cigars, with
a fourth burning in hand. His jacket was off and his
shirt collar was unbuttoned.

Hamilton was straddling the arm of another leather
chair, his own jacket off, shirtsleeves rolled up, and
a stack of papers in his hand. He was scribbling
furiously with a pencil while another stuck out from behind his ear. His eyes gleamed as he leapt from the chair
to tack another scrap of paper to the board. His enthusiasm for the topic at hand had temporarily won over
his polished demeanor, revealing a devilish, almost
reckless bearing. He'd barely even noticed their entrance.

"Ladies!" bellowed her father. "Our troops are now
fully assembled." The morning's sober countenance had
faded, now replaced by the authoritative, conquering
leadership they had all grown to admire. The unsinkable Senator Jason Maxwell was back, and ready to
take on all who challenged him. Marlena smiled at her

father. Tyler whirled around and called out a buoyant greeting of his own. A mixture of relief, hope, and energy held everyone for a moment.

"Well, now I can finally convince myself this is an election," pronounced Deborah, surveying the scene with her hands on her hips.

"Pardon me?" replied the senator, offering her a puzzled look from behind a long puff on the cigar.

"Senator, in all the years I've worked for you, the campaign never really feels under way until the board goes up and you start plotting like a general. I am certainly glad to see it up today, sir."

Maxwell laughed heartily and got up from his chair and came around the desk to take Deborah by the shoulders. As the daughter of one of his most valued employees, he had taken her in when her father had died. With her mother gone, Deborah had practically been reared in the campaign office, playing alongside Marlena. Their bond really did extend beyond employer and employee. "My goodness, Deborah, I believe you are correct. This one does feel like a war, doesn't it? I reckon this may be the worst one yet, my dear, but don't worry. Hamilton and I are on the battlefield and our guns are drawn. What we need are reinforcements."

"Take heart, General," declared Marlena, coming to her father's side with a wide smile. "The cavalry is here." She pecked him encouragingly on the cheek and walked over to the board to inspect the outlines. "What are our orders, sir?" she asked over her shoulder, poking through the layers of notes and quotes tacked up. She tried to keep her gaze from Hamilton, for he looked far too appealing in his haphazard state.

"You and Deborah pull together the press list while Hamilton and I finish up our strategy. We'll break for lunch in an hour or so."

Marlena stood still, with her hand still holding one of the papers. It was not the answer she was expecting. She wanted to be in the thick of things, not arranging the invitation list. Her face tightened up as her anger at being excluded began to rise. "Surely, Daddy, you'll want us all working on the—"

He cut her off. "Lena, honey, we've got the debate under control. Hamilton's living up to his pedigree and we have a brilliant strategy."

"But Daddy—"

"The best strategy in the world will do me no good, darlin', if there's no one out there to hear it. I need you assembling that list and persuading every reporter in shouting distance to be in my office Tuesday morning. Now, you two get working. I want those telegrams sent the minute the wire office opens tomorrow morning."

Marlena had been usurped again. Banished to the parlor to play with filing cards. Steaming, she shoved a box of cards at Deborah and turned on her heels. Deborah followed after Marlena, pulling the doors closed in silent retreat.

Once in the parlor, Marlena grabbed the box from Deborah and unceremoniously dumped it onto the floor. She sat down in the middle of the pile and began flying through the cards, flinging barbs at the two men under her breath and sorting cards into stacks. The inflection of her accusations pitched a bit higher with each card she flung down. She was grateful Deborah kept silent and simply took notes. By the time they broke for lunch, the names of over fifty reporters had been sorted and prioritized, and individualized telegraphs had been drafted for each one. Marlena felt vindicated when even Hamilton raised an eyebrow at her speed.

True to expectations, her mother did not appear for the meal. The conversation fell silent halfway through luncheon as they heard the kitchen girl taking a tray up the creaking stairs. Marlena watched her father pause for a second, then sigh as he dug his fork back into what was left of his roasted chicken. Diana and Andrea looked at each other in dismay.

Finally, Diana spoke up to break the silence. "The weather's just spectacular for riding, Daddy. Andrea jumped the west fence twice today—she is getting to be quite the horsewoman." Her voice suddenly took on a very adult tone. "Do you ride, Mr. Hamilton?"

"I do, Miss Maxwell. The style in Boston is a bit different, however. I'm afraid you might find our English tack a bit stuffy. But I assure you, the thrill of jumping a good fence is universal." Hamilton seemed grateful for the change of topic.

"You must ride with us this afternoon. I would be fascinated to see English tack," said Diana in a demure invitation.

"Now, Diana," interjected Marlena, exploiting her role as hostess in her mother's absence, "if Mr. Hamilton is not accustomed to Western tack, it would hardly be proper to expect him to jump today." She directed the comment not at Diana, but at Hamilton, in a not-so-thinly veiled challenge. *Let's see how our gentleman fares on a spirited mustang,* she thought.

Her father denied her the chance. "I'm sure it's a fine day for riding, girls, but Mr. Hamilton and I have work to do. You'll have to amuse yourselves for the afternoon, I'm afraid. Another day, perhaps."

Thwarted, Marlena rang for coffee and for the table to be cleared. The senator rubbed his hands together as his cup was poured, saying, "Hamilton, I believe we've put together a fine strategy. You've got a good head on your shoulders, but now it's time to see if you think as well on your feet."

"What do you mean, Senator?"

"I mean that you've built a fine argument, but you're

going to have to defend it to the press. I'll be making my statement and taking questions, of course, but I don't think you're going to come away from this on Tuesday without having to take your own stand. Hamilton, you're ready for the toughest test I know."

"Thank you, Senator. I appreciate the vote of confidence," said Tyler a bit smugly.

"My confidence isn't won entirely yet, son. I said you were *ready to take* the toughest test I know. I believe you're ready to face my daughter."

Marlena stopped midsip. Deborah smiled quietly as if she'd seen it coming a mile away. Tyler looked baffled. The senator continued, "Lena can poke holes through the soundest of arguments. She's got a reporter's mind."

Marlena smiled. It was her turn to be smug.

"Debating with her is the best way I know to sharpen a speech. If you can defend yourself with her, you'll be able to stand up to anyone on Tuesday."

Marlena's smile turned catlike. "Why, thank you, Daddy," she said, licking her chops. "How kind of you to say so. I'd be delighted to be of assistance."

"An excellent idea, Senator. There's not a statesman in the world who can't benefit from a little rehearsal," said Tyler, smiling at Marlena with an annoying confidence. She recoiled at the idea of Hamilton equating himself to a statesman. It made her eager for the debate.

"Well, then," said her father, darting his eyes between them with the look of someone who'd just fired the gun at a horse race, "we've a press conference to stage."

Tyler watched Marlena fold her arms across her chest as she paced behind the leather chairs in the back of the study. She fired the first question without even looking at him as he stood behind a makeshift podium on the senator's desk.

"Mr. Hamilton, why are you here in Texas?"

She certainly lost no time getting to the heart of the matter.

Tyler's grip tightened on the podium. He'd faced reporters before, and he wasn't even that apprehensive about the upcoming press conference. He found the prospect of squaring off against Marlena Maxwell, however, far more unsettling. Tyler doubted any of the press he would face on Tuesday would have such distracting green eyes.

There was another part of him that found the prospect of open debate with her exhilarating. For Tyler, debate was intoxicating. It was like a courtship of viewpoints; an intricate dance of forward and backward, testing and responding. A vigorous debate, to Tyler, was as passionate as the most sensuous kiss.

But now, good Lord, he was about to debate a woman—never mind the most impossible, exciting woman he'd ever met. His adrenaline surged and he found himself balanced on the balls of his feet—alert, alive, and ready. Very ready. And very determined. No woman, no matter who her father was, no matter how beautiful, no matter how distracting, was going to best Tyler Hamilton III at the podium.

"Why does anyone come to Texas, sir?" he returned, placing a slight emphasis on the "sir" to undercut Marlena's confidence by reminding her that she was only a stand-in. "I have come because my future is here. I believe not only my future, but *the* future is here in this state. I believe in what Jason Maxwell stands for, and if I'm to be cast as the living analogy for his views, then I will serve in that role with honor."

"Speaking of honor, Mr. Hamilton"—Marlena faced him to stare directly into his eyes; Hamilton noticed that a thin wisp of hair had strayed from its twist to hang lazily around her neck—"what would you say to all the mothers and wives and babies of honorable

Texas soldiers who lost their lives at Yankee hands and won't have the chance to vote for your candidate?" Even the senator raised a gray eyebrow.

Oh, no, you don't. You won't get away with that tactic with me, thought Tyler as he turned on the charm. "The same thing any decent human being would say. That I am sincerely sorry for their loss. That war is ugly and men die. I'm not foolish enough to believe that I can say anything to relieve such pain or grief. But all of those lives will have been lost in vain if this country cannot find a way to heal itself. To bring about the better future we all want. Change is painful. It's awkward and difficult. But men like Jason Maxwell know that change is our best chance at a future."

His eyes never left Marlena's for the entire answer, locking on her as he stood his ground. He wanted to stare her down, to force her to look away from the power of his gaze, but she refused to give in. She held his gaze just as intently. He tried to ignore the mild, confounding knot emerging in his stomach.

Marlena's fingers drummed against the chair back she was holding. Long, delicate fingers. Pale and curved. She fired her next question. "Exactly how long, Mr. Hamilton, have you been engaged in professional politics?" Since she wasn't getting anywhere with ideals, it seemed her next target would be his credentials.

"Does the length of your career, sir, indicate the quality of your reporting?" shot back Tyler, feeling as though he'd effectively sidestepped the issue.

"No, son, that won't do," jumped in Maxwell fiercely, standing up and raising a hand at Tyler. "You can be eloquent and clever, but the minute you start talking smart, we're cooked."

"But that's just—"

Maxwell stopped him short. "I know you think the

answer will harm you, but stand up and answer the question or you'll start looking sneaky." The senator sat down again. "Take your lumps, son. Don't run around them." Marlena smiled and lightly tapped her fingertips together. She was formulating the next attack. Tyler took a breath, reined in his frustration at having been rebuked, and answered directly.

"This will be my first professional post, sir. And I can think of no finer." He looked to the senator for confirmation as he added, "I consider the length of my career irrelevant." Maxwell nodded in approval.

Marlena wouldn't budge from the tender topic. She launched five more questions directed at his qualifications. Tyler answered every one, growing more direct and unapologetic with each answer. She was trying to wear him down, but instead the assault was giving him strength. Tyler watched her think as she prepared to change tactics again. Her jaw worked and the lines of her throat shifted. He could see her pulse in its hollow. She was proving a wonderfully worthy adversary. She enjoyed her control of the dialogue. She was leading this dance, not Tyler, and clearly delighted at having the upper hand. They were testing each other with equal force, building up an energy between them that both could feel. She relished meeting her match. When she looked up at him again with fiery purpose in her eyes, he swallowed.

"You spoke of war's ravages, Mr. Hamilton. Tell me, did your family lose anyone in the war?" The sweet edge in her voice let him know she was setting him up because she already knew the answer.

"I thank God that no one in my immediate family was lost, but there were—"

That was all she needed. "Then how do you claim to understand the devastating losses suffered by fathers and wives and—"

"I don't."

Tyler had shot back to stop her in midsentence, steeling his eyes and voice. "I couldn't claim to know their grief. But loss, gentlemen, is not a prerequisite for hope. If we cannot as a nation look up from our grief and move forward, then we *are* doomed." Tyler took off his glasses and locked his eyes on Marlena's.

The room became only two people, as if Deborah and the senator had vanished. "Is there no one amongst this press with vision enough to ask me about policies and ideas? Ask me about commerce and education. Ask me about jobs and the railroad. Must this election be about résumés and birthplaces? I want to talk about Texas' future!"

Marlena seemed to be losing her composure, her chest heaving, but then she went on the offensive again. He wasn't going to win her over with idealistic talk. She was relentless in her questioning, skillfully picking apart Tyler's proposals. Tyler was her match in his defense, occasionally bringing her to a defensive stance herself. There was no question it would have to be declared a draw, but each side took such obvious pleasure in the competition that neither one would back down to end the debate.

Tyler found the tension and energy between them growing almost uncontrollable. Had there been no audience, it felt as if they would have overturned the podium and chairs between them. But the heat in Tyler's blood told him it would not be blows they'd come to. The debate had roused the same passion in her. He knew it. By the time the senator finally threw his hands up and called a halt, Marlena's face was flushed and her breath was coming hard. He hoped the senator had sensed only the passion of the argument and no other. Sweet Jesus, this was getting complicated.

He was exceedingly grateful when after a few hollow

formalities and small talk, Marlena made some excuse and left the room. Deborah followed quickly behind her, leaving him thankfully alone with the senator to wrap things up for the afternoon. He didn't care to hear the senator analyze his performance. He was in no mood to think anymore. In fact, he'd have preferred to strip to his shirtsleeves and run laps around the stables until the lightning in his body calmed down. It seemed hours until, a mere half an hour later, the senator declared work done for the day and released him to spend the rest of the afternoon as he wished. Tyler was upstairs, changed, and headed for the stables with his English saddle in his hand before another quarter of an hour had passed.

⊰ Chapter Five ⊱

Deborah found Marlena at the piano, banging ferociously through a march. She sat down next to her on the bench, waiting until the overloud rendition finally stopped. "I don't think I've heard that one played quite so . . . enthusiastically, Lena."

Marlena said nothing, but charged into another piece with the same vigor.

"From the sound of it, it might take four or five of those before you play it out of your system." Marlena stopped and shot Deborah an annoyed look, then continued on a bit louder, as if hoping to drown out her friend's editorializing.

"Or perhaps I should say, before you play *him* out of your system." Marlena stopped again, then took up the next stanza on a slightly softer note, feigning disinterest rather unsuccessfully.

"I've had arguments with Daddy before. We'll get over it just as soon as this campaign season is finished," she said over the music.

"It's not your father, Lena. Remember who you are talking to. I was in that room this afternoon and these spectacles aren't *that* thick." Marlena's hands landed a little heavier on the keys.

"Whatever do you mean? Daddy asked me to debate Hamilton and I gave him a run for his money. That was all. You're reading too much into this, Deborah."

"Am I?"

"Of course. Whatever you're thinking is just ridiculous." Marlena's tempo sped up.

"And just what am I thinking, Lena?"

"Good heavens, Deb, how should I know? There's nothing. You saw two people having a passiona—spirited debate. You saw me poking every hole I could into that Yankee's politics. You saw me doing what any decent reporter would do with that character and his green credentials. You saw a press conference rehearsal. You saw nothing."

"I saw two people who couldn't take their eyes off each other for all the longhorns in Texas."

Lena missed a note.

"You saw nothing of the kind. What a ridiculous notion."

"Good Lord, Lena, Senator Maxwell could have lit his cigar on the air between you and Tyler Hamilton. He strikes your fancy, doesn't he? And you can't stand the idea. Wouldn't that just be delicious if the man who finally catches Marlena Winbourne Maxwell hails from Boston?"

"Deborah!" Marlena made another mistake and started fresh on a different piece. "That is the most appalling idea. Don't even think of repeating that to anyone. The very thought."

"He does interest you, doesn't he?"

"Go away. I've heard enough of this."

"And it's driving you crazy, isn't it?"

Marlena finally stopped playing. "Deborah, will you please—" A slamming door at the top of the stairs stopped her short. Through the parlor doorway they could see the senator storming across the landing.

"For God's sake, Claudia, how could I possibly have known? *Now* you tell me, and expect everything to halt?"

Deborah and Marlena saw the master bedroom door open again, and Mrs. Maxwell's voice came harshly: "If you cared about my feelings, Jason, you'd find a way to get him out of here. How can you do this to me?"

Maxwell turned instantly and barreled back to the bedroom. "Sweet Jesus, calm yourself! Do you want the whole house to hear you? He's done nothing to deserve this. It's too late to stop now, Claudia."

"Suddenly it's too late for the great Jason Maxwell to do something!" came Mrs. Maxwell's shrill voice, tinged with tears. "Well, I never! I won't stand for it."

Maxwell started talking over her again and the door shut to muffle their angry voices inside.

Marlena stood up, nearly knocking Deborah off the bench as she pushed it back and slammed the cover down over the keys. "This is going too far!" She cursed. "I don't see the point in any of this. None at all!" She flew out of the room, sending sheet music flurrying across the parlor in her wake.

Marlena headed for the kitchen again, shutting her ears to the raised voices upstairs. But even inside the kitchen door, her parents' angry exchanges could be heard. Cook stood over a pile of vegetables, looking up at the ceiling and shaking her head. Marlena hurried over to the cupboard to find a cup and saucer, but the horrible noises upstairs refused to cease. She banged the cupboard shut and slammed the kitchen door as she headed out into the back garden. Arms crossed, head down, skirts flowing wildly around enormous strides, she barreled across the garden toward the open fields.

The hot afternoon sun burned her cheeks and stung her eyes as she came out of the garden into the western fields. The cattle had all gone to the eastern pastures to find cooler grazing, and the field lay empty before her. Thick grass, singed from the long, hot summer, crunched under her feet. The air smelled dry and dusty.

Wiping her wet cheeks with the back of her hand, she cut diagonally across the field to a fence just below the base of a small hill and a grove of trees.

With the thoughtlessness of someone who'd done it a thousand times, she ducked under the upper fence slat. The lace of her skirts caught on the wood, and she nearly growled as she pulled impatiently at the cloth and snapped it free. She marched up the small hill and reached the shade of a thick grove. Once there, she paced from tree to tree, having reached her destination with far too much energy left to sit down and think. Marlena snapped a twig off a nearby branch and began slapping it into her hand, as if preparing to switch something or someone. She kept up her laps between the trees, swatting saplings and shrubs in a rhythm that punctuated her own inner shouts.

Why was it so important for Hamilton to be here? Was it worth alienating her mother? Why him? Why was he so damned attractive? Why couldn't all that fire have landed in a Texan man? Why did such compelling words have to come with a Boston accent? And the worst of all, why did Deborah have to notice what he did to her? She was as annoyed with herself for the way she felt during the debate—during the entire weekend, for that matter—as she was with him. If most of Austin's eligible young bachelors bored her, why had this insufferable dandy piqued her interest? Why didn't her stomach grow knots when one of those complimentary, *charming young men with such excellent futures* called on her?

Her mind replayed the encounter in the study. And those sizzling moments from the debate when they looked nowhere but at each other. She swept the thoughts from her mind, reminding herself instead of her parents' angry voices and the humiliation of being kept out of the study. Eventually she sat down, snap-

ping the twig into smaller and smaller pieces as she
looked back toward the house.

Tyler's horse, an amiable cream-colored mount,
hadn't seemed to mind the strange saddle after a few
minutes. The bridle and other tack were only slightly
different from the English tack Tyler knew well. The
saddles were what truly separated the styles. And the
clothes. For the sake of speed, Tyler had left the riding
jacket and hat back at the ranch house, opting instead
for his jodhpurs and a riding shirt and cravat.

He soon learned why English tack seemed so out of
place in Texas. Within twenty minutes, the harsh afternoon sun reminded him why most Texans wore such
big hats. The dust of the pasture gathered on his sweating neck under the shirt's high collar, making it uncomfortable, and the strong wind of the open land kept
flapping the cravat in his face. The riding jacket would
have held it in place; however, the heat made the
thought of a jacket unbearable. English style wasn't just
too stuffy for Texas, it was downright impractical. Tyler
cursed as the cravat flapped up to obscure his vision
again, and he yanked it free from the thick loops that
held it in place. Laughing inwardly at the frilly fabric,
he used it to wipe his beading forehead before stuffing it
in his pocket. He glanced down at his black boots, gri-
macing at the coating of dust that gave the once shiny
leather an old, faded look.

Scanning the horizon in front of him, he noticed how
different the landscape was from New England's gentle
green hills cut with mossy stone walls. Seas of tiny blue
flowers covered acres and acres of the near-flat land
that stretched out before him. Clumps of prickly pear,
with their amusing, unfamiliar look, thrust up between
the grasses. The salt smell was missing from the air, re-

placed with a weathered, smoky scent. Even the birds sounded different. Gone were the coy chirps of robins or chickadees; the air was pierced now and then with only the shrill cries of hawks, and far too many insect noises.

Tyler had raced for the first part of his ride, jumping fences and charging around pastures in an effort to jar the tension from his body. He'd ridden hard and fast in short laps around the ranch's eastern side, keeping the house in clear view, in no mood to explore new trails. This was exercise, plain and simple. Actually, even to call it exercise was a lie. This was distraction. He was channeling the debate's energy into another outlet so that those green eyes would leave his mind. It was working. Almost.

After half an hour or so, the long lapse since his last ride caught up with him and he slowed his pace. The horse snorted, picking its way through the paths around the ranch's east section to turn south toward a small creek. The tough, thick grasses gave way to a greener, softer sort shooting up in clumps along the stream. Groupings of short, bent trees struck gnarly roots into the ground around the water, as if trying to hold the rocky earth together. He followed the stream as it led away from the house, bending slowly toward the low afternoon sun.

Tyler thought about Harvard, about everything familiar and certain. His mind replayed his father's voice as he'd listed the various job offers. He leaned back in the saddle, comparing what he might have had if he'd stayed in Boston with what he was facing now. He loosened the reins and let the horse follow the path at its own pace. If Tyler were in Boston, he'd be sitting at an enormous mahogany desk, listening to the sounds of a city summer lilt through thickly fringed curtains.

On such a Sunday afternoon, he'd probably be smoking a pipe and visiting with Dawson Writhwood, his Harvard roommate. Tyler smiled as he imagined Dawson, who'd more than likely be ogling the carefully coifed, blue-satin ladies they would have joined for brunch at someone's mother's house. The routine was so familiar. His future was so certain.

What would Dawson have thought of someone like Marlena Maxwell? With her beauty and her station in life, it was hard to believe someone hadn't already claimed her, that she'd remained unbetrothed. *Maybe not.* He smirked as he remembered the unbelievable way she spoke to both him and her father without, it seemed, a moment's hesitation or remorse. She'd be torture as a wife. He smiled as he imagined her standing at the bottom of some stairway in the dark hours of the early morning, stamping that foot, arms folded in disgust as her husband came home from a well-deserved night's carousing with his friends. Just remember how she'd chided him for the brandy with Senator Maxwell.

His mind washed back the whole study scene before he could stop the memory. He remembered her eyes and skin as she stood against the door. That intense, slightly surprised look he'd seen creep up again during their debate. God, he hadn't even realized the debate and the moonlit encounter were in the same room until just now. It wove the two experiences together in an overwhelmingly suggestive sensation that made him spur the horse out of its dreamy trot.

When he took in his surroundings, he was at the base of a small knoll, a grassy, greener area, thanks to a grove of trees at its top. He edged the horse up the slope, only to stop and suck in his breath. There was Marlena, standing up and brushing the grass off her skirts. She'd heard someone coming, but hadn't seen him. He was thankful her focus was on the skirt when he saw her. It gave him a split second's advantage to re-gain his composure.

Her guard went up the instant she saw him. But just before it did, he saw that wide-eyed look flash momentarily across her face. When he looked at her, his mind's eye overlaid the dreamy midnight woman and the passionate debater. It was a powerful combination.

Marlena was taken aback by his disheveled appearance. The jodhpurs looked out of place, but somehow with the black boots and the formal riding shirt tugged open at the neck, he looked like a gentleman pirate. Those blasted glasses were gone again, leaving his unnerving expression naked to the world. Those eyes. They kept pulling at her, daring her to meet his gaze. He looked . . . well, the only word that came to mind was "dangerous." She checked her impulse to run away, edging up against a tree instead. She tried to think of all the reasons she disliked him, but it seemed only to make matters worse. She didn't dislike him. Just the opposite.

"Mr. Hamilton." She gave her skirt waistband a tug. "Invading our fields as well as our house?"

"I meant no intrusion, Miss Maxwell." His eyes told her he was lying.

"Well, you have. You've intruded in any number of ways. You have barely been here twenty-four hours, and things are in ruins. Tell me, Mr. Hamilton, do you have any concept of the commotion you've caused?" Marlena was talking strictly about politics and family, but regretted how much personal commotion the tone of her voice revealed.

"In terms of political uproar, why, yes, I'm well aware of the commotion. I expected it. In fact, I'm not foolish enough to think that such commotion isn't part of why I was hired." He cracked a mischievous grin. "What other commotion have I caused, Miss Maxwell?" He nudged the horse toward her a foot or two.

Marlena's back stiffened. In his present state he had a
wild look to him that did unreasonable things to her
pulse. She watched the sinews of his arms, bared by up-
turned sleeves, as he worked the reins. He was making
it hard to think. She flung her arm in the direction of
the house. "My God, man, my parents are shouting at
each other in there. Over you! Don't you care how
much your presence upsets her?" She raised her voice
and glared at Hamilton angrily. "Must you launch your
career at the expense of my family?" Her mother's reaction was hardly his fault, but the wrenching, wounded
cries from the top of the stairs echoed in her ears. She
didn't really understand why her mother was reacting
so violently—some reason she'd only just told her father, it seemed—but it didn't matter. Tyler Hamilton
was stirring up too many things and she wanted him to
stop. She turned away from him, because she needed to.
She was used to being in control.

Marlena shut her eyes tight and swallowed as she
heard him dismount. It was too hot, they'd seen too
much of each other in the debate, and he was about to
come too near. That perplexing mix of anger and attraction kept creeping back no matter how many times
she stifled it. If he came within arm's reach, Marlena
didn't know whether she'd strike him or . . . or . . .
Well, it wasn't safe even to think about that.

"I've no aim to be a walking wound to people—to
your family. But I don't let other people's opinions stop
me. Any more than you do. If you did, you'd be sipping
lemonade on the porch with your embroidery instead of
trouncing my credentials in the study. Rather soundly, I
might add."

He took a step closer. She could hear him breathing.
See his shadow as it crossed her shoe. "North or South,
you're no different from me. Or is that just too difficult
to admit, Miss Maxwell?"

"No different, are we?" She spun around. "It's hard to imagine how we could be any *more* different, Mr. Hamilton. You are so busy being charming and dashing and—and"—she searched for the words—"so *false*."

He stepped toward her again, showing a tinge of anger at her words. She sidestepped him. Anything to keep him at a safe distance while her mind flew faster than her tongue.

"You're never offstage. Everything is a speech. You're so busy spouting political positions that no one really knows why you're here."

The truth of it struck her. She stopped pacing and turned to face him. "Why *are* you here, Mr. Hamilton? Aren't there enough crusades back in Boston? What exactly is it that you want?"

Hamilton grew agitated, but Marlena wasn't letting up. She'd hit a nerve. She'd found her foothold against the power he seemed to have over her. "Why?" She raised her voice. "What do you want here? What do you want?" She stared at him now.

Then something snapped in his eyes. He lunged at her, grabbing her shoulders like a vise. She struck her arms against his chest, blocking him. The move pulled another shirt button loose. His blue eyes bored into her for one long dare of a moment. He pulled her closer, slowly, despite her resistance. Closer, until finally he brought his mouth down so powerfully upon hers that her head fell back. He kissed her hard, almost angrily, assailing her for the unwanted passion she knew she'd roused in him.

Marlena felt as if she were coming unstrung in his hands. The debate, the tension she'd felt for the last twenty-four hours, the desire she'd tried so hard to talk herself out of, all seemed to come unwound in her. Her body melted to his demanding grip, caught inside the blinding pressure of his kiss. Her mind went white like a burst of lightning. His hands stayed locked onto her shoulders, supporting her as his kiss nearly arched her backward.

Every reason not to give in to this powerful sensation left her. Her hands stopped pushing, and lay on his chest. The release of finally touching him was staggering. His kiss became slightly more tender at her small response, his mouth softening. His hands slid off her shoulders to caress her back. The gentleness evoked an even more powerful response in Marlena, and her mouth suddenly, eagerly sought his.

He pulled his head away suddenly, looking out of control. They stood there, struggling for breath, staring at each other in something short of disbelief.

Marlena pulled away, looked at him, and slapped him.

It was a ridiculous response, insincere and hypocritical, given the circumstances, but it was the only thing she could think of to do.

Tyler lurched back in surprise. He rubbed his jaw. "What the devil was that for?"

Marlena herself seemed surprised at the obvious sting she'd caused. "What do you think it was for?" she retorted, for lack of a better answer.

"For kissing you? Good God, woman, you hardly seemed to object a minute ago. Are you going to stand here and pretend you didn't enjoy that? For God's sake, Lena—"

"Don't call me Lena!" she snapped, straightening her hair and pacing again.

Tyler put his hands on his hips. "What should I say?"

"Don't talk about it. Not at all." Marlena was pacing, trying furiously to pull herself back together. "We won't talk about it. It never happened. This never happened. I'm going to go into the house now, and this never happened. Do you understand me? Never."

Tyler leaned back against a tree.

Marlena continued her pacing, grasping to put it all in place. She finally turned to look at Tyler with an oddly analytical stare.

"My God, Mr. Hamilton, how did this happen?"

Tyler laughed at her attempt at logic. Finally, he said plainly, "You asked, Miss Maxwell."

"What on earth do you mean?"

"You asked me what I wanted. I showed you."

Marlena fumed at his flippant remark. "You . . . you . . . you . . ." Unable to find a suitable word, she growled and turned to charge down the hill.

"Yankee?" Tyler called after her in an amused voice.

She hissed and kicked a cactus, sending green pads flying across the grass.

⊰ Chapter Six ⊱

Tuesday morning, everything was ready. Marlena was looking for her father to check in on him, the final preparation. She found him standing quietly at the library windows, staring out at the wet Austin streetscape. He had on what he referred to jokingly as his "press suit," a distinguished gray coat and vest that gave him the look of a man in command.

"It's all ready, Daddy," she said softly as she pulled the library doors shut behind her. The rain streaked the gray light framing her father in the enormous windows.

"I know, sweetheart. I never doubted you and Deborah would have everything in perfect order." He seemed distracted, but extended his arm for her to come and nestle against his shoulder. "I don't think the rain will keep them away today. It'll all work out just fine." He would have convinced anyone but Marlena with the carefully crafted tone of his voice.

"It's not right, Daddy. Mother should be here, not at the ranch."

Her father cut her off. "Let's just not worry about your mother today, Lena. Things will work themselves out. I've done something that hurt your mama deeply. I didn't know it at the time, but it happened. I can't change that now." His gaze drifted back out the windows.

Marlena mustered her courage. "Why is Mama so

angry? She's acting so strange. I mean, I don't care much for Mr. Hamilton either, but—"

Her father cocked an eyebrow in mock surprise, as if this were really news to him.

"Oh, stop, Daddy." Marlena poked his lapel with her pencil. "What I mean is that I . . . well, I don't hate him the way Mama seems to. Something's wrong."

Maxwell turned to face her. "Your mama has plenty of reason to hate Yankees. Yankee soldiers have done awful things to her and her family."

"But you knew that."

"I did. And I reckon I thought she got over most of it. But what I didn't know before Sunday was that the soldier . . . the brute who gave your mother her scar . . . well, he had . . . the damn savage had a Boston accent."

The pained look on his face made Marlena's heart break. "Lord! Then every time . . ."

"Every time Mr. Hamilton opens his mouth in her presence, it's like gettin' cut all over again." He looked as though he felt it was his own hand on the knife.

"Oh, Daddy. What are you going to do?"

He took a deep breath. "We're too far downstream to get out now. So I'll just keep going, and pray with all my might your mama can find the strength to get past it."

His voice lacked the trademark Maxwell self-confidence. Marlena chided herself for bringing up such a painful topic just before the press conference. But as he said, they were too far downstream to turn back now. She leaned her head against his shoulder.

"Look, Lena honey, you're old enough to understand that marriage isn't valentines all the time. Your mama and I have had our share of whopping arguments." He lightened a bit and turned to face her. "Did I ever tell you she threw dishes at me once?"

"Mama? Threw china? At you?" Marlena chuckled.

"I don't think I can picture it. What on earth were you fighting about?"

"That is just the point, Lena. I don't even remember. Doubt your mother could recall, either. I do know, however, that she packed a much more powerful arm than I had ever given her credit for." He laughed genuinely, and it relieved her to see him in good humor. Marlena thought about the look on Tyler's face when she'd slapped him. That same surprise told her Tyler hadn't expected her to pack much of a punch, either. She wrinkled her nose. Maybe her mother and she had more in common than she realized.

"Lena? What's ailing you, child?"

"Hm? Oh, nothing, Father. Too much swimming around in here." She tapped her head with the pencil. It had been a good idea to pretend Sunday afternoon on the knoll had never happened. The details of the return trip to Austin and Monday's flurry of telegrams and letters had made it easy to keep busy and stick to business. Marlena had been grateful when Hamilton refused an offer to stay for dinner Monday night, claiming he would rather go home to his apartment, "to prepare." She wondered if Hamilton knew the reasons for her mother's aversion to him.

Marlena drew her thoughts back to the matters at hand. "Well, they'll all be here, Daddy. *Star Journal*, the *Beacon*, all the major press. And, of course, our good friends at the *Austin City News*. It should be a grand time. You'll be the talk of the town by tomorrow morning."

"That's right, dear. Your ol' daddy's not outfoxed yet. They don't *make* 'em smart enough to outfox me. You just head on back to the office and make sure Arthur Stock has a front-row seat."

"Yes, sir!" Marlena pecked an affectionate kiss on his cheek and headed out the door.

Deborah met her with two more soggy telegrams. "These just came. I think that makes everyone, doesn't it?"

Marlena scanned the wrinkled sheets. "Yes, I think that's the last of the major press to fall in. Now, if the rain doesn't hold any of them up, we should have a full house. How many seats did we end up fitting in the front parlor, anyway?"

Deborah gestured toward the office and they walked together as they talked. "We could only get thirty-eight until Hewitt came up with the idea to move the melodeon. Then we could fit forty-five."

"You moved the melodeon? Well, then I guess it's a good thing Mother isn't here after all. She'd have gone into fits. Did you think to arrange for a tuner to come tomorrow morning to tune it up once we get it back into place?"

"He'll be here at ten-thirty." Deborah and Marlena smiled at their ability to read each other's thoughts. Deborah's face grew serious for a moment and she stopped walking. "It's odd without her here."

"I know. I don't like it either, but Daddy is making the best of it." She wasn't ready to share any of the news about her mother.

"What'd he say?"

"He said I was old enough to understand. He claimed he and Mother have had their share of bad rows."

"Romance and fighting. Now, you wouldn't know anything about that, would you? Not a thing." Deborah raised her eyebrows and peered over the top of her glasses.

Marlena slapped the pile of telegrams down on top of Deborah's clipboard and walked away. "You don't give up, do you? Do you want to have a cup of coffee with me before this circus begins or don't you? We've a press conference to stage, in case you've forgotten why we're here." She trotted off down the hall without looking back.

Deborah clicked her tongue and followed behind, shaking her head.

Forty-five wooden chairs stood in formation in the Maxwells' front parlor. Every member of the house staff, except the few staying at the ranch house to serve Mrs. Maxwell and the girls, was lined up in full regalia behind Deborah and Marlena. The absence of her mother and the special nature of this conference had placed Marlena back in the spotlight, and she relished the position after being put out by Tyler Hamilton for the last few days. Her father had agreed with her suggestion that it was better to keep Hamilton beside him, waiting in the wings, than to have him greeting the press.

At 10:30 carriages began to line up on the street for their turn under the town-house portico to discharge their passengers. A brigade of house staff stood ready to relieve reporters of wet coats and hats. One by one, notebook-carrying reporters began to take their pre-arranged seats. Marlena greeted each one with effortless charm. Many of them knew her by sight from her highly visible role in the previous campaigns—and she knew many by name, as well. She checked off names one by one from the door list. The event took on the odd atmosphere of a brunch party rather than the political assault it was. Treat even the most serious conflicts with graciousness and style—that was the Maxwell credo.

Marlena's nervousness grew to genuine agitation when by ten minutes to the hour there was no sign of Arthur Stock. She flashed sideways glances at Deborah as each new guest arrived, each of them failing to be the morning's most important attendee. Quickly she scribbled a note to her father and sent one of the house staff running to the library. Marlena worried about giving her father the unsettling news, but she also knew the benefit of having him prepared. At five minutes to the hour the girl returned with a note. In bold capital letters the message read, "I WAIT FOR NO ONE. LET STOCK'S EMPTY CHAIR SPEAK FOR HIM." No doubt about it, Jason Maxwell was back on his feet and shooting with both guns. Marlena smiled and handed the note to Deborah, who grinned as well before tucking it under the door list on her clipboard.

At exactly eleven o'clock, Marlena snapped her watch shut with a flourish. Leaving Deborah to deal with anyone rude enough to be late or simply delayed by the steady rain, she strode down the hall and knocked loudly on the library doors before sliding them open. Her father stood ready. Hamilton stood at his right shoulder, wearing a dark suit and white shirt. His eyes gleamed like blue beacons against the clean lines of his collar. He looked like a man who could take over a room. Marlena hoped for her father's sake that he could. She had to admit, the two men made a rather distinguished team.

"Stock?" her father growled.

"No sign of him."

"Then Arthur Stock be damned. Let's go, Mr. Hamilton." He strode to the door and took both of Marlena's hands, giving her a quick peck on the cheek.

"Good luck, Daddy."

"Luck has nothing to do with it, Lena dear," he said with a twinkle in his eye. It was the traditional exchange Marlena had with her father before every big event. It made her feel good to hear it again.

Hamilton came through the door behind the senator, looking straight at Marlena. She felt awkward, but he showed no sign of anything but smooth confidence. One had to admire the man's grace under pressure. She turned to go, but changed her mind. Respectfully, she held out her hand to him, but in such a position that requested a shake, not a kiss. It was the least she could do, given all she now knew and all he was about to face. She was pleased to see the look of slight surprise on his face as she said graciously, "Good luck, Mr. Hamilton."

"Thank you, Miss Maxwell," he said, with a broad smile. "Thank you very much." Marlena convinced herself he stood a little taller as he made his way down the hall after her father. The accent—however grating—was hardly his fault.

Marlena closed the thick velvet curtains at the archway to the parlor as the two men walked up the front aisle to take their places. The empty chair in the front row was clearly visible. Her father paused at the chair, casually glanced at the place card, and then turned it around to face the audience so that everyone could read that the empty chair was reserved for Arthur Stock of the *Austin City News*. A quiet chuckle rippled through the audience. It was a brilliant opening statement. Marlena tucked her hands behind her and leaned back against the far wall as her father cleared his throat to begin speaking.

In the hallway, Deborah stared at the one open space on her door list. It was unbelievable that Stock could have pulled such a stunt as to personally accept the invitation and then not show. But then, Deborah reminded herself, Arthur Stock wasn't exactly a man who stood on propriety.

At 11:10 a speeding carriage lurched to a stop under the portico to let out a running passenger. Deborah sighed in relief as she signaled for one of the house staff to prepare to accept another wet coat. "Damn, I'm late," cursed an alarmingly familiar voice as the soggy reporter burst through the door to stop and stare at Deborah's wide-eyed glare.

Hasten.

Stock had done worse than not show; he'd sent a reporter to cover the press conference, as if it were some minor town council meeting. And worst of all, he'd sent Samuel Hasten. And she'd almost agreed to let him walk her home on Friday afternoon. She'd forgotten he worked for Stock. Deborah pulled herself up into a defensive stance and eyed Hasten angrily.

"Good morning, Miss Edgerton," he said, offering a sheepish smile as he handed his coat and hat to the staff.

"You're late, Mr. Hasten," said Deborah, scratching Stock's name off the number-one position on the door list with a slow, nasty line. "You will have to take a seat in the rear." Under no circumstances was she going to let this man jaunt down the aisle to Stock's chair. He was lucky she was letting him in at all.

"Look, Miss Edgerton, I—"

"Good day, Mr. Hasten," Deborah shot back before he could get another word out. She handed him his packet and left the hallway, running only after she was sure she was out of sight.

Halfway through her father's opening statement, Marlena watched a sheepish young man sneak into the parlor and arrange himself noisily in the last row. She didn't recognize him, but her back stiffened against the wall when she realized the reporter was opening Arthur Stock's packet. *Of all the underhanded stunts.* It would have been better had he not shown at all than to pay them the insult of sending a stand-in. Marlena hoped her father couldn't see him from the podium. He might bodily remove the reporter if he realized the affront. While her father could stand with dignity against any criticism, insults flared his temper instantly.

The questions from the floor after the opening statement were relatively mild. It seemed the reporters were saving their nastier inquisition for Mr. Hamilton. Marlena's eyes repeatedly strayed to Hamilton, but he showed no outward signs of anxiety. Only the flawless confidence she'd seen at their first meeting. He sat perfectly calm, perfectly still.

Tyler could feel Marlena watching him. Her surprising offer of best wishes had taken him quite off guard, although he was sure he had hidden his astonishment. Sunday night Tyler had gone nearly mad with anxiety that Marlena would run to her father and relate their encounter on the knoll. It was foolish to give in to the impulse to kiss her. Surely it would mean his job. By Monday morning, as the entourage headed back into the city with the flurry of activity that followed, Tyler realized that she could no more admit the incident to her father than she would admit her disappointment at not being campaign manager pro tem. None of that changed the power he'd felt in their kiss. That moment, when he felt her soften in his arms, something happened. He knew it. She knew it.

He stole a long look at her. She was staring furiously at a young reporter in the back row. *Such fire in those eyes.* That one short spark between them served only to heighten his awareness of her. And she of him. They'd done their best to avoid each other and hide behind a sea of details, but the feel of her hands spreading against his chest would not leave his mind. They couldn't go backward now. Forward wasn't a viable option at the moment, either. They were hung in a strange state until someone thought of the next move. Tyler, usually never without a strategy, was at a total loss.

"Gentlemen," rang out the senator's voice, "I apologize to no one for my choice in campaign manager. You're darned right I intended to make a statement by hiring Mr. Hamilton. But I am not in the habit of hiring unqualified people simply to make a point. Tyler Hamilton is a brilliant young strategist. He embraces the same political ideals that I hold dear. And he's ready to do the job of beating Dickson Kenton. If you have anything further to say, you'd best say it to Mr. Hamilton directly. Gentlemen, I introduce to you Mr. Tyler Hamilton the third, graduate of Harvard University, and manager of my campaign for reelection."

Marlena watched the room shuffle as Hamilton took the podium. Again, his accent stood out against her father's broad drawl. He delivered a brief statement and then opened the room up for questions. Marlena found herself holding her breath as Hamilton recognized the first reporter.

"Mr. Hamilton, why are you here in Texas?" A satisfied smile broke across Marlena's face. She *had* known exactly which questions the reporters would raise and in exactly which order. And Hamilton was prepared for each and every one of them. He never skipped a beat on even the most scathing of comments. Hamilton was direct, entertaining, and clever. She couldn't deny that his success went far beyond the rehearsal he'd had under her fire. The man was simply outstanding at what he did. Marlena watched him with satisfaction as he answered a question about his length of professional service with a simple, direct admission. Once again, the great Jason Maxwell had called it right on the money. But even her father hadn't planned on the surprise ending Hamilton gave the event.

After it seemed every question had been answered, Hamilton looked back to his employer for a sign of approval as he said, "Gentlemen, if I may, I would like to pose only one question to all of you." Her father hesitated only a moment before he nodded.

Hamilton faced the audience and removed his

glasses. Marlena backed up against the wall again. "I put to you gentlemen the most obvious question of the morning. Where, may I ask, is Arthur Stock?"

The room shifted in surprise. Even her father raised an eyebrow.

Good Lord, thought Marlena, *what's he doing?* Then she thought again. *Of course.* Hamilton must have seen the reporter enter the room and had latched on to Stock's plan. Now he was going to call Stock's bluff. It was an enormous chance, but the potential payoff was nothing short of brilliant. Hamilton stared straight at the fidgeting young reporter trying to disappear under his chair in the back row.

Finally the man seemed to realize that he would do more damage by remaining silent than by speaking up. Surely he knew he shouldn't let Hamilton have the last word, but Marlena bet he couldn't even begin to think of an acceptable response. He stood up slowly.

"Mr. Stock felt quite confident you were aware of his position, Senator Maxwell."

Hamilton was on it instantly. His eyes melted into that irresistible smile of a man who was up to something. Marlena held her steepled hands to her lips. This was going to be first-class. The other reporters sat, pens poised, waiting for the response that would surely be the quote of the day.

"Really," he said, with an inflection that spoke volumes. "Oh, we are all quite clear on Mr. Stock's viewpoint." His smile broadened. "But I think he ought to be clear on mine. You will tell him, won't you? Or perhaps one of you gentlemen," he said, motioning to the other reporters present, "will be kind enough to fill him in." The reporters chuckled. The man turned redder than his hair. Marlena hummed victoriously. She'd stake her watch that that was not the ending note Arthur Stock had in mind. Not at all.

• • •

"You said *what*?" demanded Arthur Stock as he slammed the press packet down on his desk and glared at Samuel Hasten. "What the hell were you thinking, boy? I ought to fire your tail right out of here this minute. That's all I need. I sent you to sit in the back row and cover a press conference so I could have the information I need and still make a point by not attending. You were to be invisible, Hasten. Unseen. But can you do this? No, you end up sticking your big foot right down my mouth in front of every paper in Texas!"

"I'm sorry, sir. I never dreamed your attendance would be directly questioned. I just couldn't come up—"

"Damn right, you're sorry, son. You'll be sorrier if you don't get that thick head of yours out of my office this minute, before I fire you." Stock waved his hand as if he were shooing away a fly. Hasten fled the room. Arthur Stock held his head in his hands and closed his eyes. *Damn that Hamilton.* That green little Yankee had more spine than he had counted on. Stock had been outfoxed and he knew it. His only retaliation would be to take his lumps in tomorrow's headlines and look toward the next battle. He was cursing his luck when Jacobs entered the room.

"I take it the press conference did not go as planned, Mr. Stock?" Jacobs had a nasty habit of stating the obvious. Stock looked up and painfully recounted Mr. Hasten's poor choice of words.

"I can't think of one good reason not to fire that fool," said Stock, standing to look out the window at the heavy rain still falling.

"Actually, sir, if I may be so bold, I can think of a reason."

"Jacobs, if you tell me something about employee shortages or wage seniority—"

"Just the opposite, sir. This has nothing to do with finances. Actually, it has very little to do with journalism. It's just that I overheard Mr. Hasten saying to the copyboy on Monday how fond he was of Miss Deborah Edgerton."

"What is that to me?" Stock asked wearily.

"Miss Edgerton, sir, is Senator Maxwell's secretary. And Mr. Hasten seems to think she is fond of him as well. If they began to see more of each other, perhaps something useful could be forged out of such a relationship."

Stock turned around, surprised. "Why, Jacobs, I'm impressed. I must admit, I never thought I'd find a dark streak in you. It seems that uptight numbers-head of yours is growing a newsman's ears. Why, yes, I do believe we'll find a use for poor Sam Hasten after all. Yes, indeed. Come up with a few tasks that will send him to Maxwell's office next week."

"Certainly, sir." Jacobs smiled, proud of his newly tarnished reputation. The wicked grin looked out of place on his bookish face.

"Stop by Hasten's desk on your way out and ask him to be in my office at nine o'clock tomorrow, sharp. Scare him just enough to make him think he's about to be fired. Understand?"

"Clearly, Mr. Stock." Jacobs was enthusiastic in his new role of conspirator as he left the room.

Arthur Stock laughed as he settled into his large leather chair and reached for a cigar. The morning hadn't been a total loss. Tomorrow's press would be bearable now that he knew a much better battle was at hand.

"Now, let us see what brand of total disaster we can whip up," said Stock to himself as he bit off the end of the cigar and struck a match.

❧ Chapter Seven ❧

Marlena hummed to herself as she carried a coffee service down the hallway. The afternoon had been celebratory and frantic. The office had been packed with photographers, telegrams, packages, and reporters seeking quotes. This was the first breathing room she'd had since a brief but cheerful luncheon after the press conference.

She backed through the office door to find the room almost empty; only Hamilton stood over some papers in the far corner. Her plan to politely offer him coffee seemed overstated now that it was just the two of them. She wasn't quite sure she was ready to be alone with him. Overriding her hesitation, she strode into the room and plunked the service down on her desk. "Where is everyone?"

"The senator and Miss Edgerton went to send a driver with a message and some flowers to your mother. They should be back in half an hour or so."

Marlena wondered why her father hadn't asked her to accompany him. It was *her* mother, after all. "Why didn't he wait for me?"

"He said something to me about Miss Edgerton looking tired and upset. He thought the walk might do her good. I didn't ask, really. I'm sure it's nothing."

Uneasy that he seemed to read her so well, Marlena forced herself to brighten. "I was craving a cup of coffee. I thought you might like one, Mr. Hamilton. How do you take it?"

Hamilton smiled at her and crossed the room. He had a look on his face that, for no logical reason, made her feel uncomfortably intimate. "Black. But you take two sugars. Often three." His hand lingered just a moment as he took the cup from her.

"You noticed how I drink my coffee, Mr. Hamilton?" Some part of her was pleased that he had.

"Miss Maxwell, you are the first woman I have ever met who drinks coffee at all, much less without cream. It was among the first things I noticed about you."

The way he said "among" hinted that he had noticed much more. The look in his eyes planted a knot in Marlena's stomach as she sipped her coffee.

"Why don't you drink tea, like a proper Southern lady?" he teased.

Marlena was grateful for a polite topic. She launched into an antitea monologue to keep from thinking and saying everything else that came to mind. "I've hated tea from the day Mother taught us to drink it. It's weak. Flimsy. Most of the time it's lukewarm, and someone's always making it worse with lemon or cream or sugar or something else. I just can't bear the taste of—"

"Yes, I see. You've made your point quite clearly," interjected Tyler, holding his hand up and chuckling. Marlena forced a small laugh in reply, but then an awkward silence fell between them. Each reverted to a sip of coffee to cover the gap in conversation. Both were highly aware of being alone together.

"I find I must admit that you were really very good this morning, Mr. Hamilton. Daddy is as pleased as could be. How on earth did you know Hasten was from the *Austin City News*?" Marlena fought to keep the conversation going and her thoughts on business. She swore the temperature of the room had gone up ten degrees.

"By watching you."

"Pardon me?" Marlena flushed. Tyler Hamilton began to look dangerous again.

"You stiffened up about three minutes after he sat down. I knew only one newspaper could make you that angry. Then I saw there were no other empty place cards and put two and two together. The rest was easy." Marlena stifled the warm feeling that came from knowing he had been watching her so closely.

"You took quite a chance, Mr. Hamilton," she said, grasping at formality. She wanted him to take his eyes off her. And didn't want him to.

"It was quite a payoff, Miss Maxwell." The smile that spread across his face showed her that Tyler wasn't about to back off.

"Are you always in the habit of taking such risks, Mr. Hamilton?" Marlena had meant it to sound harsh, but it failed to come out that way. Instead it came out with a tone that spoke far more of the risk he had taken Sunday on the knoll. Lord, but he did things to her composure.

He didn't respond right away, but just looked at her. Then he set his cup down, crossed over to her, and took her free hand. He ran his thumb across her palm. "Only when I perceive the payoff to be well worth the risk." He did not let go of her hand, but stared straight into her eyes.

Marlena thought she would drop the cup. She fought back the sensation of his touch and tried to clear her head. After what seemed an eternity, she pulled her hand out of his and turned away. "Yes, well, someday you may find such a tactic will be your undoing. Some risks are simply not worth taking." She began to shuffle through some papers in a transparent attempt to get busy.

Tyler circled around and stood in front of her again. He planted his hand on top of the papers, stopping her shuffling. He didn't move until she looked up at him again. When she did his eyes were inescapable. He said quietly, intimately, "I disagree."

Marlena held her breath, only to have it rush out of her when she heard the office door burst open. He took a step away from her just before Deborah and her father strolled into the room.

"Daddy! What did you write to Mother? Did you send roses? You sent peach ones if you sent roses, didn't you? Do you think she'll be coming to Austin soon?" The questions served to cover her own fluster at Tyler's advance.

"Whoa, girl," laughed her father. He came over and kissed her on the cheek. "Don't you think I've had enough questions fired at me for one day? One at a time, please."

"All right, then. What did you say to Mother?"

"I wrote her that I felt the press conference had been a success. That I wanted her to come back to Austin. I didn't tell the driver to wait for a reply. I don't think your mother will send one right away. If I know her, she'll send me a message with a list of things for the house staff to do. We'll just let it sit for now, Lena honey. My God, child, are you drinking coffee again? You'll be banging around the house all night, at this rate. Your mother'd skin you."

"Well, I'm glad she wasn't here to see us move the melodeon. She'd have skinned me for sure."

"Did you call a—" started the senator.

"The tuner will be here at ten-thirty," said Deborah and Marlena in unison. She liked the laugh it brought out of her father.

"Well, then, I know everything is under control. It's time to close down this office. Miss Edgerton, I'll have Hamilton here see you home. Mind, you be ready in dinner dress, Mr. Hamilton, at seven o'clock sharp. We've an invitation to Congressman Powers' home for dinner tonight."

"Carleton Powers, sir?"

"That's right. Congressman Powers has invited us to his home tonight in celebration of our little victory. I trust you made no other plans?" The question was no query; it was a clear demand for attendance.

"No, sir," said Hamilton, taking down the address. "Seven o'clock sharp. I'll be there, sir. Miss Edgerton?" Marlena watched him help Deborah into her wrap and whisk her out the door.

Marlena eyed her father sharply. "Seven o'clock. Daddy, that's hardly enough time to get properly dressed. You could have said something earlier. I haven't the slightest idea which dress would be best."

"Lena, weren't you in this same office all afternoon? Just when did you think I had the time to go over our social schedule? Besides, you'll look lovely in anything. Now, run upstairs and get gussied up. Richard will be there this evening, you know. I get the sense that Congressman Powers' son is a mite sweet on you." He touched Lena's cheek affectionately.

"Oh, Daddy," Marlena dismissed her father's all-too-broad hint, "you think every man is sweet on me. Enough already about Richard Powers. All he ever talks about is cattle and railroads. I can hardly make polite conversation."

"Cattle and railroads, Lena, make Mr. Powers a very wealthy man. You'd do right to try harder to make polite conversation." He winked and sent her off with a wave of his hand. "Upstairs with you."

• • •

Marlena sat at her dressing table alternately holding a green or pink jeweled comb up to her hair. She was uncharacteristically indecisive. She knew why. Hamilton would surely have those glasses off, and she could just imagine how those blue eyes would stand out against a black dinner coat. Even more so than this morning. She put the combs down and drummed her fingers against the dresser.

Then there was Richard. Her father's guess was not all wrong; Richard Powers had shown her a great deal of attention at the last social gathering they attended with the Powerses. He wasn't unattractive. He was friendly and complimentary. It might be a good idea to divert her attentions elsewhere for the evening. Hamilton was getting far too confident for her liking. After all, November was still four long months away. She'd better do something to stave off his advances. *His advances do need to be staved off, don't they? Of course they do. Absolutely.*

Marlena settled on the green comb and slid it into the curve of her chignon. She stood up and stepped over to the full-length mirror to survey the effect. In her reflection she saw Sarah entering the room.

"Miss Lena, that color is splendid on you. You are sure to be the center of the evening's attention."

"You're kind, but I doubt it. The evening's talk is sure to be of solid politics from start to finish. Or of cattle and railroads, if I'm to sit next to Richard Powers. Would you please get these last buttons for me?"

Sarah moved over behind Marlena to finish the stream of tiny buttons running up the back of her rose-colored gown. She smiled as she remarked near Marlena's ear, "You know very well there are women in Austin who would line up to dine next to Richard Powers. Cattle make men rich. Besides, with this dress,

I hardly think his mind will be on livestock." She giggled as she secured the last button. Marlena turned and shooed Sarah away with a teasing flourish.

"Oh, please, you're just like all the rest. Daddy has you all convinced. Should I wear the black wrap or the cream one? Do you think these ear bobs are right for this dress?"

Sarah feigned amazement. "Indecision? From Marlena Maxwell? This is a surprise. Could it be that Richard Powers has finally caught your attention?"

"Hush up and help me decide. I'm thinking the cream one will be best."

"I agree. And the bobs are perfect. But Miss Lena, aren't you missing something?"

Marlena stopped midstep, her hand flying from hair to rings to ear bobs. "What? What?"

"Well, I've just never seen you go anywhere without the watch, that's all."

"Oh, my goodness, my watch," said Lena, rushing to the nightstand to fix the pearled fob to her gown. She fingered the timepiece with affection as she checked herself in the mirror one more time. "All right, I'm ready now."

"I should hope so, Miss Lena. Your father's been waiting in the study for over a quarter of an hour now. You'll be late if you don't leave soon."

"All right, all right, I'm off. Thank you, Sarah." Marlena grabbed the black wrap instead of the cream one and swished out the door in a rustle of satin.

Tyler rounded the corner a second time and puffed on his cigar again. He'd walked the length of the block next to Congressman Powers' house three times now, having arrived an unseemly twenty minutes early. The walk had served to clear his thoughts, however, and he was growing ever more resolved to steal a few moments alone with Marlena Maxwell at some point during the evening. After this morning's victory he was feeling indestructible. He was going to find a way to get her in his arms again. He took a final, long draw of the cigar and headed for the lighted portico of the Powerses' town house with determined strides. Best to arrive before the Maxwells and get his bearings.

The Powerses turned out to be as nice a family as Tyler had ever met in Boston. His accent failed to produce the raised eyebrows Tyler was becoming so accustomed to seeing. Instead, Carleton Powers remarked that one of his closest colleagues in Congress was, as he put it, "a Harvard man, so they can't be all that bad." Powers' laugh was as broad and genuine as Maxwell's, fitting perfectly with Powers' full red beard and mustache. Tyler liked him instantly.

Mrs. Powers was just as jovial, a small, round woman with an enormous bun of silver-blond hair that spilled in excited little curls around her full face. She made a warm, funny little sound when Tyler kissed her hand in greeting. "Now, Mr. Hamilton, I want you to meet my son, Richard. Richard's just come out of business school in Virginia, so the two of you will have lots to talk about." She presented Richard Powers with all the pride a mother could muster.

Richard was a friendly fellow Tyler's age, not nearly as outgoing as his father, but genuine and amiable, just the same. "You've created quite a stir, Mr. Hamilton. How does it feel to be the center of such a controversy? I'm not so sure I envy you all the attention." Richard laughed a bit in sympathy.

"I had hoped for a slightly subtler entrance into Texas," mused Tyler, appreciating the empathy.

"Where Jason Maxwell is concerned, I should think you'd know better than to expect subtle."

They were still talking when Tyler heard the Maxwells' carriage pull up to the portico. Mrs. Powers shooed the house staff away and bobbed up to the door to open it herself.

"Jason! Good to see you, my dear. We're so glad you could come to dinner tonight. I was afraid you wouldn't be able to tear yourself away from the reporters to join us." She clasped Maxwell's enormous hands in her tiny white fists.

He kissed her on the cheek and laughed. "I'm grateful for the respite, Marion. Too many reporters can be a bad thing. But I can never get enough of your hospitality." He turned past her to the congressman. "Carleton. Mighty fine of you to have us this evening. I'm glad to see you." They clasped hands.

"And, of course, Marlena, dear," Mrs. Powers said as she pulled Marlena into the foyer with a hug. "How are you? You look more stunning every time I lay eyes on you. So nice to see you again so soon after the barbecue."

Conversation involuntarily stopped between Tyler and Richard when she stepped into the foyer light. Marlena did look spectacular. The cut of her gown was more than flattering. A low-cut and impossibly tight bodice accented the alluring lines of her neck and bosom. The distracting swirls of her black hair let loose a flood of ungentlemanly thoughts in Tyler. He felt his stomach tighten at the sight of her, and his resolve to steal a moment with her doubled.

She looked toward the two men for an instant before turning her attention to her hosts. "Congressman and Mrs. Powers, how very nice of you to have us as your guests this evening. It really is a treat. You're so kind to think of us." She stood on tiptoe to plant an affectionate peck on Powers' bearded cheek. He put his arm around her and led her across the foyer to where Tyler and Richard were standing. Tyler heard Richard suck in his breath as they approached.

"Marlena, Richard's said barrels full of nice things about you since we had brunch at Easter. He's only just returned from business school in Virginia."

"Hello, Miss Maxwell. Delightful to see you again. I'm quite sorry I had to miss the barbecue this year, but I had some details in Virginia that needed tending. I would have liked to have been there."

"Why, thank you. It was a splendid evening. Wasn't it, Daddy?"

"Yes, Lena honey, it was." Tyler couldn't help noticing the looks exchanged between Maxwell and Congressman Powers. The two of them obviously liked the sight of their children together. Tyler felt himself growing defensive when he saw Marlena offer her hand to Richard in greeting. He didn't kiss it, but he took it most affectionately. Only after an annoyingly long moment did one of them remember their manners.

"Of course, you know Mr. Hamilton," said Richard. "We were just getting introduced. He sounds like a fine addition to the senator's campaign."

"Yes, of course," said Marlena, looking solely at Richard with a potent smile. "It seems we'll have quite an interesting run this year. Good evening, Mr. Hamilton." She added indifferently, "Thank you for seeing Miss Edgerton home this afternoon. I'm glad you could join us for dinner."

Tyler disliked Marlena's veiled attempt to hook him up with Miss Edgerton. "My pleasure. I wouldn't have missed this dinner for anything." *My God, but you look ravishing*, his mind added.

"Richard dear," interjected Mrs. Powers, "why don't you take Lena and Mr. Hamilton into the study and show them your jumping trophies from graduate school? Perhaps Mr. Hamilton rides, as well." She turned to Maxwell. "We're just so proud of how Richard's done at the university. I'm tickled to have him home again."

"I'm sure you are, Marion," said Maxwell with a smile. "Go on, Lena dear, Powers and I have a bit of business to catch up with, anyway."

Richard flushed. "You'd think they were twelve feet tall the way Mother goes on about those trophies. They're really not much, but I'd be happy to show them to you."

"Of course I'd like to see them," said Marlena, her green eyes focused on Richard. "I'm sure they're quite impressive. I'd like very much to hear about Virginia, as well."

"Delighted," responded Richard, clearly pleased. His tone sounded far too much like a polite afterthought when he called over his shoulder, "Do you ride, Mr. Hamilton?"

"Why, yes," said Tyler as he followed after them, trying hard not to sound annoyed as he remembered the last time he was on a horse, "I do ride. Quite fond of jumping, myself, actually."

The small talk of the evening gave way to an elaborate dinner. Pocket doors slid open to reveal a long table resplendent in golden-hued glassware and ivory bone china. A fireplace to the right of the table set the flames' reflections dancing across the glassware. Massive silverware, "in the family for generations," as Mrs. Powers put it, glittered in military rows on either side of each setting. In the table's center, a lavish bowl of yellow roses picked "just for Jason" expressly by the hostess sported tiny green fern leaves and puffs of baby's breath. Delicate lace place cards told Tyler that the lovely Miss Maxwell had been placed far down the table from him but right next to Richard Powers. He couldn't decide if her position slightly out of view and crosswise on the other side of the table was a blessing or a curse.

Just before the main course, however, a fortunate arrangement of leaning bodies offered him a long, un-obstructed view of her during a lull in his own conver-sations.

"So that's how the railroad is going to move my cat-tle," Richard was explaining, "but I'm not so sure you'd find that at all interesting. Do you?"

"Hmm? Oh, yes, well, of course I find it interesting," she replied. "The railroad . . . well, it's going to be the driving economic force of the future, I think."

Richard looked puzzled. Evidently "driving economic force" were not words he expected from a woman.

Tyler watched Marlena put on her "belle" face. It was similar to the one that she had used on the porch steps at the barbecue. "Cattle," she cooed, "now, there's something I just can't seem to take an interest in." She was pouring it on thick. "They're just big, clumsy animals to me. And, of course, occasionally they're dinner." She turned to face more toward Richard and looked up at him with doe eyes as she sipped her wine. "I'm afraid that wasn't very funny. Perhaps if anyone can explain the intricacies of cattle to me, you can. Do let's forget I ever said such a dreadful joke." Tyler nearly moaned.

"Our secret," said Richard, obviously won over. "It wasn't that dreadful, really. I'm sure I've heard worse. I've surely said worse."

To Tyler's right, Mrs. Powers looked over at her son and beamed with pride. She had the planning look of a mother with an agenda for her son regarding a certain young lady.

Tyler sighed. There was no mistaking that this was

the world in which Marlena Maxwell belonged. She seemed born to play the charming young belle in the merger of powerful Southern families. But she was lying. He had the certain, inexplicable sense that she was manufacturing her interest. It was an act. As he pondered it more, Tyler decided that this was a different act from the one she put on with the guests at the barbecue. The charm at the barbecue was impulsive, purposeful, and deliberately genuine somehow. This, Tyler knew but couldn't say why, was *forced*.

Then it struck him why. The look in Marlena's eyes as she beamed up at Richard lacked the fire he'd seen on the knoll Sunday afternoon. It wasn't there. Marlena wasn't born to just fall obediently into place. That fire belonged to him. And both of them knew it, no matter what the circumstances.

Another question from Congressman Powers dragged him back to the dinner conversation. Still, with every course, he watched Marlena pouring on more charm. By the time the men retired to the library for brandy and cigars, Richard was all but lovestruck. According to Mrs. Powers, Richard had been taken with her since Easter. Maxwell and the congressman were certainly fueling the fire, slapping each other on the back and chuckling like two salesmen who'd just closed the deal of a lifetime. Tyler drowned his annoyance in his brandy and hid his defensiveness behind cigar smoke.

He was out of his element, a welcome guest, but a— what had Lena called him?—a "novelty" to be discussed and hired but certainly not wed into the family. *Wed?* How had his mind jumped that far? He'd barely kissed Marlena Maxwell and now he was getting annoyed at not being considered betrothal material? This was going way too far.

Instead of squelching his feelings for Marlena Maxwell, the impossibility of it all seemed to feed the attraction. Each time circumstances conspired against catching a moment alone with Marlena, he grew more determined to be with her.

Near the end of the evening, the group gathered outside in Mrs. Powers' celebrated rose gardens. It was a spectacular night, warm and still. The deep indigo sky sported a dazzling array of stars. The perfect sliver of a crescent moon cast a hint of light across the paths. Powers and Senator Maxwell humored the lady of the house as she gave them an extensive tour of the roses.

Tyler, Marlena, and Richard wandered farther off toward the hedges and herb gardens. As Richard strode ahead to unlock one of the estate's many wrought-iron gates, Tyler seized his chance.

"Ask him to bring you a lantern," he whispered sharply at Marlena's shoulder.

"Pardon me, Mr. Hamilton?" She turned with an amused look on her face, and he guessed he had not successfully hidden his desire to be alone with her.

"You heard me."

Marlena glared at him. "I will not."

Tyler adapted. "Powers!" he called, striding up to the gate where Richard was struggling with the lock. "Richard, the lady is finding it rather dark. If you'd like to enjoy the evening in her company, why don't you get a lantern? I'll stay and keep watch, then I'll make my excuses and disappear when you get back." He flashed Richard a knowing look as further incentive.

It served its purpose, for Richard went straight off for the lantern, promising a swift return. With a quick look around, Tyler spied a shadowed corner of hedge near the gate and took Marlena by the elbow. She gave a small gulp but didn't put up a great deal of resistance.

He backed her into the corner, out of view. "He's not for you," Tyler said softly while allowing himself the luxury of staring deep into those captivating green eyes. A lacy pattern of moonlight came down through the leaves to play across her face and chest.

Marlena's attempt to sound sharp fell revealingly short. "How dare you!"

"Exactly." With the sense of urgency that was pounding in his veins, he wrapped his hands around her waist. She tried to push him away. He pulled her closer. "How dare I!" he whispered into her cheek, and felt her shiver. He brushed his lips against hers softly. She swiped at him in a hollow, halfhearted attempt to make him stop. He deepened the hesitant brush into a lush kiss. For a second or two, he felt her soften against him. More than before. *Sweet Lord.*

But even before Richard's footsteps could be heard, Marlena somewhere found her strength and shoved Tyler away. "Don't!" she hissed, jabbing a finger at him. "I swear, Tyler Hamilton, if you ever touch me again, I'll . . ."

Tyler smiled. In the moment she'd let down her guard again, they'd crossed the divide. He knew she felt what he did. They weren't going to be able to fight it much longer. He picked up a pebble from the path and held it up to her like a poker chip. "My wager is that you'll yield." He pressed it into her palm.

Richard was coming down the path. "I've no desire to yield to you," she growled.

"You're lying. Good night, Miss Maxwell. I'll leave you in the unfalteringly polite hands of Mr. Powers."

He marveled at her aim when the pebble struck him sharply in the shoulder as he turned to take his leave.

"Mr. Hasten, good morning or no good morning, I should think by now you would have realized you are not welcome here."

"Miss Edgerton, please," started Hasten, his foot bracing the door to prevent her slamming it, "I need to talk to you about what happened."

Unmoved, Deborah brought the heel of her shoe down on Hasten's toes and attempted to shut the door. "Go away!"

"Sweet Mother of God," Hasten cursed, yanking his foot away but catching the slamming door with his elbow. "Is that really necessary?"

"Seeing as how you and your employer attempted to insult the senator, I'd say it was rather mild," Deborah shot back in icy tones, pressing her body against the door in an effort to shut it in Hasten's face. "Now, will you please go away, or do I need to call Hewitt to come throw you out?"

"Please. Just listen to me, will you?" He finally jammed his elbow into the door and propped it open just as Deborah gave it another shove. "Ouch! I was just filling my post. Carrying out the assignment Stock gave me. I thought it was a rather underhanded thing to do, myself, but I've got to make a living, and Stock made it clear my job was in question if I didn't do what he wanted. Miss Edgerton, please, you can't blame me."

"Can't I?" snapped Deborah, disliking the quick way he passed blame on for his own actions. "I think you might need to make a wiser choice in employers, Mr. Hasten. Now, good day."

Hasten winced again as the door cut into his arm. "I'm not leaving," he said with a boyish grin. "I'm simply not leaving until you hear me out."

"Mr. Hasten, what you did was horrible. The fact that you were under orders is no excuse—"

"Oh, Lord's sake, Miss Edgerton," interrupted Hasten, "what is it you want me to do? What could possibly make it up to you?"

Deborah took a moment to ponder Hasten's question. "You have yet to apologize. To me or to the senator."

Samuel Hasten broke into a smile. "Well, I don't know about the senator, but I am mighty sorry I caused you any embarrassment, discomfort, confusion, annoyance . . . pain or suffering"—he looked up as if consulting a mental dictionary for more nouns of torment—"anguish, insult—"

"That will do, Mr. Hasten," said Deborah, laughing in spite of herself. He had a disarming habit of obliterating her annoyance with his enthusiastic charm. She wasn't sure if she minded. "Apology accepted. Please try not to become such a dreadful adversary again."

"I give you my word I'll do what I can. But I do work for Arthur Stock, you know. I can't promise anything. But in the meantime . . ." He produced a small paper cone from his pocket and presented it to her with a flourish. Deborah accepted the package and opened the top to reveal a mound of peppermint candy. She had no idea how Hasten had found out about her love of the sweets. It made her pleased and suspicious at the same time.

"My favorite. Thank you, Mr. Hasten."

"Really? I had no idea, but somehow you struck me as the peppermint type. I'm really quite glad you like them. I'm fond of them myself, actually." Deborah popped one of the delicate pink-and-white circles into her mouth and offered the cone to Hasten, who took two. His cheeks puffed out, making him look like a red-headed squirrel as he spoke. "Well, then," he said behind the mouthful, "I should be off. Don't worry, I'll be back soon. Hmm. You like peppermints, too. Who would have guessed?" He began strutting down the street singing the word "peppermints" to the tune of "Pop Goes the Weasel" in a voice far too loud. Deborah could hear him turning the corner still chanting behind the mouthful of candy. She laughed quietly, sat down at her desk again, and tucked the paper cone into her bottom drawer, where no one else would find them. But not before she popped another into her mouth and hummed the same tune.

A few hours later, the office door opened slowly to reveal Marlena and the senator returning from the ranch house. Hamilton looked up from adding figures, surprised to see the pair back so soon from gathering Mrs. Maxwell and the girls. Neither Marlena nor her father said hello. She headed straight for an empty desk, flinging a stack of newspapers down on it. Maxwell made straight for his office, shutting the door behind him with his daughter's characteristic slam.

The two had obviously been arguing. Tyler wondered what could have set them off. Maxwell had been ecstatic this morning over the coverage—and, thought Tyler defensively, had exhibited obvious pleasure over Marlena and Richard being together. Tyler caught Miss Edgerton's eye and raised an eyebrow in silent inquiry. She shrugged her shoulders and shook her head, as if to say she was as baffled as he. Neither one seemed brave enough to venture a question to the Maxwells.

Tyler lowered his eyes to the column of figures again and pretended to continue calculating. The room grew so silent that Tyler actually heard Miss Edgerton chewing the last of her peppermint. He was momentarily distracted by how many of the sweets he'd seen her consume in the last half hour, and wondered where they had come from.

"Well?" Marlena suddenly snapped into the quiet. Tyler looked up. "Isn't *someone* going to ask me what in God's name is the matter here?"

"Miss Maxwell—" started Tyler, and was instantly

sorry he'd responded instead of letting Miss Edgerton jump into the fray.

"You! You, Mr. Hamilton, are what is the matter here. Your presence. Your employment. Your press coverage. This campaign. Must I elaborate?"

"Lena . . ." started Miss Edgerton, attempting to squelch the storm before it gathered too much force. "But this morning it all seemed—"

"Yes, didn't it?" retorted Marlena angrily. "It all seemed perfectly wonderful. Everyone was won over by Mr. Hamilton's *exquisite* rhetoric yesterday morning. Everything glossed over with just a few clever remarks." Marlena tossed her stack of newspapers onto the floor and shot a slicing glance at Tyler. "But not everything can be remedied with a silver tongue. Some problems just don't go away, do they, Mr. Hamilton?"

Tyler was getting his back up already. "Miss Maxwell, I'm afraid I don't know what you're talking about. If there's something I've done to—"

"*If there's something you've done?* My God, Mr. Hamilton, how much more can you do? Perhaps you would like to shatter two or three families before you would consider your work here finished!" Marlena spun around and paced toward the windows.

"You don't mean she's not—" Miss Edgerton said in a quiet voice.

"Yes, I mean she's not!" Marlena shot back as she turned around to face her. "That's right, Mother and the girls are still at the ranch house. They're not . . ." Marlena caught her voice for a moment. "They're not coming home right now. Mother says she cannot bear to be under the same roof as our living metaphor Mr. Hamilton, here. Tyler Hamilton, I wonder if you realize just what Mother has been through—"

Maxwell's office door was flung open and Jason Maxwell stood ominously filling the doorway, red-

faced and angry. "That's *enough*, Marlena!" His boom-
ing voice stopped her midsentence. She froze, bit her lip
for a moment, and flew out of the office, slamming the
door behind her. Miss Edgerton winced.

"Senator . . ." began Tyler in as sympathetic a tone as
he could muster following the tirade.

"Later!" boomed Maxwell as he slammed his own
door.

Again the office went still with expectation. Tyler,
half fuming, half dumbfounded, considered his options.

"Miss Edgerton, I believe it would be best if I left for
a few hours."

She seemed to think it was as good a response as any.
"Yes, Mr. Hamilton, perhaps that would be a good
choice, given the circumstances."

"Good day, Miss Edgerton." Tyler left without another word.

Storming down the street, mentally listing the unreasonable characteristics of one Miss Marlena Winbourne
Maxwell and perhaps her entire family, Tyler found
himself heading not to his apartment, but in the other
direction, toward the tavern at the corner. The same
tavern where he and the senator had toasted their newfound partnership only six days before. Six days that
seemed months ago. After a moment's pause, he decided an ale was as good a response as any to his need
to kill a few hours out of the Maxwells' presence. A bit
early for brandy, but an ale at two in the afternoon
wouldn't raise anyone's eyebrows. Tyler laughed at
himself. Now he seemed to be overcompensating for his
newfound ability to start arguments by his mere presence. Still, he thought as he plunked down the coin and
took a slow draft of the foamy brew, some part of him
thoroughly enjoyed the controversy. It was such a refreshing change from his Northern life, even if it did

have a few rough edges of late. *Rough edges like hot-tempered, unreasonable Lena Maxwell.*

He ordered a sandwich. *Face it, Hamilton,* thought Tyler, *you want her anyway. All the social conventions don't mean a thing in the face of it.* Tyler took another long swallow of his drink and leaned back in his chair. *Ah, but she's not lining up at your feet like all those good-natured girls from Boston, is she? Is that why you want her so much? She's right about one thing, Hamilton: Down here, you're a foreigner.*

"Now, there's a gloomy face for someone in such a spotlight!" came an amiable voice, accompanied by a rowdy slap on the back. As if by some miserable cue, there stood Richard Powers above the tavern table. "With that melancholy face, you couldn't have been reading the same papers I was this morning. You're the talk of the town, Hamilton. I'd have guessed you'd be celebrating, but you surely don't look it." He watched the barkeep put a sandwich on the table. "Don't they feed you at the Maxwells'? It's a bit early for supper."

Tyler was glad for the company, even if it was Richard Powers. At least someone was happy to find him in a room. "I'm afraid not every voter has cast their ballot in my favor, Richard. Things are a bit . . . shall we say 'tense' . . . at the senator's office. I thought it best to steer clear for a while." Tyler pulled a chair out for Richard. "What brings you to this part of town in the middle of the afternoon anyway? Surely no one's cursing your existence these days?"

Powers laughed and sat down, motioning to the barkeep to add another ale to the table. "Not that I know of. I was supposed to meet a friend here, but the cad hasn't shown. I was just about to call the afternoon a total loss when I caught sight of your pitiful figure at the table."

"Ah, the very sight of me."

"Let me see if I've guessed this right. Mrs. Maxwell, good press or bad, doesn't see eye to eye with the senator regarding his choice of campaign manager, does she?"

Tyler wished he didn't need a friend so much at the moment. He wished Richard weren't so friendly. It would make it easier to hate him. Tyler nodded and bit into the sandwich.

"Mr. Hamilton, you do have a problem. No doubt the senator is immovable on the subject. Lord, I don't envy you a bit on this one. I don't believe I'd get between the senator and his wife for all the cattle in Texas. I'd better get you another ale. No, wait. I've a better idea."

Tyler laughed in spite of himself. "I am certainly open to suggestions."

"It would probably be best if you disappeared for a while, no doubt. Am I right?"

"I think that might be a wise course of action," said Tyler, remembering the searing way Marlena had looked at him.

"I believe I have just the thing. My friend and I were going out to the ranch to do a bit of riding. You said you ride, didn't you?"

"Yes."

"It's settled, then. I'll get my driver. We can stop by your apartment and pick up your tack if you've got any, or you're certainly welcome to borrow anything from our stables."

"I'm just around the corner. And my saddle is feeling rather neglected of late. But I've found my English riding jacket to be a bit of a nuisance in this Texas heat. I'd be obliged if you could introduce me to some more . . . well, *local* attire."

"Good God, Hamilton," laughed Powers, adding a

cowboy accent to his already pronounced Southern drawl, "we'll have you in chaps and spurs by sunset. And eatin' a mite better grub than this here waterin' hole provides."

"Well, that'd be mighty fine," countered Tyler, in a most laughable Southern-drawl-cum-Boston accent. The combination was pathetic. The two men stomped out of the bar like gun partners from a dime-store novel.

❧ Chapter Eight ❧

Marlena stood at the far end of the hallway, facing the closed door to her father's offices. She crossed her arm over her chest and fingered the pocket watch while she stared at the door. It had been over a week, and the tension had hardly let up from the day she and her father had made that terrible ride back from the ranch. No matter what the ideology, her mother took Tyler Hamilton's continued employment as a personal affront. Mama had asked—pleaded, even—that Hamilton be removed, as a personal consideration of her feelings. As a wife. As a woman who had been brutalized. In the name of the sanctity of marriage and the love and loyalty of a husband.

Her father, for matters of principle and fully knowing the cost to himself, had refused. Out of conviction. Out of genuine, sacrificial love for the future of his country and the personal pain it would take to move it forward. Marlena didn't know who was right. She had no idea what to do. And she was very afraid that things would never be the same between her parents again. The thought glared at her every time she sat at her mother's chair in the dining room, passed her closed dressing-room door, or even looked at her father. Despite their many disagreements, she missed her mother and the organized, gracious atmosphere she gave to the Maxwell household. Marlena didn't much care for having to fill those shoes.

They'd managed to hide Mother's absence from those outside the family, but it was hard work. Marlena was grateful when friends believed the smiling lie about her mother "wanting to stay out of the fray for a while." But how much longer would they believe that? Marlena was angry with her father for his stubborn will. She was angry with her mother for holding on to such bitterness when Tyler had done nothing to hurt her. And she was angry at Tyler for keeping her father so close to him when she felt so far away.

She turned away from the door and paced down the hall a few steps. Tyler seemed to be everywhere in her life she didn't want him to be, and nowhere she thought he ought to be. Over the last week, Tyler had neatly slipped into the gap now spread between her and her father. He had taken her place as the senator's confidant and right hand. She heard them conferring late into the night in the library. Sometimes she would wake in the small hours of the morning to the sound of the family carriage taking Tyler home after a marathon session at the office.

Worse yet, he hadn't paid a lick of attention to Marlena since that swashbuckling attempt at a kiss in the Powerses' garden. It was as if he had thrown down the gauntlet and now waited for her to respond. Well, she wasn't ready to respond. She wouldn't give him the opportunity to win his wager. Truth be told, she couldn't guarantee she wouldn't "yield" if Tyler kissed her like that again.

Worst of all, and by far the biggest surprise, was that he and Richard Powers had become fast friends. Richard was supposed to be her territory. She didn't

much care for that Yankee honing in on the attentions
of everyone in her life. He was unpredictable.

So am I, Marlena decided. In that moment, she made
up her mind. Marlena Winbourne Maxwell wouldn't
give up and she damn well wasn't going to yield.

The hall clock chimed 11:30. Within seconds
Marlena had her plan. On Fridays the senator had
lunch with a colleague, and Deborah usually took the
opportunity to go out. With a smile on her face,
Marlena headed for the kitchen door. She was going to
show that braggart Mr. Hamilton that no one wagered
on her emotional fortitude.

She swooped into the kitchen. "Sarah, please serve
luncheon for Mr. Hamilton and myself in the library today. We have work to do. Have Hewitt send for Mr.
Hamilton when lunch is served." She swooped out before Sarah could answer, the acknowledgment merely
echoing to Marlena from the other side of the swinging
kitchen door.

"Excuse me?" Tyler's surprised expression only
intensified when he took off his glasses to blink at
Hewitt. His pencil was still poised in midair over a sizable ledger.

"Yes, sir. Miss Maxwell has requested that you join
her for luncheon. At twelve noon exactly. That would
be in ten minutes, sir. Shall I tell her to expect you?"

Tyler drew his hand over his chin, not quite sure
what to make of the invitation. Not only was it mildly
improper for a young lady to invite a man to lunch,
but highly uncharacteristic for the distant Miss
Maxwell he'd seen this past week. With the senator
already gone for lunch, Tyler glanced over to Miss
Edgerton for some help in interpretation. She kept
her head down, humming "Pop Goes the Weasel"
again. No assistance would be coming from that corner,

despite the fact that Tyler knew she had heard every word.

"Sir?"

"Well, Hewitt, I think you had better tell the lady she can expect me. This doesn't sound like an invitation I ought to decline, wouldn't you say so?"

"That would not be for me to say, Mr. Hamilton," said Hewitt, unhelpfully proper as usual. "Luncheon will be served in the library."

"The *library*?"

"Exactly, sir. The library. Good day."

Tyler stood up, removed his sleeve garters, and walked to the corner coatrack for his jacket. He waited for a comment, but Miss Edgerton kept her eyes glued to her paperwork. If Tyler wanted some assistance, he was going to have to solicit it.

"What do you make of this, Miss Edgerton? Is this an olive branch or an ambush?"

"That would not be for me to say, Mr. Hamilton," she parroted, her voice colored by a smile.

Hamilton let out a slow whistle as he buttoned his jacket. "Ever so helpful as usual, Miss Edgerton. You are truly indispensable."

"Why, thank you, Mr. Hamilton. I'll be leaving for lunch now, as well."

"Of course, Miss Edgerton," said Tyler, with a wide grin. "Perhaps it would be wise to leave the building."

She smiled. "That would not be for me to say, Mr. Hamilton." She flung on her shawl and nearly whirled out the office door, locking it from the outside. Tyler watched her head off down the street, obviously laughing. He straightened his tie, adjusted his cuff links, and took a deep breath as he pushed open the inner door to the household.

"Good afternoon, Mr. Hamilton," Marlena said precisely. She sat regally in a glowing mint-colored dress at the end of a small library table that had been elaborately set for luncheon. She enjoyed the not-quite-concealed bewilderment in his eyes. So far the plan was working. "Thank you for joining me."

He responded with equal formality. "Good afternoon, Miss Maxwell. I was delighted at your invitation. Such a refreshing change from the formal dining room."

"Quite."

Marlena nodded to Sarah, who stood in the corner. The girl began to serve. Throughout the salad course, Marlena watched Tyler wait for her to speak. She remained silent. She would occasionally look up at him with an enigmatic smile, then continue as if a luncheon for two in total silence were the most normal meal one could imagine. She noted with pleasure that Sarah began to fidget in the corner.

By the soup course it seemed Hamilton had accepted her culinary equivalent of a stare-down. He too would occasionally smile, but did not offer conversation. Suddenly, he reached into his pocket. He placed a pebble on the table between them. The pebble she'd thrown at him Tuesday night. The pebble he'd held up to her like a poker chip, a wager that she would surrender to his charms.

I will not yield, Marlena reminded herself. She set her jaw in determination. She certainly wasn't about to give him the satisfaction of unnerving her.

The third course came and went without so much as a word. Neither side flinched. In the forced silence, Marlena found herself increasingly aware of Tyler's presence. Not just his attendance in the room, but the *presence* of him. The strength of his charisma, the force of his determination—even if it was just in a childish standoff—became palpable as the meal went on. She looked at the pebble and remembered his challenge.

What would she do if he kissed her again? If given no resistance and no fear of discovery, what kind of kiss would he give her? Long, slow, and searching? Or powerful, urgent, and breathtaking? The pebble sat, posing the question amid the table setting. It wove an irresistible spell over her. She blinked, recapturing her wandering thoughts. Her aim of standing him down was becoming surprisingly more difficult than she'd planned.

Instead, she noticed how his jaw moved when he ate. How the muscles in his arm worked when he cut his meat, the way his fingers curved around a glass. *You are a foreigner, a guest—no, not even a guest; you are an employee. We do not belong together.* The aversion and the attraction melded together inside the silence to create a disarming sensation. Again.

Marlena noticed Sarah's hands shaking when she served dessert. The tension in the room had rendered the girl nearly incompetent. Neither she nor Tyler had even acknowledged Sarah's presence in the last two courses.

Marlena picked up the long silver parfait spoon like a drawn sword. Slowly, carefully, with an almost languid quality, she ladled up a spoonful of the dessert and ate it—no, she relished it—without taking her gaze from Tyler for an instant.

They were debating all over again, this time without words, armed only with parfait spoons and glances. The library clock ticked. She took another luxurious spoonful. Then a third. All without blinking an eye.

Marlena heard Sarah's feet shuffle. The girl paced as if she would run from the room at the first opportunity. Marlena noticed Tyler's jaw tighten almost imperceptibly as she licked the dessert off her spoon with particular enjoyment. *Good.* She swore she saw him fight harder to maintain a calm, icy expression. *Excellent.*

She wanted him to know all the frustration she'd felt in the last week. She wanted to make *him* yield.

That was the lethal side effect. The intensity she was channeling at Tyler reflected back at her in the form of sensuality rather than triumph. It woke up a deep, unwanted desire, just as the debate had done.

Marlena made a conscious effort to slow her breathing. She reminded herself that until Tyler's appearance, *she'd* run the campaign. She narrowed her eyes and drummed up her fury to squelch the creeping glow in her stomach. But somehow it seemed one emotion only fed the other. Her smile widened eerily when she heard the gentle clink of her spoon hitting the bottom of the glass. It widened further still when she realized Sarah had thrown duty to the wind and fled the room. *I won,* she thought, not realizing she'd turned the dessert into a slow race.

But Tyler hadn't entered the race. He hadn't finished his dessert. In fact, Tyler had stopped eating altogether. He was simply sitting there, fingering the damnable pebble, staring at her with a smoldering look in his eye. Once again he'd managed to unnerve her, and she couldn't be at all sure that she'd managed to unnerve him.

Marlena put her spoon down. She took a sip of water, peering at Tyler over the gold rim of the stemware. When she set the glass down again they eyed each other for at least a minute. Testing and parrying with hints of expressions rather than debate rhetoric. Invisibly calculating a next move.

Marlena placed her napkin on the table and began to stand. Tyler shot upright in the proper response, beating her slow rise. Her eyes narrowed. The library clock struck one o'clock in a lone, echoing chime.

"Mr. Hamilton" was all she said, in a tone that

hinted at nothing and everything and anything. Still, her eyes could not and would not leave his. He responded by inclining his head in the smallest of nods, his eyes locked on hers.

Without comment or closure, Marlena headed for the door.

But not before Tyler's broad hand latched on to her elbow. In an instant he spun her around, locked the other hand around her waist, and drew her in. He pulled her face so close she could feel his breath spill across her neck. His hand caressed her elbow while the other pressed her hips into his with a force that made it difficult to breathe. He moved his lips a hairbreadth from hers. For a lingering, expectant moment, he hovered just above her lips. Not quite touching, but so very close.

Then, suddenly, he released her and stepped away, flawlessly calm and collected, as if what had just transpired had never happened. Marlena's eyes flew open the minute she realized they had fallen shut. She glared at him, finding passion, anger, daring, and a million other emotions in his eyes. The damned veneer was up in a flash and she had no idea what had just happened. Tyler offered a polite "Miss Maxwell," snatched the pebble off the table, and quit the room before Marlena could draw another breath.

The glass didn't shatter half as much as she'd intended it to, when it struck the library door.

Tyler flung himself through the office door, glad to find the room empty. For a moment he paced around the office, his hand running through his hair. *Damn this baffling, unnerving, irrational, spectacular woman.* His body flexed as he remembered the feel of her small frame against his. The look in her eyes as she wove that

spell over him during dessert. He had nearly let loose
his desire just then. Dear God, what a match she was.
He admitted to an insatiable hunger to have her. And it
was far beyond physical.

This was not at all what Tyler Hamilton III was used to
in women or work. This was an incalculable risk. Could
he pursue her openly? There was no telling what the senator's response to such a courtship would be. Tyler
doubted, however, that it would be encouraging. Perhaps
after the campaign, but now was unwise, inappropriate,
and downright dangerous. But she was so wonderful. So
sharp and daring. Suddenly there were so many gray areas
in places of his life where, previously, black and white had
been so easy to distinguish. Could he work with her on
the campaign and not fall prey to her charms? Two weeks
ago he would have said yes. Just now he wasn't so convinced. Tyler Hamilton was losing control where control
had never been a problem. He checked his reflection in
the glass doors covering the bookshelves.

Satisfied that the disarray was only on the inside,
Tyler calmed himself by sitting down at his desk to face
the ledger again. He took a deep breath and spread his
hands slowly across the large green paper, taking in the
smooth predictability of columns and figures. The black
and white of arithmetic, where sums were purely right
or wrong. He put on his glasses and grasped the pencil
tightly, as if holding the wood and lead were a balm.

The pencil snapped as the interior office door swung
open and Marlena marched through it. *My God,*
thought Tyler, half in exasperation and half in panic at
being alone with her again, *doesn't she know when to
leave well enough alone?* He made sure Marlena saw
only a smooth, calm facade.

"What just happened?" she asked angrily, with her
hands on her hips, as if she hadn't just been in the library.

Tyler thought the question a ridiculous one, even though he'd asked it of himself only moments ago. He forced a wry smile. "Must I explain?"

"Don't toy with me. I know perfectly well what happened." She was attempting to appear calm and collected, but failing. Tyler found her efforts strangely endearing.

He noticed the flush on her cheeks and neck. How deeply she breathed. It made him wonder what her face would look like if her passion were fully aroused. Her hair spread out on a pillow . . . *Stop that. Stop that!* He fought back the image and tried to clear his head. "A young lady just invited a bachelor to an unchaperoned luncheon. And then refused to speak to him the entire meal."

"You are skirting the issue."

So she wanted to discuss the real issue. Or so she claimed.

That was all the encouragement Tyler needed to get to the heart of the matter. He pulled the small rock from his pocket and sent it bouncing onto the desk. He was annoyed and frustrated at both himself and Marlena. The situation was getting out of hand. This was going to have to be settled once and for all before things went any further.

"And exactly what is the issue, Marlena? What you and I were both feeling, have both felt for a while now? Perhaps that I called your bluff?" Now that he'd finally given himself permission to talk about it, the words came rushing out of him. He came out from behind the desk. "Or is this more about the fact that I won't settle for shallow displays of charm like the ones you pour on poor Richard Powers? Sad fellow, I don't believe he has any idea of the thorny path you've led him down just for your own amusement."

Marlena's face lit with anger at his accusation. "How dare you bring Richard into this!"

"How dare *you* bring Richard into this. Don't you think I saw everything that night at dinner? Richard is a decent, honest man, and you were reeling him in like a helpless fish. Not that you really care for the man. It was all I could do to sit back and watch you lavish feigned affections on him until he couldn't see straight. I like Richard. He's the only friend I seem to have in Austin, and I don't care to see you hoodwink him for your own entertainment."

"How do you know I don't care for him? Richard is a—"

"Because I can see it. The difference in the way you look at him." They were going to face this, and they were going to face it here and now. "The difference in the way you look at him and the way you look at *me*." She took a step back. Tyler pressed on. "The way you look at me, Lena." He used the name intentionally. "Admit it for once, and perhaps we can get on with this. As much as it's impossible, as much as you think you hate me, you cannot deny what's between us any more than I can."

Marlena simply stood there. She had dropped her sharp demeanor for just a moment, and through the chink in the wall Tyler saw a collection of emotions that made his heart skip.

He knew with every bone in his body that he shouldn't, that the senator or Miss Edgerton could come in at any moment. He knew to get close to her again would be dangerous, that he'd be undone by his desire for her. It would go beyond a test of wills. Yet he watched his fingers pick up the pebble. He watched his feet walk over to her. He placed the stone in her palm and wrapped her fingers around it. An unexpected tenderness flooded him. He wrapped his hand around hers. He almost shook her slightly as he spoke in a hushed tone. "Yield." He realized at that moment he didn't know if he was speaking to her or to himself.

She gazed at him, wavering. Her eyes. Dear God, her eyes could make him beg. They did things to him no woman had ever done. He gave in to the bone-deep yearning and leaned in to kiss her. But she surprised him. She kissed him first. Lips parted, she met him with an eager, seeking mouth that stopped his pulse and sent Tyler's defenses tumbling down. Her hands slid into his hair. Her kiss was passionate and reckless. He gave in. He yielded, himself, and he was glad of it. His arms wrapped around her and he pressed his mouth so powerfully upon hers that her head fell back against his arm. Lena's hands slid down his neck to clutch at his coat, pulling him closer. With a low moan he let his tongue wander, tasting the trifle on hers. He poured his kiss across her mouth and down her neck, caressing her back with deep, possessive strokes. Marlena melted under his hands. For a few brief, breathtaking moments, the world consisted of only two people, coming together in spite of the tremendous risk.

Tyler pulled away first and rested his forehead on hers. "Lena," he said simply. It was delicious, intoxicating, to say her name.

"Oh, God," said Marlena, her own voice breathy and quiet. "What do we—"

Tyler put his thumb to her lips. His words came in short, heavy spurts between deep breaths, much as they had done in the study that first night. "Don't. Not now. Go. We'll find a way to talk later."

Her eyes took on a panicked look. "Tyler . . ."

His name.

She had said his name.

Tyler had never heard her use his first name, and it

threatened to destroy the thin thread of control he had left. He shut his eyes tight and gripped her arms. "Go. Go right now. I swear to you, I'll find a way for us to talk later. But you *must* leave this instant."

Marlena pulled away and ran for the door. Tyler stood there, listening to her footsteps race down the long hall. Inch by inch Tyler fought back his emotions to put up the front he needed. Twenty minutes later, he had not moved from the spot, but Senator Maxwell had absolutely no idea anything was out of the ordinary when he came through the door and Tyler turned to greet him.

⇥ Chapter Nine ⇤

The hall clock sent a single chime out into the darkness. With a backward glance, Marlena stole toward the library door and pushed it open. She stepped into the room, exhaled, and pulled the door shut behind her. Peering about, she found Tyler sitting on the window seat, his features whitewashed in the moonlight. He held a bottle of wine in one hand, with two wineglasses threaded through the fingers of the other.

"Hello," he said softly, warmly. Marlena's stomach lurched as it had done every time she'd thought of him since this afternoon. Even his voice was enough to send a glow throughout her. He had a way of saying complete ideas in a single word. She watched him pour the wine into the glasses, the red liquid looking blue-black in the cool light.

She took a step. "Tyler, I've been thinking. I am not so sure this—"

"Myself as well." He set the bottle down. The light sent a silvery cast through his eyes and hair.

"This is such a risk and so much could—" Her words were speeding up.

"A huge risk. Enormous." Tyler's words came on top of hers. He stood up and began walking forward.

"I'm not at all sure Daddy wouldn't react very badly."

"It could very well cost me my position." He reached her.

Marlena's fingers were knotting together. "And this isn't the time. The campaign is at a critical—"

"Completely. A vital juncture. I couldn't agree more." He took a sip of wine and handed her the other glass. She took it in both hands. Marlena fought the impulse to drain it in one gulp.

"Tyler, you're not listening."

"I am listening, Marlena," he said. She felt as though his eyes were devouring her.

"Well, I want to know why you don't sound nearly as concerned as I am. I am trying to tell you I'm having second thoughts, and you are standing there looking at me like some lovestruck schoolboy."

Tyler smiled. Then he reached over, and as he smoothed a stray hair away from the side of her face, the smile disappeared. Just his slight touch against her cheek made her suck in her breath. "I'm frightened to death, Lena. More scared than I can ever remember."

Marlena squeezed her eyes shut for a moment. "I'm relieved to hear it." She opened them again. "Tyler, I'm serious. Sneaking around like this is disconcerting. We really ought to think this through—we're intelligent people."

"Marlena Maxwell, you are the most intelligent woman I believe I've ever met." His hand hadn't left her cheek.

"Then you can understand what a very unwise thing this is to do. We've got to find a way to deal with this sensibly."

Tyler put his glass down on one of the small tables that flanked the armchairs. "The sensible thing to do would be to ignore our feelings." He spoke matter-of-factly, but his eyes betrayed him.

"I agree," Marlena replied. The touch of his fingers

was making *sensible* a very unattractive option at the moment.

"We should be able to work together without becoming involved. Both of us are strong enough to overcome an unfortunate bit of chemistry."

Marlena set her wineglass next to his. But not before taking two more healthy swallows. "Tyler, I think we're making a wise choice here. You need to keep your attention focused on the campaign. We both do."

"I completely agree." He was so close to her. He obviously didn't agree one bit.

"I'm glad we've come to an understanding." He was easing closer. *Oh, Lord.* "It will be so much easier now, don't you think?"

"Not at all." He slipped his hands around her waist and drew her into a quiet, tender kiss. A slow, savoring kiss. *Oh, dear Lord.* It wasn't even worth resisting. There were a dozen solid arguments for why they should not pursue this relationship.

And Marlena was perfectly ready to ignore them all.

They stood with their foreheads together, eyes closed. "It is impossible to just ignore this, isn't it?" she whispered. She felt Tyler's nod. Suddenly he began to hum, and to sway. His pitch was so inaccurate—and that was a kind term—that it took a moment for Marlena to realize he was humming the first waltz from the barbecue. She picked up the melody and they danced a small, intimate version of the steps, keeping close. He was strong when he danced. Solid. Something to draw strength from.

She pulled back and looked up into his eyes. "Isn't there some far more judicious girl back in Boston? Someone your mother would be so pleased with?"

Tyler chuckled. "Yes, as a matter of fact, there is. But I can't seem to recall her name just now. And I no more want to be dancing with her at this very moment than you want to be dancing with Richard Powers."

Marlena sighed. "Richard." She pulled Tyler close
again. "Good Lord, Tyler, how are we going to do this?"

"I haven't a clue." She felt his chin settle on the top
of her head. His arms tightened around her. "At least
not yet." They swayed in silence for a minute. She felt
him lift his head and scan the library. "When is the last
time you read *Romeo and Juliet*?"

"Tyler, we hardly qualify as 'star-crossed lovers.'
And, might I remind you, nearly everyone ends up dead
in *Romeo and Juliet*."

"My point exactly. Best to know what *not* to do."

"Tyler . . ."

"One day," he murmured, running a finger along her
forehead, tracing her hairline, "I am going to unleash
this hair and lose myself in it. Your hair invades my
thoughts, Lena. It could drive a man to distraction."

He has a tender touch, Marlena thought. She hadn't
expected it of him. She imagined there were a lot of unexpected things in Tyler Hamilton. "Remind me to
wear it down next time we debate," she teased. "It'll
seal my victory."

"A dirty trick. But a delicious defeat. I'd concede in a
moment—a wise man knows his limits."

"Concede?" Marlena ran her finger along his collar
and watched the muscles there respond to her touch.
"That'd be a hollow victory. I'd much rather best you in
a fair fight." She enjoyed sparring with him. He was
challenging. A victory over him was a true victory—he
wouldn't patronize her or condescend. He wouldn't water down his views or his arguments just because she
was a woman. Nor would he expect her to keep her
opinions to herself just because of her gender.

"If you let your hair down, it will not be a fair fight."

She ran her finger down to his chest and poked
him. "And I suppose you took off your glasses during

our debate simply to clear your vision? Tyler Hamilton, I could best you with my hair shorn clean off my head."

Tyler grimaced at the vision. Then a wave of affection washed over his face. "I believe you could. That's what I find so attractive about you." He tapped her head. "I'm as fond of what's under that hair as I am of the hair, you know."

The fact that he enjoyed her intelligence was more attractive to Marlena than Tyler's spellbinding eyes. "Telling a woman you admire her intellect?" She poured on her Southern-belle drawl. "How insulting. Why, Tyler Hamilton, that's usually a man's last resort when he cannot think of a thing to say about her beauty."

"I can think of any number of things. Where would you like me to start?"

Tension filled the office with the morning light. Senator Maxwell crumpled a paper and threw it against the wall, slamming a fist against the door frame and cursing. Hewitt had brought the message only minutes before, and stood at the door awaiting a reply. He waved Hewitt off abruptly and closed himself in his office by banging the door shut. Without reaction, Hewitt dropped his silver tray to his side and began to leave. Tyler could hear the senator's voice railing against whatever news had been delivered.

"Hewitt?" asked Tyler as he looked up from the day's papers. "May I ask from whom the message came?"

Hewitt, usually poker-faced even in the most delicate of situations, looked slightly uneasy. "That would not be for me to say, sir." His response told Tyler this message was no piece of ordinary bad news or poor press.

"Of course, Hewitt, forgive my impertinence,"

replied Tyler. "My concern is purely for the senator's well-being."

"Naturally, sir." Hewitt turned on his heels and went back into the house through the interior door. Tyler started for Maxwell's door.

"I don't think that would be wise right now, Mr. Hamilton," said Miss Edgerton. Tyler stopped in his tracks. In the past two weeks he'd come to rely on her keen intuition where the senator was concerned. She had an uncanny sense of the nuances of his campaign and personal life.

"What do you mean, Miss Edgerton? He obviously is quite angry, and perhaps I could help."

"I don't think you can offer any assistance in this matter, Mr. Hamilton. Did you happen to notice the paper?"

"What paper?"

"The paper on which the message was written. The stationery on Hewitt's tray."

"Good heavens, no. It looked like any other message."

"It was on cream paper. With a light blue border."

"I'm not following you, Miss Edgerton. What does the paper have to do with the message?"

"It has more to do with the sender, Mr. Hamilton. That paper was Mrs. Maxwell's personal stationery. I would venture that this is not an issue where your involvement would be welcome. In fact, if you'll forgive me, I'd venture the message was about you in some respect. Going in there right now would be . . . well, uncomfortable at best."

"Good Lord, what's she done now?" railed Tyler, pulling his hands through his hair and sitting back down at his desk. He was beginning to feel the weight of Mrs. Maxwell's prejudices these days.

"I'd imagine it's what she *hasn't* done that has the senator so angry," she replied. "I don't think Mrs.

Maxwell is going to back down on this, Mr. Hamilton. Our senator seems to have quite a fight on his hands."

"Lucky me, I'm the battleground. Why couldn't I have chosen to cut my teeth on a nice, quiet, unchallenged incumbent race somewhere uncomplicated, like New Hampshire? Miss Edgerton, why on earth did I come to Texas?"

She smiled and pulled the now ever-present cone of peppermints from her desk drawer, popping one in her mouth and offering the cone to Tyler, who waved it away. "That does seem to be the key question, Mr. Hamilton. Or, more precisely, why did Jason Maxwell *bring you* to Texas?" She took off her glasses and continued, her speech garbled slightly by the candy. "I'd be willing to bet that if you just keep your mind set on the larger issue here—the idea, not the people, mind you— you'll do just fine. No matter how messy things get. Mrs. Maxwell is surely a handful, but you don't marry a man like Jason Maxwell without being able to hold your ground. That man would swallow up a lesser woman whole. Much as I don't care for this argument—or how serious it's getting—I can't imagine the senator married to anyone with less spine."

"It is getting serious, isn't it?" Tyler asked.

"As serious as I've ever seen it get, Mr. Hamilton."

"Let me ask you, Miss Edgerton, are you worried?"

She sucked on the peppermint for a moment. Then she put her glasses back on and looked at Tyler in complete seriousness. "Yes, Mr. Hamilton. I'm worried. Very worried."

"But surely you've got to consider—"

"No." Senator Maxwell held up a hand toward Marlena as she followed him through the office door after lunch.

"Certainly there's a way to—"

"No!" He was heading for his office, fleeing her pursuit. "Lena, I'm telling you—"

"Daddy, you're not listening to me." She was right behind him, undaunted.

The senator spun around so that Marlena nearly slammed into him. "I *am* listening to you. I've heard each and every blasted thing you've said, and I'm telling you, if you don't back off this minute, young lady, I'm going to banish you from this office. Now, git!" With that he stormed into his office and gave the door a Maxwell slam that shook the cabinet glass.

Marlena stared after him, foot tapping, fingers drumming against her hips. Tyler took refuge behind a newspaper. Miss Edgerton found an excuse to rummage through her bottom drawer. It was getting to be a bit of a routine around the office.

"Banish, my foot!" muttered Marlena, flinging through the day's mail. "If he weren't such a pigheaded old horse married to such a stubborn old hen, they'd . . ." She continued in such a colorful collection of murmured name-calling that Tyler finally had to look up and laugh.

"Good afternoon to you too, Miss Maxwell," he greeted politely, taking care to hide the surge of attraction that happened now at the mere sight of her. It was excruciating to be in the same room with her and not touch her. Especially when she was full of fire. Dear God, she was exquisite when she was angry.

Suddenly, Marlena gave a small yelp of surprise. "Who on earth convinced Vincent Boardman to be a precinct captain? We've been courting him for months!"

Tyler smiled. "It's amazing what can happen when you spend an hour complimenting Mrs. Boardman's dogs. They are *dogs*, aren't they?"

"Those snippy little things? Yes, they're dogs—and

you should live as well as those dogs. Mr. Hamilton, I've tried going through Mrs. Boardman. I've even tried going through those beastly little animals, and I've gained nothing." She hesitated for a moment before adding softly, "I'm impressed."

Tyler's smile broadened. "Sometimes," he said warmly, "it is easier to woo an old lady when you are a young man."

Her eyebrows shot up. "Well, yes, there is that."

He reached into his drawer, extracting a short stack of cards. "Speaking of which, Miss Maxwell," he began, coming out from behind the desk, "I can't seem to find the right ending for the Cattlemen's Club speech for Thursday. They're old men. Would you mind giving it a young lady's perspective?"

"Of course," she replied. "I'd be happy to help." Tyler handed her the cards. She sat on the desk edge, flipping through them. "You've got nothing in here about railroad access. They won't let him go without addressing that issue. And you had better include at least two compliments to Anthony Dorlan. If you don't stroke that man's ego, he goes home and complains to his wife and it will be all over town by sundown." She tapped the cards against her fingers, her brow twisted in thought. "The ending needs to be about cattle's future, and how it can't be separated from Texas' future. These men consider themselves the backbone of Texas economy, and in many ways they are. They need to know Father has their interests at heart." She tapped the cards into a neat pile against the desk before handing them back to Tyler. "And one more thing, Mr. Hamilton. You'll regret it if you don't strike that remark about pork. Frederick Brown owns more hogs than cattle."

"Indeed."

"In other respects, it's rather good."

He took the cards from her, but slipped something into her palm as he did.

A single, innocent pebble. Like the one she'd thrown at him when he kissed her. Like the one he'd placed on the table at lunch. It had now become his secret display of affection. From the look on her face, it was clear she understood his code. It seemed a century before tonight, when they'd meet again. *One at a time,* he thought. *One at a time.*

Tyler sat waiting on the window seat again, his attention focused on the library door. The night was hot and dark, bereft of moonlight.

The library doors slid silently open. Marlena turned to close them carefully behind her, and then flew noiselessly into Tyler's arms. Her touch ignited him instantly. He kissed her hungrily at first, satisfying the need to be near her that had driven him to distraction all afternoon. He felt her melt in his arms. She nuzzled her face into his neck and closed her eyes. Tyler leaned his head back against the window frame and breathed in the way her body snuggled next to his. His hand wandered luxuriously through her hair. He kissed the top of her head and curved his other hand around her cheek. "Do you know why I didn't have a single cup of coffee this afternoon?"

Marlena lifted her head to meet his gaze. "Why?"

"You've ruined it for me." He stroked her cheek. "I taste it and I think of you. Of the taste of coffee on your tongue. Then I think about kissing you, and I'm done for. I tell you, you've ruined a perfectly good beverage."

"Well," she replied, settling herself into his lap. "You've done some damage yourself."

"Surely not I." He traced the curve of her ear.

"Oh, yes, indeed." She stuck her chin up. "I shan't be able to walk up the drive with a clear mind ever again."

"Hmm?"

"All those pebbles. I see a pebble and I think of kissing you. Imagine that long driveway filled with millions and millions of wicked, sinful pebbles." She purred the words out.

"Remind me to show you the miles and miles of stone walls in New England."

She chuckled. "It's very different up there, isn't it?"

Tyler nodded. "In a thousand different ways. The people, the landscape, even the air."

"Tell me about your family," she said, weaving her fingers through his. "What did they think of your coming here?"

"They weren't very happy." Tyler sighed. "I'm not sure they knew what to make of it. Mother got this rather disappointed look on her face, as though I'd done something intentionally to hurt her. Father was . . . well, puzzled. I couldn't give him a solid reason why I was going, because he wouldn't have understood why I chose to do it, anyway. I couldn't really tell him I did it to get away from the family, now, could I?"

"Get away?"

"Being from a prominent family has advantages, to be sure, but don't you ever wish just once that you could meet someone who had no idea who you were? Go someplace where no one expected you to act like a Maxwell?"

"That's just it," Marlena mused, "no one *does* expect me to act like a Maxwell. Just some watered-down version of a Maxwell, suitable for wives and daughters. Every time I start acting like a Maxwell, I invariably get into trouble."

Tyler brought their interwoven hands to his lips. "You get into quite a lot of trouble." He liked that. He admired her defiance.

"I don't see why I should." Marlena sat up straight.

Tyler watched that spark in her eyes ignite again. *Here she goes.* When she got herself onto a topic, it was like blowing on an ember—things fired up in a thousand directions. He enjoyed watching the flame catch. "It seems ridiculous. Medieval. Having a brain and wearing a skirt should not be mutually exclusive. Why, I'd even run for office if they'd let me. I'd be a better legislator than some of those half-brains puffing their egos up over the most shortsighted little things. As if trousers were a prerequisite for common sense!"

"You'd get my vote," offered Tyler. "Skirts notwithstanding. You could debate circles around half the fellows I knew in law school."

"You see?" Marlena shot back, nearly on the edge of the cushion now. "You say that as a compliment. Mother would say it as though it were a vice. I'm so tired of being told I've overstepped my bounds. Having an opinion—especially when I'm right—is not rude, it's—"

Tyler clasped his hand over her mouth.

"*Yes,*" he said on top of her ongoing speech, "Texas is very different from Boston. And about my family . . ."

Her eyes looked up at him, contrite, from above his hands. Deep, wide, and so very green. Brilliant and gemlike. He told himself again they were the most amazing things he had ever seen. One day he'd buy her emeralds that exact color.

"I did start this by asking you to tell me about your family, didn't I?" she said, after prying his hand off her mouth. Her penance was a collection of small, feathery kisses across his palm. It was an unnecessary incentive for forgiveness.

"Did I look as if I minded?"

"Having an opinion is not rude. Not letting you speak yours *is* rude."

"Well put."

"I yield the floor to the gentleman from Boston," Marlena declared, making an accompanying gesture.

"I've told you most of it. I wanted to escape the expectations. To make my own name for myself, not be just the third installment in the Hamilton family credo. My family is delightful, well respected, all the sorts of things people wish for in a family. But it's all rather stifling. Everything is different here. Loud. Up-front. I am the unknown quantity, and that feels rather refreshing." He fingered the hefty signet ring on his right hand.

She touched the golden initials. *TJH.* "It's lovely."

"I'm fond of it, too. It just fits rather tightly at times."

The next two evenings, events conspired to keep them from meeting. Tyler couldn't always find a plausible reason to stay late into the night at the Maxwell house, and neither one was ready for Marlena to venture out of the house for a meeting. The pair of days felt like months, and Tyler grew hungry for Marlena's touch. She must have felt it as well, for she nearly knocked him over with her first kiss when they finally met again.

"Show a little mercy, woman!" he teased. In reality, Tyler loved her unabashed physicality. Her desire for him was honest and unhindered. It made it difficult at times to keep his control. "I've no wish to bed you in the library window, Marlena."

"No wish?" she purred into his neck.

"Wish, well, that's a—*you'd better stop that*—perhaps I ought to say I have no *business* bedding you in the library window. But you're making it rather difficult to be honorable, Lena."

"Yes, honorable. All that upstanding Hamilton blood ought to count for something."

"It might, if you'd stop heating it up all the time."

"Well, if your circulation needs cooling, you'll get your wish. I'm going out to the ranch tomorrow."

"I heard," said Tyler, stroking her arm. He hated the thought of her being so far away.

"He wants me to try and talk to Mother."

"What are you going to say?"

Marlena let out a sigh. "That's just it; I have no idea what to say. They're both as stubborn as mules, and neither one is right."

Tyler stopped his caress. "What do you mean, 'neither one is right'?"

Marlena looked at him blankly. "It's just that . . . well, I can see her point of view, that's all."

A cold chill chased down Tyler's spine. "Your mother is hanging on to bitter grievances, staunchly denying Texas any real future in the Union, and you can see *her* side?"

Marlena pulled away from him. "You don't see it, do you? Tyler, this isn't a political argument. This is about my parents' marriage." She stood up. "I'll admit you've done nothing yourself to harm Mother, but you've got to know by now, your mere presence is painful for her." She looked at him, then began pacing. "You don't know, do you? How like my father not to tell you, to think it unimportant. Dear God, Tyler, do you know where that gash on her cheek came from?"

Tyler sat up straight. "Yes, damn it, I do. But it didn't come from me."

"No, it didn't. But the beast who gave it to her, he had a *Boston accent,* Tyler. He spoke like you."

Tyler saw where this was going, and he didn't like it. He stood up. "And . . ."

"And every time she hears you speak it's like everything is happening to her all over again. It isn't logical.

It's not about public policy. This is emotional. You can't just switch it off because it's impolite."

Tyler spoke coldly, slowly. "What are you saying, Marlena?" He watched her expression change. She had heard the anger rising in his voice. Good. He wanted her to hear it.

She selected her words carefully. "I am saying that I understand the way Mother is reacting. It's not right, but she's been through so much, and I can understand her feelings. I can understand why she asked Father to"—she stumbled over the words—"to remove you."

Tyler said nothing. He let the silence hang uncomfortably around her. After a long moment he growled, "She is wrong. She has no right to ask that."

"Whether she is wrong or not doesn't matter. He's her husband. She has a right to have her feelings come first with him. I'd expect to come first with my husband. Isn't that what it's supposed to be about? Man and wife? One flesh? It's not as if—" She cut herself off.

"Say it!" Tyler snapped, wounded. "It's not as if there aren't dozens of good Texan boys who could do the job. Say it." He narrowed his eyes. "I want to hear the words coming from your mouth, Lena."

He'd hurt her. He'd meant to. Her voice grew wounded. "Tyler, all I am trying to say is that I can see her side. I know what he's trying to do; I know he thinks it is what he has to do. And he's right to do it." She groaned, frustrated. "They're both right. They're both wrong. It's complicated."

"Your father is asking your mother to look beyond her personal pain and reconcile with the future. No one's saying it's not difficult. But how can he ask everyone in Texas—people who lost husbands and sons and fathers—when he won't even ask it of his own family? My God, Lena, can't you see that?"

"Of course I can!" she hissed, pacing.

"Do you believe in this? Tell me, Marlena, are you as pleased to have me here during the day as you are at night?" He wanted to shake her. His hands fisted at his sides.

Marlena whirled around, throwing her hands in the air. "You can't just pretend that where you come from doesn't matter here. It's not that simple, and you know it."

"Of course it matters. It is the whole *point* of the matter. Tell me this: Why are you going to the ranch tomorrow to convince your mother to come back to Austin?"

"You know perfectly well my father asked me to."

Tyler walked over to the bookshelves and leaned against them, facing away from her. "That is not reason enough."

"What on earth do you mean, 'that's not reason enough'? They are my parents, Tyler. I care about them. This is tearing them apart. Far apart. I'd expect my husband to put our marriage above anything else. At any cost. Why do you think I haven't settled for a husband yet, Tyler? I want *that* kind of love. Total. I want it to be worth that much to me. To him." She paused. "My parents used to be like that." He could hear the catch in her voice and feel her glaring at his back. "What is it you want to hear, Tyler?"

He turned to face her, not bothering to hide his pain. "I want to hear that *you* think *I* am the best choice for your father's campaign manager. That you agree with the principles that drove him to hire me. That you believe in what he and I stand for. In what *I* stand for. That my coming from Boston is not evil or bad or extreme or even just novel. That it is irrelevant and I am the right man at the right time."

"You can't expect an entire society to ignore years of war and heartbreak and—"

Tyler lost control. "I don't give a damn about an entire society; I care about what *you* think!"

"My God, Tyler, quiet down. If anyone knows you are here, all this won't make a bloody bit of difference!"

Tyler crossed over to her. He clamped his hands on either side of her face and leaned close to her. "Don't you see? This," he said, shaking her head slightly, "*this* is what I want on my side. I want your *reason* as much as your *passion*. Answer me: What are you going to say to your mother tomorrow to convince her to rise above this? How are you going to tell her I am the best choice for your father's campaign manager?"

Marlena struggled against his grip. "I don't know! I can't think."

Tyler kept his hold on her. "You shouldn't have to give it much thought. If you believed it, you would be able to give me a razor-sharp argument in a heartbeat." His voice became alarmingly calm and quiet. "But you don't, do you?"

"I don't know what I believe."

He dropped his hold. A deep disappointment refueled his anger. "You are not some ruffle-laden belle. You have a heart *and* a mind." Tyler headed toward the door. "And I've no intention of settling for only half."

"Tyler—"

"Good night, Lena." He stormed out of the library without looking back.

⊰ Chapter Ten ⊱

"There is really not much to tell aside from the standard sad story," said the mealy-looking man seated in front of Arthur Stock. His finger picked at the edge of the file in his hands. The nervous twitch made Stock want to reach out and whack the hand with the paperweight he kept on his desk. The man continued, his words spurting out at a nervous pace. "Her father was a longtime and loyal employee before he died; her mother died when Deborah was six. Taken in as a dear family friend, she lives in a modest little boardinghouse and doesn't go out much. There's just not much to the story, sir."

Stock fingered the paperweight. "What about her other family? Any aunts or uncles?"

"None." The man stared at the paperweight beneath Stock's hand. As if guessing his intentions, the fidgeting finger flattened out against the file. His face paled a bit more. "She made a long visit to some family friends seven years ago, but that's it."

"Anything on her father? Drinking, gambling? Affairs? A man without a wife has got to find his pleasure somewhere."

"No, sir. Straight as an arrow. Not to say I haven't tried to find something. I've made exhaustive inquiries. It's simply that no one seems to have a bad thing to say about the man. And he did die some time ago, sir."

Suddenly he straightened up as if he had just remembered some juicy detail that might save him. "I did learn something I'm sure you'll find interesting, however."

Stock's hand left the paperweight. "Excellent."

The man leaned forward and hushed his voice. "It seems, sir, that she has been spending a great deal of time with one of your employees. A junior reporter named Hasten. I've seen them together quite a few times." The man's face split into a smirk and he seemed quite proud of himself. "They appear to be romantically involved," he said as if revealing a dark secret.

Stock let out an exasperated sigh. "Good God, is that all? I goddamn well already know that! Why in the world do you think I'm having you look into her?"

The man sat silently, deflated.

Arthur Stock glared at him. "Dig more."

The man gulped. "Yes, sir, but I have already asked around quite a bit. I'm concerned continued probing might raise suspicions."

Stock was unimpressed. "That is your problem, not mine. Find the story without ruffling feathers, or I'll find someone else who can. Earn your fee, and don't come to me with heartwarming fairy tales. I want something I can use."

The man stood, straightened his ill-fitting jacket, and quickly stuffed his files into a flimsy attaché. "Yes, sir, Mr. Stock. Right away, sir."

"Now, out of here. I can't have you seen in this office too often, for God's sake. Send word to Jacobs when you have found something useful. And not before."

"Of course, sir."

Arthur Stock took a deep drink from an enormous mug on his desk after the man scurried from the room. He'd hoped for better results. Something had to be there. No one lived through Deborah Edgerton's tragic little life without stepping in a few ditches. But there was some truth to not stirring up too much dust or he'd give himself away.

Stock perused the morning's front page again. The smell and feel of a freshly printed edition never ceased to give him pleasure. The ink's strong scent, the cool and dusty feel of the newsprint between his fingers, and the shine of the large letters spelling out *"Austin City News"* were like opiates to him, addictive reminders of the press' power and the power he wielded through it.

The news this morning, however, failed to give him much pleasure. Maxwell seemed to be pulling ahead in the campaign. Here it was, already into August. As the late summer sent everyone into slow gear, it would be difficult for Dickson Kenton to make a strong move. He would have to wait until interest picked up again in September, which might very well be too late.

Unless, of course, thought Stock, *some news comes out in September that is so damaging that it has a terrific impact.* If Stock could dig up something sufficiently horrible, and play its release out over the first two weeks in September, that might not give Maxwell enough time to respond effectively. A mere six weeks just might not be enough time to overcome some truly damning information. Then Maxwell would be coming from behind for the last weeks of the campaign. Stock smiled as he folded the paper shut. That was a scenario he would enjoy. To break the story that would break Jason Maxwell would be the pleasure of a lifetime.

His reporter's instinct told him again that Maxwell's secretary was the key. If this pathetic little detective couldn't bring him what he needed, then he'd be forced to rely on Hasten. Hasten was only a fair reporter and a worse businessman. He'd have no trouble convincing him that there wouldn't be another job for him within a hundred miles. But Hasten had to have the needed information first.

"Give him more time to court the girl," Stock mused to himself. "Let him get good and hooked. Give him reason to be more than a bit afraid for his job. Then apply the pressure." It was an easy recipe for a senator's downfall. Expose some terrible truth about a member of his staff, play that into a lack of ability to judge character—which should be a cakewalk after the Hamilton fiasco—and run it home. Stock smiled and leaned back in his chair. He did love this job.

Marlena stared blankly out the window the entire trip to the ranch. She was tired, having barely slept after her scene with Tyler the night before. It was ungodly warm for so early in the day, and a menacing wind repeatedly pushed walls of hot air in through the carriage window. Her fingers strayed to the pocket watch at her waist. *What would Grandfather think of this mess?* Would he have approved of Tyler? It was nearly impossible to say. Marlena found she could make arguments for her grandfather taking either side, for or against hiring Tyler. He certainly would have discussed it with her first. He still, however, might have chosen the same tactic as her father.

But Tyler had become more than a tactic. Far more. More to her, more to everyone else; the man meant a dozen things—good or bad—to a dozen different people. Whether she readily admitted it or not, he was coming to mean a great deal to her. She thought about him constantly. She found herself wanting to ask his opinion of things, to dissect the issues of the day with him.

She was too practical to deny his effectiveness as a campaign manager. He'd done an astounding job at the press conference. He'd managed to turn his "foreignness" into an asset—people took appointments with him just to see what the controversy was all about. And yet he never stole the focus from her father. Tyler Hamilton was damn good at what he did.

All of that had very little to do with how he made her feel. How she enjoyed his intelligence and nearly bombastic determination. How he met her, match for match, parry for parry, as an equal. How the ground fell out from under her feet when he looked at her a certain way. His passion for life, politics . . . and his passion for her. Tyler wanted every last ounce out of life, good or bad, and she loved that about him.

The word brought her up short. "Love." She felt differently about Tyler than she had about any other man she had ever met. There was a hunger there, a craving to be near him that was physical, but far beyond physical. With a sinking, surging feeling, Marlena admitted to herself that she was falling in love with Tyler Hamilton. It did feel so much like falling—very, very far down. And she thought he was falling in love with her, although neither had spoken of it.

What kind of future could there be for this relationship? She couldn't possibly marry Tyler, could she? For goodness' sake, this household could barely stand the notion of his being an employee, much less a member of the family. What would her father think if he knew about Tyler and her? Given all his political rhetoric, would he welcome the idea? And even if he did, what did that matter in the face of her mother's reaction? In any case, her father had his hopes set squarely on a match between her and Richard Powers.

Ah, Richard. Kind, amusing, indisputably proper and appropriate Richard. She really did like him, but *like* was as far as it went. Nothing near that slow, smoldering knot that crept into her stomach every time she was with Tyler. The way her skin would seem to catch fire anywhere he touched her. Or even when he looked at her.

None of that happened with Richard. He hadn't even kissed her. Richard was so thoroughly proper he hadn't even tried to steal a kiss. Not even in a moonlit garden, with their parents practically cheering them on. Truth be told, she hadn't missed it. Certainly not after what Tyler had done to her just before he left. She couldn't really imagine what it would be like to kiss Richard. He just seemed to be more the hand-holding sort.

So where did passion come into a marriage? Was this, she wondered, feeling scandalous, why she'd heard about proper Southern women marrying good-standing men and taking secret lovers?

With a gulp Marlena realized she'd done just that—taken Tyler as a secret lover. Well, not exactly in the complete sense of the word, but some nights when Tyler let his hand linger down the side of her bodice to brush just slightly against her bosom, and her whole body ached to have nothing between them, her mind wandered to the possibility. Marlena let her head fall back against the seat and felt a wave of desire sweep over her body the way it always did when she thought of being with Tyler. No, she certainly never felt this way when she thought of Richard Powers, no matter how much her parents adored him.

It was all just impossible.

The familiar turn into the Double X's long front lane failed to produce the usual thrill in Marlena as the trip came to an end. She felt too drained for her task. She contemplated staying a few days. It might do some good to stay away from Tyler for a while, until she had her thoughts sorted out. Marlena sighed and wiped more stray, sticky strands of hair from her forehead as the carriage lurched to a stop outside the ranch's front door.

The conversation at the dinner table sparked the three Maxwell sisters' usual rivalry. Mrs. Maxwell held

court at the head of the table, dressed impeccably despite a noticeably gaunt complexion. She hardly spoke
as Marlena and her sisters taunted each other about
who was the better horsewoman, whose jump over the
west fence had been the most daring that afternoon, or
whose horse had the finest gait. The evening was almost
pleasant, her mother's troubling distance almost forgotten, until Diana again brought up the thorny subject of
the campaign.

"So, Lena, how do you think Father's campaign is
going?" Diana's voice had the air of forced maturity.
Marlena noticed her mother's spoon stop momentarily
as she stirred her tea. She neither looked up nor spoke,
but Marlena could tell her mother was listening atten-
tively for whatever answer she was about to give.

She chose her words carefully, trying not to be too
obvious as she monitored her mother's reaction. "You
all know it has been a tough race. I don't believe it will
get any easier. Kenton's going to run hard in the fall,
and everyone at the office is preparing for a very close
contest." She deliberately stayed away from the subjects
of Tyler Hamilton and the now-famous press conference.

Diana foiled her plans. "What about Father's new
campaign manager? How do you feel he's faring?"

Before she could stop herself, Marlena shot an annoyed look at Diana for bringing up exactly the wrong
subject. But the question had been asked, and to not answer it would make matters worse.

Again Marlena chose her words carefully. "Hamilton
has had a rough time. Some people are taking to him
and like his ideas. But there are still a lot of folks who
don't think Daddy should have ever hired him for the
job. Deborah thinks he is doing very well. As near as I
can tell, Daddy seems pleased with his work." It seemed

trite and uninformative, but it was the most conciliatory answer Marlena could create on the spur of the moment.

As if determined to create a scene, Diana posed still another awkward question. Marlena was grinding her heel into the carpet underneath the table, wishing it were digging into Diana's foot to shut her up. "What do *you* think, Lena? You've been at the town house all this time; you must have been watching him work, the way you spend so much time in Daddy's office. How do you think he's faring?"

Marlena took a long sip of coffee in an attempt to buy more thinking time. "Diana, it's just terribly complicated. Hamilton is very good at what he does. But"—she hesitated, trying to find the right words—"this is one of those situations where 'very good' simply may not be enough." She glanced at her mother for a clue to her response. None came.

Unaware of the weight of her questions, Diana went right along eating her cake as if she and Marlena had just discussed yesterday's weather. "Hmm," she said, dismissing Marlena's answer while thoughtlessly running her fork through the buttercream icing.

Mustering her courage, Marlena followed her mother through the front foyer when she left the table after dessert. She stopped her mother as she was heading up the stairs.

"Mother, could we spend the morning together tomorrow?" It sounded abrupt and clumsy. "I . . . want to talk," she added. It was obvious to both of them that Marlena had come here for the express purpose of talking to her mother. Couching it in small talk seemed condescending.

Marlena could almost see her mother decide to play along. Her thin hand reached out to rest on top of her daughter's on the stair rail. "Of course, dear. It will be nice to catch up. We'll talk in the morning." She patted Marlena's hand with her own. Marlena saw the coldness return to her mother's eyes as she allowed herself the luxury of a cutting remark. "It *is* why you're here, dear, isn't it?"

Marlena stood there, stunned by her mother's unusual frankness. She watched her turn and glide up the staircase. Tomorrow morning seemed entirely too soon.

An entire morning with her mother brought Marlena no closer to her goal. Dozens of attempts to steer the conversation toward the great rift growing larger between her parents were met with only avoidance and denial. Marlena was angry and frustrated by the time lunch was served. Somehow, though, she sensed that an outright confrontation with her mother would only make things worse. Perhaps what her mother needed more than anything else was time. Time to cope. Time to come to grips with the situation. Time for both of her parents to come out of this stubborn deadlock they'd created and find a way home to each other.

Marlena locked herself in the study after lunch, seeking some peace. It was a mistake. The sight of the room sent her imagination flying to the night she had encountered Tyler in there. She remembered the look on his face as he pinned her in the doorway. The way she wanted so much to reach out and tunnel her fingers through his flaxen hair.

None of that changed his heritage. No matter what persuasive words he would say, they would still come in a Boston accent. His presence would never be anything less than a painful, ugly reminder for her mother. A thorn her father was knowingly driving into her side, no matter how noble the reason. Despite what she felt for Tyler, Marlena wasn't sure it was worth the high price.

And yet those feelings were so strong. Wasn't love supposed to be worth a high price? Was that why the kind of love she wanted seemed to be so rare—because only a very few people were brave enough to pay the high price? What kind of price would her parents pay for each other now?

Sometimes very good, she quoted herself, *is simply not enough.* The impossibility of the situation pulled at her like an undertow. Tyler had sided with her father in putting political ideals before consideration of one's wife. That was certainly not what she wanted. She wanted a man who would love her at all costs. Perhaps Tyler couldn't be the kind of husband she had been waiting for. Perhaps it wasn't love, just infatuation. "Chemistry," she reminded herself as she had done the morning after the barbecue. "It's pure chemistry and nothing more." She couldn't afford to love Tyler.

Marlena stood up and headed for the stables.

She was a skilled enough debater to know she wasn't convincing herself, not even in the slightest.

Marlena rode most of the afternoon, the clear skies and sweeping landscape working their balm on her spirit. By late afternoon she sat in her favorite grove, mulling things over. But even this grove, her own private place, held potent memories of Tyler Hamilton.

From between the veil of trees, she saw it. She thought at first maybe she was imagining it, and blinked her eyes, but there was no mistaking the silhouette of the rider thundering up the ridge.

She had no idea how Tyler had gotten out to the ranch house or how he knew she was in the grove. It didn't seem to matter. She didn't speak. She made no move to leave. He slowed as he came near.

His appearance was disturbing. Tyler's shirt was stuck to his muscled back and his neck gleamed with sweat. He'd been riding hard. Wild, windblown hair added ruggedness to his already powerful features. Atop the sizable horse, he was so high that she had to strain her neck a bit to meet his gaze. A dark, intense edge to his expression made her afraid to ask him what he was doing here. Marlena closed her eyes for a moment, fighting the impulse to back away.

"Richard Powers wants to marry you." His voice was tight and thick.

"I . . ."

"He told me today he wants to ask for your hand."

Marlena brushed back the hair that insisted on blowing in her face. She chose not to respond.

"You don't love him."

Marlena wasn't really surprised by his directness. "Richard?"

"You don't love him. You love me."

It struck her like a physical blow to hear him say it, churning up everything she'd tamped down all afternoon. "Tyler—"

"He doesn't even love you." Marlena sucked in her breath as Tyler swung himself down off the horse. "Not really you. He hardly knows you, just your pedigree. He wants a well-behaved, charming wife. To provide him with a respectable number of sons and daughters to pass on the precious family name. That's not you, Lena." Tyler was coming nearer to her. Marlena backed away.

"Why are you acting this way?"

Tyler kept walking toward her. "I sat there in his parlor, sharing his goddamned fine whiskey, listening to his vision for your lovely, respectable life together, complete with a gaggle of redheaded Powers progenies. It made my blood boil to think of it." He pulled her into a private shadow, backing her up against a tree. "I don't want him to have you," he growled.

Marlena stopped breathing. Tyler was inches from

her. She could smell the sweat and the whiskey and the power of him. "No one *has* me," she countered. "Stop this."

"I'll stop if you look me in the eye and tell me you love Richard Powers."

Marlena just stood there.

In an instant Tyler came up against her and seared her with a kiss that seemed to crush her between the sharp edges of the bark and the solidness of his chest. His kiss was demanding and possessive, his tongue plunging into her mouth to wrap itself around hers and steal the breath from her body. He was lighting her on fire, but this wasn't going to change anything. She shook her head and leaned away from him.

"Damn you, Lena!" came Tyler's alarming roar, as he was suddenly behind her pulling her hands behind the tree. Her eyes flew open. She was drawing her breath to scream when she heard the slap of leather and felt what had to be Tyler's belt cut into her wrists. Tyler was tying her to the tree with his belt. Fright mixed with the desire he had kindled within her. Before she could gather her wits enough to scream, Tyler's mouth was back upon hers, more passionate than before. He kissed her forcefully, almost painfully, as she struggled, refusing to let her go.

It was a total, desperate, absolute kiss. She felt him surrendering to it, felt the fight and the anger and the denial give way inside him. His embrace melted into a slower, smoldering passion that overwhelmed her. His hands locked around her shoulders and slid slowly between her back and the tree trunk, pressing her to his chest so that she could scarcely breathe. He pulled away, his face an inch from hers. "Tell me you love me."

"It's not enough . . ." She couldn't finish the sentence, trapped by her own passion.

Fiercely he sent his tongue scorching down her jaw-line, sweeping the curves of her neck, and dancing across the scooping neckline of her gown. He lingered until she moaned quietly and arched against him.

"Tell me you love me," he growled huskily into her neck. She was afraid if she said it, there would be no going back.

His hands played over her until they found the first button on the back of her gown.

"Tell me," he whispered into her shoulder as his lips traced a torturous line.

When no response came, he loosened the second and the third.

"Tell me." His voice was thick and labored.

Marlena could only let out a tiny cry as his hands pulled the gown from her shoulders and roamed across the exposed flesh. Her mouth sought his shoulder, his neck, his jaw, any part of him she could reach. Tyler's tongue strayed down below her neckline, inching down the shift that just barely covered her bosom. Marlena knew she didn't want him to stop. She wanted him to take her, to remove the burden of choice and give her an excuse to surrender to him. She hardly even felt his hands circle behind her and loosen the belt from her wrists.

"Run away, Lena," she heard Tyler say, as if he'd read her thoughts. He wouldn't settle for her surrender to his own will. He wanted her to *choose* him. "Run away to Richard Powers and everything your family wants." Tyler pressed up against her harder so that she could feel every inch of him, every muscle.

Marlena chose.

Her hands flew up to bury themselves in his hair. Her breath came in gasps.

"I won't run," was all she could whisper against the tears that came.

"No, you won't, because you love me. You love *me,* Marlena Maxwell. *Me.*" Tyler lavished her with kisses with every word.

It was one thing to think it. Another to admit it. But it was altogether something else to hear him say it. To need it of her the way he did. Marlena felt the emotion and the conflict come surging out of her. "I do," she whispered into his ear, clinging to him as if the ground were slipping away under her feet.

Tyler engulfed her in his embrace. "I couldn't stand it. I sat there listening to him, and it was like something exploded in my chest. I ached for you down to the darkest part of me. Not just in body. In soul."

Marlena's fingers dug into his shoulders. "You matter to me," he continued, his voice heavy with emotion. "Everything else is just . . . useless, empty if . . . I need you beside me." His face suddenly changed and he smiled tenderly. "Dear God, I've not even said it." He tilted her head till she was looking up at him. His eyes were flooded with an affection so deep it defied words. "I love you," he said, the words choking in his throat. He said it over and over as he covered her face with tender kisses. The words washed over her like exquisite music.

"I love you, Tyler."

He made an indulgent, satisfied sound deep in his throat. "Say it again."

"I love you, Tyler Hamilton. And there doesn't seem to be a blessed thing I can do about it."

"As near as I can see, there's only one thing to do," he murmured into her neck.

"What would that be?" She smiled and tilted her head back.

"We'd best yield." With that, he kissed her beyond reason.

She pulled at his shirt, craving a physical intimacy to

match the emotional one. She wanted his skin under her fingers, wanted to feel his chest against hers. When her bodice fell away under Tyler's hands, she let it. Even the thin cotton of her shift seemed too much between them.

Tyler's hands glided across her skin, exploring, asking. Marlena tugged his shirt open and slid her hands up his chest. The feel of his naked skin was bliss. He put his hands on her waist and gave her room to touch him. Now it was she who explored, she who asked, *How far?* The smolder in his eyes, the strain in his muscles, the catch in his breath, gave her the answer.

Looking deep into her eyes, Tyler ran his hands up to the top of the corset. He paused. Lena pulled him closer. Slowly, he let his hand come up over the fabric to the softness of her breast. With a gentleness that tore her heart open, Tyler kissed her, caressed her, shared an intimacy that seemed so profound she thought she might weep. This was love. This was everything.

"We can't," he said raggedly when they began to feel as though their desire would get the best of them. They were both losing control quickly.

"No, we can't. Not here. Not now," Marlena said, catching her breath.

"Dear God, I want to," groaned Tyler, his lips lingering over the spot where Marlena's heart beat wildly. "I want to," he repeated, slowly sliding her shift back onto her shoulder.

"I know."

They held each other in silence for a long time, until the quiet was broken by the distant clang of the kitchen bell calling the ranch hands in for supper. Marlena leaned back against the tree and took a deep, quivering breath. She asked the question that refused to go away. "Tyler, what now?"

"Well, now that we've done the difficult part, I imag-

ine the rest will be easier." The unsinkable grin returned
to his face.

"The rest?"

"Now we simply have to conquer the world. We're
up to the challenge, don't you think?"

Marlena came back into the house a while later to
find her things packed. She was returning to Austin
whether she liked it or not—or more precisely, she was
being returned. Like a tidal wave, the polite firmness of
her mother swept her through an early dinner, a collection of short good-byes, and into the waiting carriage.
Claudia Maxwell, it seemed, was as immovable as her
husband.

⇥ Chapter Eleven ⇤

Marlena walked straight over and plunked herself down in front of Deborah's desk the next morning. "Miss Edgerton, I require your presence at Millington's. Immediately."

"Mmm. Shopping sounds nice, but I'm knee-deep in work."

"Ah, but I've taken care of that. Daddy has just given you the day off, with strict instructions to spend it with me." Marlena displayed the mock pout that had convinced her father. "I need someone to talk to."

"You're crafty. And I don't need much convincing. I'll just finish up this letter and—"

"Uh-uh. Right now. Or I won't give you"—Marlena brandished a sizable box of chocolates—"this box that came to our front door for you a few minutes ago."

Deborah's eyes widened. "What is that?"

"You know very well what it is. I want to know who sent it to you. And you're not getting it until you come with me this instant and fill me in on what's going on here." Marlena got up and made for the door, waving the box over her head.

"Fine. Fine. I'm on my way," said Deborah, grabbing her wrap and stuffing her papers into the top desk drawer. "Good-bye, Senator. Thanks for the day off," she called.

Marlena was practically running down the hall to

keep a few steps ahead of her taller friend's pursuit. "Could I please see that?" demanded Deborah.

"In good time, my dear. Hewitt!" Marlena called, passing the box from hand to hand and spinning around to dodge Deborah's outstretched arms. "Could you please ready a carriage to take Miss Edgerton and me to Millington's? Ouch!"

Deborah had pinched Marlena's arm and nabbed the box from her. She ran her hands over the cover and smelled the wrapping. "Don't worry, I'll share," she teased.

"I'm sure they're delicious, but it's not the sweets I'm interested in, and you know it. I want to hear it all, Deborah. Who's sending you chocolates, and why? How long have you been walking out with someone? And why didn't I know about it?"

"Well . . . I . . . it's all so—" Deborah started, only to be shushed by Marlena when Hewitt entered the room.

"A shopping trip, Miss Lena?" said Hewitt dryly, far too observant not to know the carriage was only the means to an end. Marlena was in the habit of shopping only when she wanted to get out from under her parents' watchful eye for some reason.

"Why, yes, Hewitt. The fall dresses are in from Paris."

"Indeed, Miss Lena," Hewitt replied, unconvinced. "I'll have a carriage brought around immediately."

When they were settled in the carriage and safely out of earshot, Marlena leaned back with her arms crossed. "Start from the beginning. Who is he?"

Deborah smiled and offered Lena a chocolate. She'd already read the enclosed card and clutched it to her breast. "How do you know it's a he?"

"Only men send chocolates to women. Out with it. What's his name?"

Deborah took a deep breath. "Samuel Hasten."

Marlena's eyebrows furrowed for a second; she recognized the name but wasn't able to place it right away. When she did, her jaw dropped. "Hasten? The reporter from the *Austin City News*? *The one from the press conference?*"

"Yes, that's him."

Marlena opened her mouth to begin a slew of objections.

"Now, before you get yourself in a tizzy, let me tell you that it started before the press conference and he's apologized for his actions since then. He was simply following the instructions of his employer."

Just the reference to Arthur Stock was enough to get Marlena riled up. Deborah shot her a look and Marlena lifted her hands up in defense. She calmed herself before responding. "All right, all right, so he works for *the enemy*." She glared at Deborah with the last two words. "It's already bad. But tell me the rest. And don't leave out a single detail."

Deborah told the tale with dreamy eyes. He'd been seeing her heavily once he won her over after the fiasco of the press conference. Deborah's continual supply of peppermints had been his doing. They were meeting frequently in the public gardens, and it had become serious.

Halfway through the story they'd arrived at Millington's. Marlena poked her head out of the carriage window and called to the driver to go around the park again a few times. Baking in the August heat, the driver had grumbled but complied.

"Good gracious, Deborah, I had no idea. Although I did wonder where all those peppermints were coming from. You look . . . well, you look so happy. I am glad for you, but it's so dangerous. Still, all the secrecy and intrigue sounds quite romantic." She chewed on a chocolate for a minute. "Well, we know he has good taste in confections." Marlena looked at her friend. "Do you really love him, Deb? Already?"

"Oh, Lena, I do. I really do." Deborah's face more than confirmed her words. She reached out and grabbed Lena's hand. "He's proposed. I've wanted to tell you about this for days."

"Why didn't you?"

"Honestly, I was afraid of how you'd feel about Samuel."

"You were right," replied Marlena. "For goodness' sake, Deborah, you couldn't have picked a more difficult situation. He works for that snake. He was Stock's mouthpiece at that press conference—and a mighty poor one, at that. Heads would roll if Daddy ever found out. What are you going to do?"

"Wait, I suppose. Until Samuel finds another position and the campaign is over. He wants to ask for my hand, right and proper. I told him the senator is the closest thing I have to family. He certainly couldn't ask now."

"Good Lord, no. Daddy'd eat him alive, and I don't know what he'd do to you. We're going to have to keep this a secret for now. If you've been seeing him so much since the press conference and no one's caught on yet, I suppose it can be done." Marlena leaned toward her friend. "Listen, Deborah, this is a dreadful risk. Are you sure he's worth it? Really, really sure?"

"Absolutely."

"Well, all right, then, that's enough for me. I'm glad you told me. I only wish you'd told me sooner. You should know me better than that."

The driver's wilting voice came from the carriage front. "Around again, Miss Lena?"

"Yes, please." Lena smirked at Deborah, plucking another chocolate from the box.

"As you wish, Miss Lena."

Deborah leaned back in her seat. "I know you better

than you think, Marlena Maxwell. I am not the only one in this carriage with a secret. I want to know what *you're* going to do about it."

Marlena stiffened. "Do about what?"

"The fact," said Deborah slowly, licking chocolate off her finger, "that you are in love with Tyler Hamilton."

Marlena nearly choked on her chocolate. "Deborah!"

"Don't waste your breath trying to deny it. I've been watching the two of you."

Marlena was broadsided. A dozen emotions must have shown on her face. Had Tyler told Deb?

"Tyler said nothing," interjected Deborah, reading Marlena's thoughts. "Not a word. I only guessed. Actually, it wasn't that hard to see. You two were so busy trying to hate each other that it was too clear. Lena, you *are* in love with Tyler Hamilton, aren't you?"

"Yes. No. Yes. Oh, Deb, I don't know." Suddenly all the pressure and turmoil of the past few weeks came spilling out of her and she told Deborah the entire story between sniffs and distracted bites of chocolate.

"What are you going to do?" said Deborah as she moved over onto the seat next to Marlena.

She put her head on Deborah's shoulder. "I don't know. It's so wonderful, and yet it doesn't make any sense. I don't see how we could possibly be together."

Deborah thought for a minute. "I don't think love is supposed to make sense. It doesn't seem to be about logic. Samuel and I, for example. We shouldn't be together, either. But when I see him, or he touches my hand . . ."

"Don't. Just don't talk about that."

"My goodness, but he really has gotten to you, hasn't he?"

"He told me things that made my knees come out

from under me. He said we could conquer the world."
Marlena stopped her imagination before it strayed any
further. "Look, we're coming around to Millington's
again. I'd better come home with a few packages after I
pleaded with Daddy this morning." She knocked loudly
on the carriage roof.

"Excellent, Miss Lena" came the dreary voice from
above them.

Deborah frowned at the change of subject. "I suppose if you're going to go conquer the world, Lena, you
might as well be splendidly dressed for it." She put the
chocolate box on the seat and allowed Marlena to dis-
embark first. Marlena shot her a look, grabbed the
chocolate box off the seat, and took it with her as she
exited the carriage.

"They'd probably melt in this heat. We can't have
such fine chocolates go to waste, can we?" she called
back to Deborah.

"Good heavens, no," said Deborah under her breath
as she followed Marlena, who had already sailed into
Millington's.

Arthur Stock ran his fingers across his bookshelf. He
had not yet even looked at the man sitting on the other
side of the desk, although he could hear him squirming
under the weight of questioning.

"I had hoped for some progress. I'll assume your
presence here means you have something to report."

"I believe I am quite close to finding something, sir."

"Quite close? You came here to tell me you are *quite
close*? I don't want to hear your strategy. Just tell me
what you've found out. I'm not a patient man."

"You'll have your story by the end of the month, if
not sooner. And I'll be the only one who can get it for
you."

"The end of the month may be too late. Rumor has it

the Powers boy is going to ask for the hand of that pretty little daughter of Maxwell's. That'd make for one mighty alliance come election time. Not to mention the funds it would add to Maxwell's campaign coffers. Or the coverage it would get from the damn social press. I can't wait until September or October anymore; I need something appalling and I need it now!" Stock slammed his fist against the bookshelf, shaking the crystal in the next cabinet ominously.

"I promise you, sir. You'll not be disappointed."

"I'd better not be. You don't want to see how mean-spirited I can be when I'm disappointed."

"Yes, sir. I'm sure I don't, sir."

"Fine, then. Quickly, is that understood?"

"I'll do my best, sir."

"Not 'I'll do my best, sir,'" thundered Stock, turning around to stare the man in the eyes. "You'll have that information for me fast or you'll never get another piece of useful information in your miserable little life again, is that understood?"

"Clearly, sir." Sweat beaded on the man's forehead.

"And another thing, Hasten."

"Yes, sir."

"If I ever hear you speaking of this to anyone, it'll be the last words you utter. Is that clear?"

"Quite, sir."

"Quite, sir," Stock parroted in a simpering voice after Hasten had left the room. God, he hated being depen-dent on this spineless little creature for such important information. Everywhere he turned, he was surrounded by spineless little creatures who didn't have the guts to get their jobs done. The world was full of spineless little creatures. Everywhere.

"Exactly how did these pebbles get on my bureau?" Marlena held out the evidence in question.

"You were extraordinary with that reporter today. You charmed more quotes from him than even I imagined you would." Tyler pulled a pin from Marlena's hair.

"You are evading the question. What about the ones that found their way onto the piano?"

"That idea of having the garden-club ladies receive yellow roses when they came for the tea. Really an excellent strategy. I can see why Ogden Mathers let you have your say so often." Four more pins fell prey to Tyler's fingers.

"Flattery may be a strength of yours, Tyler, but I want to know about the pebbles inside my book this morning."

"I really couldn't say." Tyler pulled the last pin from Marlena's hair, feeling the rush that came over him when the kohl cascade came pouring down around her shoulders. "Your hair will be my undoing."

"A clever pun, seeing as you've just undone mine." She shook the stunning mane out, her voice practically a purr as she ran her hands through it.

He never ceased to be entranced by what the moonlight did to her hair. The intimacy of seeing it down, the utter pleasure of being the one to release it. "I should like to do this every night for the rest of my life."

Marlena turned to him, her eyes playful. "Be my chambermaid, my dresser? Tyler, that's rather beneath your qualifications."

"Come here, and I'll discuss my unique qualifications." He took both her hands and pulled her to him. He loved having her so near. The shape of her face as she tilted her head to look at him, her hands resting on his chest, sent a surge of desire through him.

"I have impossibly high standards. You'll need to submit to vigorous testing."

"Sounds delightful." He leaned down to kiss her.

"No," she teased, stopping him. "Now I'm afraid I must be quite serious about this. An interview is absolutely essential."

Tyler groaned. "A test? I've not studied."

"That's best. I want honest answers." Her eyes narrowed in thought. "Let me see . . . ah, I've just the start." She readjusted herself against him. "Question one: Do you find thunderstorms frightening or exciting?"

The question couldn't have been further from what Tyler was expecting. "I'd have to say exciting. Provided I have proper shelter."

"Excellent answer. We'll move on to something more challenging. Do you open your Christmas presents on Christmas Eve or Christmas morning?"

Tyler laughed. "That is the more challenging question?"

"It's less open to debate." She pointed a finger at him. "There are frightfully few ways to compromise on this."

"Christmas morning." He brought the finger to his lips and kissed it, watching the pleasure mist over her eyes as he did. "But I must say, it wouldn't take much convincing to persuade me to open one or two on Christmas Eve."

"A very diplomatic answer. I'm impressed."

"I'm impatient. When do we get to the end of the test?"

"Soon enough. Compatibility is not an issue to be glossed over."

"We are compatible, I've no doubt." He ran a finger along the side of her neck, watching the muscles flutter at his touch.

"You are not cooperating, Mr. Hamilton."

"I am not feeling very cooperative at the moment." He ran his hands down her sides, feeling her inhale and stretch up to him.

"Forbearance, Mr. Hamilton. This next one is quite important. Should women have the right to vote?"

Tyler smiled. "I would have bet my last dollar this question was on the test."

She drummed her fingers against his chest. "You're evading again."

"Very well, then. Yes, but only the smart ones."

"Unenforceable. Not to mention all the dim-witted men you'd have at your throat."

"I'd rather have you at my throat," growled Tyler, leaning in.

She eyed him menacingly. "You may get your wish if you don't answer the question."

Tyler threw up his hands. "I've already given you an answer. Yes, I believe women should vote. You should know by now I'm not given to thinking of women as chattel."

"Thank goodness."

"Then we're done?" Tyler wrapped his arms around her again. Her petite size astonished him all over again.

"Patience. I've only one more question."

"Then for God's sake, let us get this over with." Tyler took a deep breath, then exhaled. "Ready."

"Are you the kind of person who prefers sunrise or sunset?"

Tyler rolled his eyes. "You cannot be serious."

Marlena brought her hands up to circle his neck. It was hard enough to think before she started touching him. "Oh, indeed I am."

"Sunset. By far."

Her smile took on a wicked tinge and she ran her hands across his shoulders. "Congratulations, Mr. Hamilton. I do believe you've passed with exceedingly high marks."

"I'm so pleased to hear it." Tyler lifted her up so that her face was close to his. "What do I win?"

A fire burned in her eyes. "Your heart's desire."

"What my heart desires presently"—Tyler made no effort to hide the huskiness in his voice—"would require at least two bottles of very fine champagne and no less than three hours of uninterrupted privacy."

"Oh." The look on her face nearly sent Tyler over the edge. She would be a voracious lover. It showed all over her body. It made him hunger for her all the more. Tyler let his hands trail down her hair, her neck, her shoulders. He swept her into a slow, tender kiss, feeling the ground fall away from under his feet as he held her. She deepened the kiss, roaming her hands over his shoulders and around his neck. Tender devotion gave way to passion, her hands lighting a fire under Tyler's skin. Her touch infused him with life. He knew, deep to his core, that this was how it was supposed to be. Not a marriage that merged great families, but a passion that fused hearts and souls. Lena and he were meant to be together, and he would ensure it, no matter the course of events.

His conviction must have echoed in his kisses, for she clung to him with all the more passion.

"Whoa, girl," whispered Tyler against her lips, his voice velvety and low. "You're making it difficult for me to be a gentleman."

"I belong with you," she said, gazing into his eyes. She kissed him again with intensity. "I want to be with you."

The look in her eyes sent Tyler reeling. "Are you saying that you don't *want* me to be a gentleman?" He was breathing hard.

Lena took his face in her hands. He brought his hands up to rest on top of hers. "Yes, I am," she said, taking one of his hands and placing it on the neckline of her gown. She moved their hands together until the gown's edge slid off one shoulder. Tyler sucked in his breath and drew her nearer. He lavished the milky shoulder with a flurry of soft kisses.

Tyler raised his head to look into her eyes. Those infinite eyes. He drew in a deep breath. "You've no idea what it does to me to hear you say that."

Lena smiled and dropped her gaze to below his chest. "Oh, I think I do."

Tyler rolled his eyes. "I'm attempting to be honorable, and you're not helping."

"Me? Not help? What an awful thing to say."

Tyler tightened his embrace. "Lena Maxwell, will you please be quiet and let me finish?"

Lena nodded.

"Though I want . . . very much . . . to the contrary," he said, grazing a hand along her back, "*very, very much,* I'll not—yet. You mean too much to me."

"I don't care what the others might think."

"It's not about what others might think. I don't want to bed you in secret. I don't want to make love to you if I can't wake up next to you in the morning. Every bone in my body wants to have you, right here, right now, but I don't want some frantic coupling." Of course he could take her right now. She'd as much as asked him to. But something deep in his chest told him it would be no mere coupling. She had a hold on him that he'd never experienced. He knew, in the dark, unopened part of his heart, that when he bedded Lena Maxwell it would be forever. That couldn't happen now, not yet.

But Tyler couldn't think of how to tell her. Did he want to marry her? Subject her to the kind of pain it might cause? Take the risk of alienating her from her mother, if not her whole family and perhaps her community? It was no small step. He had to be ready, to be certain.

"Believe me"—he kissed her shoulder and raised the gown's edge—"*believe* me when I tell you I'm feeling *very* dishonorable right now. Downright despicable. You tempt me beyond reason, woman."

"I'm glad of it." She pulled him into another breath-taking kiss.

"And," he added, reaching for the last shreds of his control as she ran her fingers down his chest, "I'm revising my former plan."

"You are?" She kissed his palm, sending a ripple of shivers down his back.

"I am," he asserted, pulling his hand away and shaking it. "It will now take *three* bottles of very fine champagne, not less than *six* hours of uninterrupted privacy, and two boxes of exquisite chocolates." He let out a faltering groan and swatted away the hand that was roaming up his chest. "Show a little mercy, Lena."

"We will be together, Tyler Hamilton. I feel it."

"I feel like I'd best dunk myself in the well for three or four hours."

The column of figures on Tyler's desk refused to behave. He'd been staring them into submission for the last half hour, to no avail—they simply refused to add themselves into the necessary total. He'd been working on an analysis of campaign expenses for two days. It needed to be on the senator's desk by the end of the week. Yet for the past two days his mind had refused to stop thinking about Marlena. He'd been rendered bloody besotted. He loved her. Over the last two days he'd become more sure of it than he'd ever been of anything in his life.

"Are you really sure, Mr. Hamilton?"

Tyler's glance flew upward; he suddenly feared he'd been thinking out loud. Miss Edgerton stood before him with a stack of reports, looking somewhat amused at his lack of attention. It was evident she'd been standing there for some time and that Tyler had totally ignored her questions.

"What? Oh, pardon me, Miss Edgerton. What did you ask me?"

She looked at him over the top of her glasses like a disapproving schoolteacher. "I was asking you if you're sure you want to see July's campaign expenses. They were included in your previous report. I'd have thought you needed to see August's midmonth figures."

"Yes, of course. I was looking for August's. You're correct, as always, Miss Edgerton."

"Well, these are July's figures. I'll put them back and pull the others right after lunch, if that will be all right. I have a luncheon engagement I'd like to keep, if the figures can wait until then."

"After lunch will be fine. If I can't even request the correct figures from you, then I don't see how I have any grounds to ask you to work through lunch. I've got the senator's stump speech to finish until then anyhow. Go off and enjoy yourself."

Miss Edgerton started to turn away, then stopped. "Mr. Hamilton," she said rather softly, "are you all right?"

Evidently it showed more than Tyler liked to admit. "I'm fine, Miss Edgerton. Working a bit hard, but fine. Why do you ask?"

"Nothing, really. You just look . . . distracted . . . these days. I trust everything is all right?"

Tyler looked at her, mentally applying his warm, charming veneer again. "Nothing a third term in office won't fix, Miss Edgerton. Just give me a campaign win and I'll be fine."

"A campaign win and the lady of the house back home." She smiled wistfully and set off to her desk.

Why, thank you, Miss Edgerton. I was so busy getting caught up in the love of my life, I quite forgot how my presence seems to be destroying my employer's marriage. How kind of you to remind me. I feel so much better now. Tyler would have banged his head on his desk if he thought no one would see. Instead, he forced himself to stare at the column of figures until Miss Edgerton waltzed out the door, obviously happy about wherever she was going. As the door shut he rubbed his eyes and decided that getting out was perhaps a good idea. He certainly wasn't getting any work done. A walk might clear his head. He didn't have much of an appetite for lunch anyway. *Imagine that,* Tyler thought, *Tyler Hamilton III not having an appetite. It must surely be love.*

One lap around the block failed to produce any results. Turning into the public gardens, he breathed in the smell of grass and the slightest hints that fall was not so far off. A touch of nature might snap him out of it. He even bought a few sweets from the old man by the fountain, amused that his appetite seemed to be returning.

Tyler wandered through the hedge maze, not paying much attention to where he was going, but simply crunching the candies and taking in the peculiar textures of a Texas August. Amid the myriad of sounds, Tyler heard a laugh. Not an extraordinary laugh, but a familiar one. Not knowing many people in Austin, Tyler found that strange, and moved closer to investigate. The laugh was not loud and jovial, but quiet and intimate. Tyler certainly didn't know anyone who would be rendezvousing in the public gardens in the middle of the day. Intrigued, he moved closer.

The laugh came again, and as he bit down on a peppermint he realized the laugh he heard was Deborah's.

He stole closer to the sound, peeking gently through the hedge to a shady, secluded corner, where, lo and behold, Deborah Edgerton sat holding hands with a red-headed gentleman Tyler could not quite see. Her back was to him, but he knew it was her by the dress and hat she was wearing, and by her laugh. In her free hand she was holding a cone of what was sure to be peppermints. *So that's where her endless supply of mints has been coming from,* thought Tyler. Now he knew the reason for her glowing disposition of late. But what of the secrecy? Why meet in such a desolate corner of the park? And why hadn't the fellow called for her at the office, as a proper gentleman would?

When Deborah accidentally dropped the candies and bent over to retrieve them, Tyler got his answer. Decades couldn't have erased that face from Tyler's memory.

Deborah was walking out with Samuel Hasten.

The reporter from the *Austin City News.* Arthur Stock's lackey at the press conference.

Sweet Jesus, what on earth is going on here?

Tyler walked as calmly as he could through the hedge. Miss Edgerton whirled around, surprise evident on her face.

"Mr. Hasten, I wonder if you might allow me a word alone with Miss Edgerton."

Her eyes narrowed. "Samuel, don't leave."

Tyler took a step closer. "I've no wish to cause a scene. Please, Mr. Hasten, as a gentleman, allow us a bit of privacy."

Hasten took Miss Edgerton's hand. "I think it may be better to speak with him, dear. Better to have this conversation here than in the office, don't you think?"

"I don't want to have this conversation at all. Samuel—"

"Hasten, I'd consider it a personal favor." The tone in Tyler's voice was not one of request.

Hasten kissed her quietly on the hand and took his leave.

Miss Edgerton stood up. "Of all the boorish, under-handed stunts! Following me like some kind of criminal! Mr. Hamilton, that is simply beneath you."

"I did not follow you here. I decided to take a walk and I had no idea you would be here."

She crossed her arms. "I'm not sure I believe that."

Tyler let out an exasperated sigh. "In any case, I don't think I need to tell you what a problem this could be. Mr. Hasten is a most unwise choice of suitor at the moment, Miss Edgerton."

"I do not see where my choice is your concern, Mr. Hamilton. Perhaps it is not wise, but I have a feeling love and wisdom keep little company these days."

Tyler wasn't at all sure what she meant by that. "Are you seriously involved with Mr. Hasten?"

"Again, is this really your concern, Mr. Hamilton?" She began pulling on her gloves. "I don't believe this has any bearing on my professional—"

Tyler cut her off. "It has a great deal to do with this office, and you know it as well as I. Look, Miss Edgerton, I asked Hasten to leave because I consider you a friend. I don't want to embarrass you in front of him. You've been very valuable to me and I don't want you or this campaign to get hurt because of any false affections on Mr. Hasten's part."

"His affections, as you call them, are not false." Her voice grew angrier. "If you must know, Mr. Hamilton, Samuel has asked me to marry him when the situation is more suitable, and I have accepted. We are not school-children. We are both aware of the . . . difficulties . . . of our current situations. He won't be at the *Austin City News* forever. Once the senator's won his race and Samuel has a new position, he has every intention of asking for my hand properly, and publicly. But for now I'll thank you to respect my privacy." She turned to leave.

Tyler caught her arm. "Don't you see, Miss Edgerton, I do respect your privacy. And you. Otherwise I'd be speaking to the senator, not you. And I don't intend to bring it up with him if I can just make you see how inappropriate this is. Please be sensible. Sit down and let's discuss this."

She stood there for a moment, fuming, then sat down slowly. "Miss Edgerton," Tyler began more softly, "it's no secret the senator is dear to you, nearly family. Think of him. I don't mean to be cruel, but have you considered that Mr. Hasten's affections may not be genuine? That he may be using you to try to obtain information about the campaign that could be twisted against Senator Maxwell? I know it isn't pleasant—"

"No!" she snapped. "That simply is not the case, Mr. Hamilton. I'll admit it would be a possibility, but Samuel . . ." She hesitated. "Samuel *loves* me, Mr. Hamilton. Of that I'm sure. And I love him. Of course it's not appropriate and the timing is less than ideal. I am fully aware of that."

"Miss Edgerton, please listen to me. Don't force my hand in taking this any further than between the two of us." It came out a little more like a threat than Tyler had intended.

"For heaven's sake, Mr. Hamilton," she shot back angrily, "I don't see how you are in any position to condemn!"

Tyler looked at her. She couldn't possibly . . .

"I know," she continued. "I know all about it. I guessed it long before Lena ever said anything."

Tyler froze. "Just how much has Lena said, Miss Edgerton?"

"I know enough," said Deborah quietly. "The rest was easy to guess."

Tyler rested his elbows on his knees and looked out at the hedge's sculpted corners. "Not much escapes you, does it?"

He heard her sigh and shift her weight, as if shrugging. "Occupational hazard, I suppose."

Tyler faced her, all his efforts at playing the role of manager dissolved. "What was it you said, 'Seems love and wisdom keep little company these days'?"

"Indeed." They sat for a moment in silence. "You love her, don't you, Mr. Hamilton?"

Tyler didn't answer.

After a moment, Miss Edgerton said simply, "She loves you."

Tyler closed his eyes again and leaned back on the bench.

"You can't be certain the senator would object, even with Mrs. Maxwell's response. I'll admit your situation is far from perfect, but somehow I just don't see a man like you backing down in light of a few obstacles."

"Then again, he could fire me," Tyler countered.

She stood up and put her hands on her hips, as if she were scolding a child. "She's worth it, Hamilton."

Tyler stopped short. "She is." The truth of it rang through him. She was. She was worth anything. "For a courteous secretary, you certainly can pick a fight."

Her face was intent. "Are you going to conquer the world together or not?"

"Excuse me, but this conversation was supposed to be about *your* inappropriate romance."

"I prefer to call it complex."

"Fine, then. Complex, it is. Since you have given me a piece of your mind, let me suggest something to you."

Miss Edgerton crossed her arms. "I'm listening."

"Let me call on Hasten and assure you—and my-self—that his intentions are genuine."

"Well, I . . ."

"You said yourself that Hasten wants to be very proper about all this. Well, he can't very well state his intentions to the senator right now, can he? If he loves you as much as you say he does, I doubt he'll need any encouragement to profess it to me. Seems to me that Mr. Hasten needs little encouragement to talk about any subject, much less his undying love for you. If nothing else, it would make me feel better. Humor me, Miss Edgerton."

She took a moment to consider it. "All right, then, I agree."

He smiled. "You're eminently sensible for an irresponsible woman, Miss Edgerton." He held out his bag of candy. "Peppermint?"

"Occupational hazard. And no, thank you, I have my own."

⊰ Chapter Twelve ⊱

Things continued to grow more and more tense at the campaign office in the next days. Another visit to the ranch had only resulted in escalating arguments between the senator and Mrs. Maxwell. Hopes rose when she and the girls returned the next afternoon, only to have her leave again after another heated discussion with the senator. On the political front, the race was still neck and neck between Maxwell and Kenton, with Kenton even showing a small lead.

Late in the week Richard Powers appeared at the office door with an enormous smile and an even larger box. Marlena had effectively stalled Richard's attempts to push any courtship forward, citing campaign pressures. Ignorant of the real reasons, Richard continued to be friendly with Tyler. Tyler found himself grateful for the friendship, despite the circumstances. He had painfully few friendships in Austin; he couldn't afford to forfeit Richard's, even if it felt somewhat uncomfortable.

"Here." Richard laughed, thrusting the box at Tyler. "I was out buying a waistcoat and I couldn't resist."

Tyler looked inside the box, and laughed. He pulled out a cowboy hat. Richard had somehow managed to find a dignified, sleek Stetson that Tyler might even have chosen for himself. It was a thoughtful gift, and just like Richard to think of it. Tyler felt grateful and a trifle silly when he tried it on. While it looked and felt a bit odd, Tyler did have to admit it suited him somehow.

"It's grand. I couldn't have chosen better myself," said Tyler, clasping Richard's arm in friendship. It was such a paradox to be so fond of Richard and yet begrudge him his intentions.

Miss Edgerton came in from the house and stopped in her tracks. "Splendid hat."

Tyler laughed. "A gift from Richard. One has to admire his taste—and bravery—in gifts."

"Indeed." She raised an eyebrow at Richard. "We'll make a Texan out of him yet, don't you think?"

Richard responded with a broad laugh. "With that accent, it will take far more than a hat, Miss Edgerton."

Her eyebrow stayed arched. "I couldn't agree more."

"You gave me the story, Hasten. It's exactly what I wanted. Why the hell are you asking me to kill it now?" Arthur Stock tossed a stack of papers on his desk.

Samuel Hasten stood his ground. "I've got a better story for you, sir."

"A better story than the shady past of Deborah Edgerton?" Stock sighed and sat down. "Look, Hasten, you did what I pay you to do. You got the story. So you wooed the lady and won her confidence and you feel bad, but it's a bit late for a guilty conscience. Take your doubts and go home. I haven't time for this."

Samuel swallowed. He'd betrayed Deborah to Stock. But he hadn't counted on it eating at him the way it had. Now, in order to protect her, someone else had to fall. It didn't really matter who, as long as it wasn't Deborah. And everything had a price. Now was no time to get sheepish. "You don't have time to bring down Claudia Maxwell?"

Stock paused for a moment. He reached into his drawer and pulled out a cigar. He lit it slowly and carefully, encouraging the burn. "Talk."

"I've developed a bit of a hobby over the years of collecting old journals. Soldiers, tradesmen, settlers, and such."

Stock shook out the match. "Skip the history lesson, boy, and make your point."

"I own one from a young Union soldier involved in the invasion of Galveston. He made a rather vivid record of an incident." Hasten dried his palms on his pants legs.

Stock took a long, menacing draw on his cigar. "Your point, Mr. Hasten?"

"I didn't connect the journal entry to Mrs. Maxwell until Deborah—ah, that would be Miss Edgerton—spoke about some trouble brewing between the senator and his wife."

Stock's interest was piqued at that. "Maxwell's having marriage problems?" He took another long puff on the cigar. Hasten could practically hear the gears turning.

"The journal records an incident at a town house just after the occupation," Hasten continued. "Involving a lady of particular prominence. He goes into rather gruesome detail about cutting her on her face."

Stock let the smoke out in a precise stream. "Down her left cheek, I imagine?"

"Yes." There. It was done. Almost.

"So you've unearthed the diary of some Yank who cut up a lady who could be Claudia Maxwell. I fail to see the story in this, Hasten. There had better be more."

"There is."

Stock reached for a pen and a sheet of paper. "Keep talking."

"Haugh-ved."

Marlena scrunched up her nose and tried again.

"Hah-vud." They'd stolen a rare moment alone in the daytime out behind the gardens because Marlena and her father were heading off to the ranch for another attempt at reconciliation.

"No, you need to broaden out your vowels. Haughved. Harvard University." Tyler leaned against the garden's back wall.

"Hah-vud Uni-vuhsity."

Tyler shook his head. "Impossible."

Marlena placed her hands on her hips. "I don't believe you are in any position to make judgments. Especially wearing that monstrosity of a hat Richard gave you yesterday. You look ridiculous."

"I've decided I'm rather fond of it." He ran his finger along the brim and adopted a gunfighter stance. "Ma'am."

Marlena laughed. "That's one affectation you'd best keep from the public eye, Tyler Hamilton. You need all the credibility you can muster. With so many people supporting Dickson Kenton, Daddy cannot afford more trouble. You could not fathom the difficulty I had today convincing Pastor Beckett to even consider endorsing Daddy." She picked a bloom off a nearby vine, twirling its tiny five-pointed white flower between her fingers. "In any case, you make a perfectly lamentable cowboy."

Tyler drew a fictitious gun. "Maybe I should 'git' me a gun and challenge poor old Sam Hasten to a draw tonight."

She rolled her eyes. "You've lost your senses."

Tyler swaggered up to her. "I've been thinkin', ma'am." At Marlena's wince he dropped the earsplitting clash of accents. He took her by both shoulders. "Marlena, I think we should tell your father."

Marlena stared at him, surprised. "Heavens, Tyler, I'd like nothing more than to stop all this creeping around, but . . . I don't know. . . ."

Tyler's hand ran down her cheek. "I'll admit it's a risk, but what if he approves? How much better would it be for us?"

"And what if he doesn't? Tyler, he might fire you. It's not as if you'd easily find another position in Austin. You might have to go back to Boston. I'd lose you." Her hands clutched his shirt.

"Even if your father tries to have me hanged for treason, you will not lose me. What I would give, Lena, to kiss you without wondering who might be watching. To hold your hand. Walk down the street with you on my arm. I don't want to wait anymore to do those things."

Marlena felt his chin settle on the top of her head. "Well, you know, I've been conducting some research, Tyler."

"Have you?"

"Did you know that three men from Massachusetts gave their lives at the Alamo?"

"As a matter of fact, I did." She heard a smile in Tyler's voice.

"Did you also know that the fence for the new state capitol building came from Ohio?" Her finger circled a shirt button. She could feel his breathing when she was pressed against his chest like this. She loved the strength she felt in him, the strength it gave her. *Conquering the world.* Maybe it wasn't impossible. A future with Tyler was worth any price.

"That is, if I recall, another one of those states of 'Northern aggression,' is it not?"

"It is." Marlena chuckled. "If one looks hard enough, one can find a daunting list of things that connect Austin to the North."

Tyler held her at arm's length. "This? From the woman whose first words to me were, I believe, 'I don't care if angels brought him from heaven; he's a Northerner!' Such transformation!"

"But don't you see? It's been decades since the war. I've changed. Others could. We could convince them." Tyler obviously needed no convincing. He was running his hands up her arms. He had a look in his eye that was melting her from the inside out. "We love each other. Maybe that's enough." Tyler's hands were rounding her shoulders, playing across her bare collarbones.

Tyler's voice grew hungry as his hands played up her neck and into her hair. "I'd take on the world for you. How difficult could one hardheaded, single-minded, forward-thinking Texas senator be?"

"You've done wonders for his hardheaded, single-minded, forward-thinking daughter. That ought to count for something."

"I love you, Lena." There was a sudden surge of emotion in his voice, the playful bantering replaced by an urgent seriousness. "To the very bottom of my Northernly aggressive soul." He held her face in his hands and kissed her tenderly. "My God, I love you."

"What if we can't convince them?" she asked, feeling tears well up in her eyes in response to the transparency of his emotions. "I need to know," she added quietly.

"We'll be together. At any cost, and no matter who objects." He seemed unable to say more.

She had no need to hear more. "Marry me."

Tyler's eyes flew open wide. "What?"

"Marry me."

"I heard you the first time." His arms dropped and he stared at her, wearing a look of utter amazement.

She was so sure of it. She'd turned the idea over in her head a thousand times, coming up with the same answer each time. Tyler had become her life, her center. They had come to work side by side on her father's behalf. How could her father reasonably object? And what did it matter if he did? This was what she wanted more than all the other things she used to think were important. When she'd realized it, the certainty of her knowledge gave her a solid, unshakable conviction.

So why wasn't he answering her? "Why the devil don't you answer me?"

Tyler's arms stole back around her. He pulled her to him so that their faces nearly touched. His eyes blazed with an ice-blue fire. "Marlena Winbourne Maxwell, I love, honor, and cherish you. I want you to be my wife. I want to spend my life with you. But I'll be God-bloody-well-damned if I'm going to let *you* do the asking!"

Marlena let the fire in his eyes vanquish her. "Then ask me."

His answer was a kiss burning so fiercely with commitment that tears fell from Marlena's eyes. The reverence in his earlier kiss gave way to a heartrending hunger. Pressing her up against the solid coolness of the brick wall, he kissed her as if to claim her for life. To meet her soul and forever cleave it to his. Her own hunger roused, she met his ardor with the power of her own.

"I have never . . ." he breathed into her ear, clutching her, "in all my life . . . in my dreams, even . . ."

"I know." She let the tears come over her cheeks now, not holding them back. "I know."

He smiled and kissed her wet lashes. "Dear God, Marlena Maxwell, I want you as my wife more than I want the air I breathe, but I'll not ask you today, not now."

"Why not?" Marlena pretended to look angry, but she'd already been given the vow she needed.

That dashing grin of his, the one that reduced her defenses to ashes, spread across Tyler's face. "Because you've enough of the upper hand as it is. A man's got to stand his ground somewhere."

• • •

Later that night, Tyler settled into the tavern chair to face a rather inebriated Samuel Hasten. "I'm here on behalf of Miss Edgerton."

"Mighty fine of you to do so, Hamilton. Have a drink. I'm celebrating."

"Look, Hasten, I'll speak plainly. Your relationship with Miss Edgerton could get you both into considerable difficulties. Your affections could cost both of you your positions. I want to be certain of your intentions for both professional and personal reasons." Tyler immediately regretted how he phrased that as he saw Hasten's back go up.

"Personal? You'd better not have designs on Deb—"

"Good heavens, no, man, quiet down. She's a good, decent woman and a valued coworker. And invaluable to the senator, I might add."

Hasten calmed. "I know all that. Hamilton, what is it you want from me?"

"I want assurances that you are not taking advantage of her for some political gain."

Hasten stared at him for a moment. "What is it to you?"

"Miss Edgerton has no family, and we are friends. And, professionally speaking, this relationship could be highly dangerous to the senator's campaign. The two of you are taking a tremendous risk."

Hasten hoisted his mug. "Ah, that's love for you, my good man." He took a sloppy gulp and wiped his lip with the back of his hand. "Deborah does have family, you know. It's just—well, that's beside the point." Hasten fell silent and looked straight at Tyler. "No, I can't vouch for my intentions."

"What?"

Hasten grinned, proud of having startled Tyler. "Who could prove love? How do you verify matters of the heart? I love her. Of course it doesn't make sense. How do you make sense of it all, anyway?"

Tyler found his drama irritating. "There's no need to—"

"I've got a question for you, Mr. Hamilton."

Tyler wasn't sure why, but he humored him. "Yes?"

"Why did you come down here and stick yourself into this nasty fight when you could have stayed safe and sound and prosperous in Boston, or wherever it is you came from?"

Tyler was beginning to wonder what on earth it was Miss Edgerton saw in this man. He constructed the briefest possible answer. "To make a point."

Hasten pointed at Tyler with his mug. "To make a point. Something noble, is that it? I didn't think there was anyone left like that, Hamilton."

Hasten raved on about nobility and honor. It struck Tyler that perhaps Hasten had done something dishonorable that was making it hard for him to live with himself. Hasten was drowning himself in ale and self-pity, not celebration. Perhaps Tyler had better find out why.

He put on a charming smile and tapped his mug against Hasten's. "You strike me as the noble sort," then he added, "Sam."

"Ah, now you're warming up. I knew we could be civilized, even if we're on opposite sides. No sense in being unfriendly."

"Just as long as you know you're on the losing side. We're going to win this campaign, and you can't stop us."

"You just keep thinking that way, Hamilton, and you'll do just fine." Hasten drained his mug. "Were I you, though, I'd have an escape plan in my pocket, just in case you lose."

"Now, why would we lose?" Tyler probed. "Maxwell's got years of experience in the Senate and he's beat Kenton before. His record is exemplary."

"It isn't all in how you vote, Hamilton. You ought to know that." He straightened in his chair. "The press can play a very powerful role in a campaign. You ought to have a lot of respect for the likes of me. The wrong press can stop a campaign in its tracks."

"It's a good thing we're friendly, then, isn't it?"

"We're still on opposite sides. My boss is still out to get your boss." Hasten laughed and almost slid off his chair.

"He is indeed. I imagine he's looking everywhere for the story that could break Jason Maxwell. The trouble is, no such story exists. But you already know that, don't you, Hasten. You're a sharp fellow. I'd imagine if there's a fly in this ointment, you'd have found it weeks ago. Every reporter lives for the kind of story that will make him front-page material. I suspect with your skill that it's only a matter of time before everyone is reading your name."

Hasten chuckled. "Sooner than you know, my good man."

The hair on the back of Tyler's neck stood up. "So they've got you working on more than just the Maxwell campaign? You really must be talented. There's no such story in our office, so what other scandal have you had the time to unearth? You're better than I thought, Hasten."

"I *am* a damn good reporter, aren't I?"

"I can't imagine all that charm hasn't landed you some enviable inside scoops. The way you've charmed Miss Edgerton, I'd imagine you've been able to coax many a juicy story out of some poor, innocent girl. You've got quite a talent for wooing, Sam. I could learn a thing or two from you."

"You just might, at that." Samuel was slurring his words now. Tyler thought Hasten would slip any second if he could just keep playing up to the fellow's enormous ego.

Tyler raised his glass. "So, Sam, what should I do?"

Hasten took another long gulp. His eyes were nearly glazing over. "What do you mean? You mean if I were you?"

"Yes. If you were me, what would you do?"

Hasten began to chuckle. He tried to stop himself but laughed all the more. He put his face very close to Tyler's. Tyler caught his breath at the stench of alcohol emanating from Hasten. Eyes wide, as if whispering a great secret, Hasten blurted, "I'd get the hell out of town." He burst into hysterical laughter, and would have fallen out of the chair if Tyler hadn't caught him.

Tyler played along. "Now, really," he said, laughing as hard as Hasten, "why would I want to leave a town like Austin, with so many beautiful Southern belles in it? They all seem so flawless. So pristine in all those bustles and buttons."

Hasten laughed louder. "Oh, Tyler, you've got a lot to learn about women. Some of them ain't as pure as they look. 'Specially the high-and-mighty ones. Sometimes they have the biggest secrets of all."

"Sam. Sam . . . is there something I ought to know about those high-and-mighty Maxwell ladies?"

"Sure, he sent me to dig up dirt on Deborah. And I found some, too. She's so goddamned sweet, though. And she just kept gettin' under my skin, you know? 'Course you know. I just couldn't let him run the story."

"What story?" Tyler was sweating.

Hasten continued on as if he hadn't heard Tyler. "So when she said about the scar and I remembered the Galveston journal, well, it was the only way to save Deborah, you see? I had to give him a better story. He's a hell of a man, that Stock. Mean."

Tyler wasn't understanding much of this gibberish, but he'd heard enough to make him afraid. "What's happened, Sam?" He fought the urge to take the fool and shake him.

"Well, I suppose you ought to know now, 'less, of course, you'd rather read it on tomorrow's front page.

Seems Mrs. Maxwell had quite a run-in with some Yankees." He cocked an eyebrow at Tyler. "It's why she hates the likes of you, you know."

Tyler was growing impatient. "Go on," he said as calmly as he could.

"He cut her up good, didn't he? The bastard cut her up even after she told him. No damn honor. None at all. He threatened to kill her if she didn't tell about the blockade-runners—figurin' the senator knew and all, so she did, too. And she did. She told him. She told him where the boat was and when it was running. And he cut her up anyway." He wiped his nose on his sleeve. "Those ugly Yankees, they went and got that boat, but it didn't have guns on it, just lots of innocent people. Well, lots of people died, didn't they? Mamas and babies, grandmas and grandpas. Ugly, messy deaths."

Tyler closed his eyes.

Hasten poked him in the arm. "Makes for one damning little piece of press, don't you think? A traitor for a wife? Your boss is finished."

"Are you sure this is true? Are you sure she was involved?"

"It doesn't really matter, now, does it, Tyler, my boy? Yessir, Madame Maxwell's nasty little secret is going to be front-page news by tomorrow morning, and your boss' character won't be worth the newsprint it'll be maligned on."

It didn't even require a moment's consideration. Tyler stood up and landed such a blow to Hasten's jaw that it sent him crashing through two tables. He didn't even bother to see who was watching as he stormed from the tavern and threw himself into the first coach he saw.

"*Austin City News* offices. *Now!*"

Tyler's thoughts went speeding as fast as the coach as it careened toward the *Austin City News* building. For all his alcohol and ego, Hasten was right about one

thing—even the implication of treason would lose the
campaign for Maxwell in such a close race. Even if
her involvement wasn't true. But Tyler wasn't really
thinking about politics. He was thinking about the
Maxwells. How the senator would feel betrayed if he
didn't know. And Tyler was guessing he didn't know.
He didn't dare think what the story would do to Mrs.
Maxwell, and Lena, in its wake. All would be lost. And
Deborah—to know what Hasten did would devastate
her. With a single headline the lives of nearly everyone
Tyler cared about in Austin would be shattered.

He had no idea what he was going to do as the coach
pulled up to the front steps of the *Austin City News*, but
that didn't seem to matter. At this point there wasn't
anything to lose. His pulse quickened as he tossed the
fare to the coachman and looked up to see lights burning in the large corner office he knew must be Stock's.
Dear Lord, Stock must be salivating in anticipation of
bringing down Maxwell with such a scandal. Tyler
didn't even notice the rain as he stepped up to the burly-
looking man standing just behind the *News'* doors.

"What's your business?" demanded the large fellow.

"I'm here to see Arthur Stock," said Tyler. There
seemed to be no point in dealing with underlings.

"He ain't here. It's nearly one in the morning. Come
back tomorrow."

"He's here. I'd venture he's not leaving the building
until tomorrow's issue hits the streets. I want to see
Stock, *now*. Just send word that Tyler Hamilton is here
to see him, damn it." Tyler cursed again under his
breath and stepped away for a moment. This was no
time to lose control. Behind him he heard the man yell
for a copyboy to send word up to Stock's office. *So he is
here. Of course he is.*

"What was your name again?"

"Hamilton!" shouted Tyler, then he clenched his fists

and regained his composure. He spoke clearly and quietly. "Tyler Hamilton."

A heavy rain started as Tyler stood on the steps waiting for the boy to return. It seemed hours before the lad came back down the stairs. Tyler turned slowly, his seamless control having returned.

The boy muttered something in the doorman's ear. The man turned to Tyler. "Mr. Stock will see you in his office." He cocked his head toward a long narrow staircase behind him. "Upstairs, end of the hall."

As Tyler started up the stairs, he was surprised by his own composure. He hadn't given a thought to what this story might do to his own career. He hadn't even considered how such a scandalous campaign loss could destroy his future. His thoughts had been only of Lena, of her family, of the devastation that was about to tear through their already unraveling lives. The senator would go down. A twelve-year career of extraordinary work would be erased by his own wife's perfectly human attempts to keep from being killed. And that was if it was at all true. A marriage shredded, if not destroyed altogether. And him? All Tyler would lose was a line on his credentials; nothing the upstanding Hamilton name couldn't overcome. Nothing he wasn't already willing to risk for Lena's sake. By the last stair, Tyler knew what he was going to do.

Stock's office was smaller than it seemed from the street below. Papers were piled in dozens of stacks everywhere. Amidst a cloud of cigar smoke, a massive chair stood facing away from Tyler. Two booted feet rested on a low bookshelf below the window, and an extended hand held a brandy and a fat cigar. The brandy was nearly empty and the cigar half-gone. Arthur Stock was already celebrating his victory. When he finally turned, his broad smile couldn't brighten what Tyler thought was the most bitter-looking face he had ever seen.

"Hamilton. Maxwell's protégé pawn from up North. What the hell are you doing here at this hour?"

"I imagine you already know that, sir."

Stock raised an eyebrow at the "sir." His face took on a snakelike appearance as he narrowed his eyes and smiled again. "And how would you know what my presses are running tonight?"

Tyler controlled his anger. "Samuel Hasten's smooth tongue is all too easily loosened with ale."

Stock crushed out his cigar. "Hasten. The runt's served his purpose now, in any case. It hardly matters."

"You've substantiated Hasten's tale?"

"Tales," he said, emphasizing the plural. "What does it matter? I intend to play it for all it's worth, true or not. There ain't nothing for you to do here, son. Get home and pack your bags."

Tyler stood his ground. He took a deep breath. "I've come with a proposal."

Stock laughed into his brandy. It was an unpleasant, hissing laugh. "You and Hasten both. Who the hell are you to be making proposals to me?"

"Someone who can offer you a better story. Substantiated by a direct, written statement."

"Funny, that's just what Hasten said. Hamilton, there isn't a story on earth that could make me stop those presses. Get out of here." Stock started to turn his chair around to face the window again.

"It's no accident that I'm not running a campaign in Boston. No one in Boston will hire me." Tyler was surprised at how easy it was to lie. "My father bought my graduation and bar exam when I was caught cheating. He used his influence to keep things quiet. Why do you think he agreed to my coming here despite all the controversy?"

Stock kept laughing. "Come, now, Hamilton, you could make up a better story than that."

"I'll sign a statement verifying those facts. Maxwell would never have hired me if he had known. I fooled him. I fooled everyone. There's your story, Stock. If I'm going to go down, let me go down showing what a great scam I executed."

"You're more of a fool than I thought, Hamilton. I ought to run all three stories just to crush you to the ground. That would be, of course, if I believed you. Noble of you, son. Stupid, but noble." He took a swig of brandy. "Someday I may even ask you how you got it out of Hasten, if you live that long. Matthews! Come escort our guest out the door."

The enormous man appeared in Stock's doorway. "What third story?" demanded Tyler. Hasten's ramblings were starting to make sense now. The third story was something about Deborah Edgerton. Hasten had given Stock a better story so he wouldn't run it, but the snake was going to run both anyway. Tyler felt sick with fear and hate.

"Matthews, make sure Mr. Hamilton receives a copy of the front page before he leaves."

"Stock—"

"I want him out of this building *now*!" howled Stock as Tyler was dragged down the stairs. Matthews grabbed a sheet of newsprint off a stack and shoved it in Tyler's face as he pushed him out the door.

There, smearing in the rain, were a gruesome pair of headlines: CLAUDIA MAXWELL BETRAYS GALVESTON and SECRETARY HIDES BASTARD BABE.

⊰ Chapter Thirteen ⊱

Tyler ducked into the next doorway, out of the rain, and read the articles. Stock had lost no opportunity to insult, condemn, and malign the senator, Mrs. Maxwell, Miss Edgerton, everyone. Tyler had expected something terrible, but this went miles beyond his worst imaginings. Stock accused Mrs. Maxwell of treason against the Confederacy, of deliberately leaking damaging information to Union soldiers. The paper called for the senator to withdraw from the race. Stock made no attempt at being reasonable or fair. The only shred of hope Maxwell had was that the story was so obviously an attempt to bring the senator down that some readers might consider it contrived. Even that was a very, very slim chance. Tyler realized his wet hands were holding the knife that would pierce the senator's heart and destroy him, professionally and quite possibly personally as well. The punched feeling in his gut revealed how much the senator and his family had come to mean to him.

Lena. Dear God, how could he get to her? With a surge of nausea he remembered where she was. If God was kind, the family had reconciled and they were still at the ranch. The Maxwells deserved one night of hope before all hell broke loose.

Thinking of what Marlena was about to face, Tyler was flooded with the yearning to be near her. To hold her and comfort her through the tidal wave that was about to destroy her life. He wanted to be there for her, no matter who objected. Nothing would keep him from her now.

It wasn't far to their town house. Tyler ran the distance, his feet accelerated by fear. A prayer of thanksgiving gushed out of him when an inspection of their stables found the carriage still gone. He roused the groom and took the fastest horse, opting for the speed of an unfettered animal over the comfort of a hired coach, despite the rain.

Tyler pushed the horse beyond sense, but it was still nearly three in the morning by the time he reached the ranch house. Soaked to the skin, and cold, he was grateful to see a fire burning in the room off the barn where the stable hand slept. Eager as he was to get near a fire, he still hadn't figured out how he would explain his presence to the stable hand and get Marlena out to meet him.

He didn't have to wonder long. His solution presented itself when he opened the door to find the young man in an ardent embrace with Sarah, the housemaid who had served Lena and him at that memorable luncheon. They were more than surprised.

"Mr. Hamilton!" gasped Sarah as she hurriedly pulled her blouse back onto her bare shoulder. Tyler was grateful he hadn't arrived twenty minutes later, or from the looks of things it would have been truly awkward. But such an embarrassment served his purpose perfectly.

"Sir . . . I . . ." stammered the stable hand. The couple looked duly frightened at being discovered in such a compromising spot.

Tyler capitalized on the moment. "I haven't time to waste, so I'll need to be direct. If you'll help me, I'll forget I ever saw you. Agreed?"

Sarah and the young man glanced at each other. "Agreed," said the stable hand, hurriedly stuffing his shirt back into his britches. Sarah simply nodded her head as she tried to repin her hair.

"Sarah, I'm going to need your help. Can you get Miss Lena out here to the stables without the rest of the house knowing?"

Sarah nodded. "I think so. She'll get awfully wet in this rain, though, and I don't expect she'll care for it much." Tyler was amused at the girl's sense of detail in such a pinch.

"Somehow I think she'll consent. Tell her that I am here to see her and the matter is of the utmost urgency." He stopped Sarah with his hand as she rose to go. "Now, Sarah, it is absolutely essential that no one knows she is leaving the house. Do you understand?" When she nodded again, he smiled. "Then this will be our secret. No one will know I came across you and . . . your friend, here." Sarah grabbed her cloak and exited into the downpour. A lightning bolt flashed across the sky and the horses shuffled and snorted in their stalls.

The stable hand stood nervously by the door. Smiling, Tyler offered, "She's very pretty. You're a lucky lad." The stable hand stared at him, at a loss for how to respond. "What's your name?" Tyler held out a hand.

Baffled, the young man gulped out, "Alan, sir," and shook Tyler's hand.

"Alan, I'm going to need your help, as well. I need some time alone with Miss Maxwell. Can you find someplace else to be for a few hours until daylight?" Tyler knew his words would be taken the wrong way, but he didn't care at this point.

"Yes, sir." The lad managed a sheepish smile.

Tyler tossed him several coins. "That's for your trouble." Alan nodded and bumbled from the room.

Another flash of lightning illuminated a steady rain

against the roof. The fire crackled in the small corner stove and the horses whinnied softly beyond the wall. With a moment's peace to consider his situation, Tyler exhaled and slumped on Alan's meager cot. He didn't care for the questionable appearance this meeting was giving, but in a few hours it wouldn't matter anyhow. All hell would break loose once the *Austin City News* hit the streets, and these petty details would be lost in the chaos. All he knew right now was that he needed to be with Marlena.

Tyler shivered. Suddenly it dawned on him that if he was wet, the copy of the *Austin City News'* front page he'd folded into his coat might be wet, as well. He fished it out to find it had been soaked around the edges, but the majority of it was still dry enough to read. He folded the newsprint and placed it on the table near the cot. Peeling off his dripping coat, he unfastened his collar. Even his shirt was soaked from the ride. He took it off and draped it over a chair to dry.

Tyler poked the fire. He stood staring at the flames for a long time, waiting for Marlena, the anticipation of seeing her seeping through his body, the full weight of the night's events pressing on his heart.

It was nearly half an hour before he heard the latch lift on the door, and Marlena came into the room. Tyler expected he would rush to her when she came in, but somehow he just stood there, his back to the fire, and looked at her. Her hair was down, and wet with the rain, clinging to her shoulders and neck in dark waves. She wore a hastily donned gown over a shift with the bodice half undone. Breathless, she let her wet cloak drop to the floor beside her.

Marlena was not prepared for the shock of seeing Tyler, soaked and tousled, standing shirtless in front of the fire. It flashed through her like the lightning overhead. Firelight glistened in the drops on his chest and played on the outlines of his muscles. The look in his eyes was hard and urgent, his shoulders braced as if for battle. Something was wrong. She wanted to rush to him and yet couldn't. They stood for a long moment before she whispered, "Tyler."

Something flared in his eyes when she spoke his name, and he came to her. He wrapped her in his arms and kissed her fiercely. She felt as if he were devouring her, and yet there was a dark brooding in him. He was fighting something as his hands ran hungrily over her body. There was something more to his being here, but she didn't care. It was a welcome devouring. It was enough just to be here with him, to be here for him, to give to him whatever he needed and whatever he wanted.

A powerful bolt of lightning split the sky, an instant crash of thunder, shaking the stables and spooking the horses. Marlena jumped and Tyler caught his breath. Startled from their moment of abandon, Tyler just held her, breathing her name over and over. She looked up to see a sharp pain in his eyes.

"What is the matter?"

Tyler held her face tenderly. After a moment, he said very softly, "Lena, things are going to get very bad in a few hours. I'd give anything to save you—to save us—from this, but I can't. I don't know how."

"Tyler, what happened? You're frightening me."

Tyler took her hand. "Sit down, Lena. I need to show you something." Without leaving her side or taking his eyes from hers, he reached behind him to grasp something from the nightstand. He handed it to her. It was a newspaper. The front page of the *Austin City News*. It said . . . dear holy God, it said . . .

Marlena's breath left her as she scanned the headlines. Reeling, she read accusation after hateful accusation about her mother, her friend, her family, and even herself. How Deborah had borne an illegitimate child.

How her mother had provided Union soldiers with classified information, enabling the slaughter of innocent Texans. How her father was a deceiving schemer who didn't deserve the people's trust. Her head began to spin. "My God, my God," was all she could whisper, as the words seemed to grow worse with each paragraph.

Then the anger began, cold and sharp and bloodthirsty. Her hands shook with the blind rage that crept up her body. She glared at Tyler in disbelief. "He can't do this!"

"He can. And in a few hours, he will." The resignation in Tyler's voice made Marlena livid and more than a little afraid.

She grabbed Tyler's shoulders. "Stop him! He can't do this! They're lies!"

"I tried. The paper will be out by dawn, if it's not out already. And Lena, dear God, I don't know how else to say this: We don't *know* if they are lies."

Marlena threw the paper at him. "Of *course* they're lies. Lies! He's slandering my mother, the snake. Some horrible, made-up tale to make her seem evil, all in the name of a blasted election! And as for Deborah . . . it couldn't be true. I would have known. She would have told me." Thunder rumbled across the sky.

Tyler saw Marlena lurch toward the door, lashing out in her anger. He lunged after her, holding her struggling body back.

"I swear I'll take a knife to him myself! I'll slice his lying face to ribbons!" She was like a wild animal. He held her tight while she fought to free herself. Everything in Tyler wanted to calm her, to tell her it would all be fine. But it wouldn't. In truth, for the first time in his life, Tyler didn't have an answer. Instead, he let her rage pour out in a torrent of curses and flailing punches until she slumped against his chest, panting and tearful.

"It can't be true," she said between clenched teeth. Tyler didn't know how to respond. "Tell me it can't be true."

He couldn't lie to her any more than he could stop his pulse. "You know I can't say that."

"Mother . . . Daddy . . . Deborah. I—how do I . . ." She pushed away from him and began circling the room, grasping for an answer. "Dear God, what am I going to do?"

"What are *we* going to do, Lena. I'm going to stay by you through this and *we'll* find a way." He grabbed her arm and spun her to look straight at him. "Somehow, some way, we'll get through this. I love you, and that's all that matters. We'll get through this. We *will* survive this. Now look at me, Lena. Look at me and tell me you love me."

"I love you." It did manage to calm her some, for the wrath in her eyes softened a degree.

"Say it again."

"I love you." The set of her shoulders gave a bit.

"Better." Tyler kissed her forehead. "The next twenty-four hours will be the worst."

"Oh, God, I don't know how to fight this."

"You'll find a way. You're a fearsome lady. I've faced you in debate, remember?"

Marlena winced. "Debates are supposed to be fair fights."

"This fight is anything but fair, but we'd best not dwell on that now. First order of business is to get you smuggled safely back into the house. I'll catch an hour's sleep here and then show up at dawn on the doorstep, hopefully just before the newspapers arrive. We'll improvise from there."

"No."

"Lena?"

"I'm not running back to the house to pretend everything is all right. I'm staying right here with you until dawn." Her glance flew around the room, taking stock. "And then you and I are going to walk up that drive *together.*"

"Is this really the time to take that stand, Lena?"

Marlena sat down on a stool. "I can't think of a better time. I need you beside me, Tyler. Now."

He pulled her up off the stool and sat her down beside him on the cot. He kissed her forehead. *She needed him.* He hadn't realized until this moment what a powerful thing that was. The firelight danced in her wide green eyes. She looked so small, so delicate, so precious. He was overcome with the desire to protect her. Tyler held her, touched her, comforted her in the only way he could: to let her know she would not be alone. Not now, not ever.

Marlena responded hungrily to his touch. They needed each other, needed to grasp at the good things in order to find the strength to fight the bad. Tyler felt the coolness of her wet skin under his fingers. The way she was drawn to his touch. She clung to him, her fingers digging into his back. She needed him. Now. The feeling of her skin on his—the urgency in her hands—lit fire to his desire. *She's mine,* he challenged the world. *I won't let you hurt her.* He kissed her face, her jaw, and let his urges take his mouth roaming down her throat. This was not just some physical urge, but a fierce desire to claim her as his own. To give her his strength. To let his body say what words failed to express. To comfort her. Now, before the rest of the world caved in.

He eased her down on the cot, covering her body with his. The feeling of her underneath him was exquisite. She made a low moan and wrapped her arms around his neck, open and willing.

Tyler's desire surged beyond his control. He poured his hands over her, relishing her responses. He pressed his hips into hers as she curled and arched beneath him. She fit beneath him perfectly. They were meant to be together. Every inch of him knew it, wanted it, craved it. With a deep, slow kiss, he slid the shift from her shoulders.

She gave a silky gasp and pulled him closer. His body was taut with want, the breathtaking friction of her legs against his pulling him under. Her hands gripped his shoulders while her mouth raced over his chest. He could tell she wanted him as much as he wanted her. The knowledge was potent. The weight of the moment was an alluring call to take her now. She'd have him. She needed him. He surrendered to it, pulling her shift open. Her cries of pleasure, sweet and desperate, called him further. *Now*, his body told him. *Now*. His hands wrapped around her hips and began to loosen her skirts. She clung to him. *Now*. He lost himself in her, calling her name.

As her fever pitched, she suddenly pulled sharply from his grasp and skidded up the cot. "Oh, God, Tyler," she panted, "we can't. We can't. I want to. Oh, dear Lord, I want to, but it's for all the wrong reasons. We can't."

"Why *not*?" Tyler responded huskily. "What the devil is left to worry about now? I want you. You want me. I'm not going to let your father or that snake Stock or your mother or anyone keep us apart. Not now, not tomorrow. What wrong reasons could there be?"

"Tyler," she said, looking at him, "here? Now? A rushed coupling on a stable cot? Think of what you've said to me before. Is this really what we wanted?"

Now was a mighty frustrating time for Marlena to get sensible.

"What I *want* is to make you mine forever. Now. No matter what else happens."

Marlena sighed and set her shift to rights. "This

won't do that." She let her head fall against the wall. "I want us to be together as well, but don't you see? If we do this now, it's just defiance. Sneaking as if this were something wrong. It gives Daddy and everyone else an excuse to see us as forced together by a misdeed, by some regrettable indescretion."

Tyler blew out a breath and arched an eyebrow. He didn't see how that was bad.

Marlena faced him, rising to her knees. "I don't want them to have an *excuse*. I want them to see the *reasons* why we should be together, and agree with them. If you 'compromise' me here, now, we'll always just have backed my family into a corner. We'll never know if they truly wanted us to be together. I don't want that, and neither do you."

Tyler let his forehead rest against hers. He let out a tortured groan. "You picked a fine time to wax philosophical on me."

Her hands came up to hold his face. "I picked the best time. Besides, you know I'm right. It's what you've been saying all along. Tyler, I want to make love to you out of *love,* not desperation."

"What does it matter, as long as we end up together?"

"Tyler Hamilton, I know that's not the way you think."

"I don't want to think at all at the moment. I can't think." Tyler slid his hands on top of hers. "Damn you, woman." But he was smiling. It occurred to him just then that she was his other half. The key to the best part of him. "I love you. And when I bed you, Marlena Maxwell, it will be long and slow and sweet and goddamned worth the wait."

Now she smiled. "Indeed. Now, in the name of philosophy, I'll do up my bodice if you'll put your shirt on. Best not to tempt, hmm?"

"Oh, Lena," grumbled Tyler as he reached for his shirt. "I am so far beyond just tempted."

And he was. So far it hurt.

The dawn split the sky with the clear colors of an after-storm sunrise. Buttery gold rays found their way through the barn's only window to rouse Tyler and Marlena from a fitful dozing. Tyler's shoulders felt sore and strained. From the expression on Marlena's face, he looked as bedraggled as he felt. He watched her try to smooth her tousled hair with her fingers as he ran a hand across a day's growth of beard. His hair had probably dried in all directions as he slept.

"I'm hungry."

She stared at him. "You're not serious."

Tyler laughed at himself. "All hell can break loose, the dead could rise from their graves, life itself could come to an end, and somehow I'd still find my appetite."

Marlena's face was tight and strained. "It's going to take a barrel of coffee. No, more. You can get a wash and shave at the house, and I've got to get myself dressed."

Tyler tossed a few more coins onto Alan's bed and they started up the drive, hand in hand.

"There's nowhere else to start but with your father. Find the papers and find him. Let's just take it that far. After that . . . well, we'll deal with that when we get there."

Marlena led them past the front of the house, heading instead for the kitchen door. "The papers will be with the house staff. I'll get Daddy after I'm dressed."

Marlena put her hand on the door handle and took a deep breath. She pushed it open to find Hewitt standing over the stove. The look on his face told Tyler the papers had already been brought from Austin and Hewitt had seen the headlines.

"Miss Lena! I was just wondering what on earth was the best thing to do, given the circumstances. Good heavens, you've been up all night from the looks of you."

Marlena said nothing, but pushed the door open farther to let Tyler come into the room. Hewitt stared at him only a moment before handing a cup of coffee to Marlena. "Miss Lena, I'm certain you need this."

He turned to Tyler. "Mr. Hamilton, how fortunate you're here. Have some coffee. I'll see to providing you with some water and a shaving kit." The extraordinary man never missed a beat. Tyler held up a hand.

"The coffee I'll welcome. The rest can wait until I've spoken with Senator Maxwell. My appearance will not change the news."

Hewitt stopped and looked at Tyler sympathetically. "I suppose not, sir." He breathed a short sigh before handing Tyler a cup of coffee. It was the closest thing to a display of emotion Tyler had ever seen from the man.

Marlena drained her cup and held it out for Hewitt to fill again. "I'll go wake Daddy before the rest of the house and ask him to meet us in the study. Hewitt, can you have breakfast and coffee brought to the study?"

"Of course."

"I'll take the papers with me," Tyler interjected.

"Burn them if you'd like," said Marlena in disgust. She picked up the front page Tyler had given her and climbed the back stairs. Both men stared after her, neither one envying what she was about to do. Hewitt turned to Tyler.

"Mr. Hamilton?"

"Yes, Hewitt?"

"It's indeed very fortunate that you're here." The

smallest hint of a smile crept into his eyes. "Miss Lena needs you, hmm?" He raised an eyebrow at Tyler.

Tyler paused, baffled. Hewitt—usually expressionless—bore an expression that was too clear to miss. Unless Tyler was gravely mistaken, Hewitt had just revealed that he knew much more than it appeared regarding his relationship with Marlena. As if that weren't surprise enough, it seemed that they had an ally in Hewitt.

It was an odd time for Hewitt to reveal such information, but then again, not odd at all—at such a time one needed all the friends one could get. Such a tiny turn of events in their favor bolstered Tyler's spirits. He attempted a smile. "Fortunate indeed, Hewitt. Fortunate indeed."

Hewitt's face returned to its stoic expression as he deposited the stack of newspapers into Tyler's hand. He nodded and turned to open the cupboards. Tyler shook his head, filled his cup again from the stove pot, then went into the front hallway.

He slid open the doors into the now familiar study with a tinge of sadness. So many things had happened to him in this room. He ran his hands across the bookcase, remembering the gossamer image of Marlena in the moonlight. The scent of the senator's cigar smoke hung in the air, and he was again reminded of how fond he had become of the man. He drained his coffee and stood in the middle of the room, facing the doors until they slid open again in front of Jason Maxwell and his daughter. Maxwell was holding the newsprint page.

"It's awfully damn early to be visiting, Hamilton."

Tyler couldn't reply. The senator was keeping himself in tight check, and Tyler guessed it wouldn't hold for long.

"Goddamned weasel!" Maxwell walked over to the desk and picked up the paper. "Who the hell does he think he is? What's the meaning of this?" The senator let out a string of expletives—daughter or no daughter in the room. "What do you know about this?" he roared, turning to Tyler.

"I learned it was coming out a few hours ago. I thought it best to come right away."

"How did you learn of it?"

"From Samuel Hasten, a reporter." Tyler thought it best not to elaborate just yet.

"Hasten . . . Hasten . . . He's that measly little wretch who stood in for Stock at the press conference, isn't he?"

"Yes, sir."

"Well, how the hell did you find it out from him?"

Tyler improvised. "I came across him in a tavern late last night. He was drunk and boasting about 'the story of a lifetime.' I plied him with questions and he told me to get out of town before the papers were out this morning. Then he told me about your wife. That's when I punched him." Tyler was grateful when the senator didn't seem to want any more details.

"Punched him? I'd have shot him. Stinking little coward didn't even have the guts to get credited for the story. There's only Stock's name all over this piece."

"He'll be disappointed, to say the least."

The senator covered his face with his hands. "Claudia. Lord have mercy, Claudia. Oh, Claudia." He drew his hands down slowly. "And Deborah."

"That can't be true," said Marlena.

"I hope not," added Tyler, "but we can't be sure. No one has spoken with Miss Edgerton yet. I'm afraid after I punched Mr. Hasten I didn't stay around to find out how he got his story."

The senator just looked at Marlena.

She picked up on his silence. "Daddy?"

"It is true. Deborah had a child. A boy. When you

thought she went away to her aunt's for a year. Well, they weren't really her aunts. The child was given up for adoption."

"You *knew*?"

"Yes, but no one else did. Not even your mother." Stunned silence filled the room, until the senator finally boiled over. "Your mother's . . . *damn* him! This is the most insulting excuse for journalism I've ever laid eyes on! How dare he print this! How dare he do this to my wife! I swear to God Almighty, Hamilton, I'll rip him apart with my bare hands."

Maxwell went over to the window and slammed his fist against the wall. "This could be it. I am undone. Lena honey, your mother won't survive this. We were just . . . Oh, Lord Almighty." He let out a horrible groan. "Lord."

The senator stood staring into space for a moment, looking as though someone had just punched him in the stomach. He took a breath. "All right, Hamilton, you've done the right thing. Now just leave me alone for a bit. Lena, you, too. I had better figure out what on earth I'm going to say to Claudia." He waved Tyler away. "Go get a shave or something, man. You look terrible."

"Senator . . ."

"Daddy . . ." Marlena grabbed his elbow, but he waved her away, as well.

"What's done is done. Just leave me be for a bit." Maxwell turned away to face the window again.

"I'll stand by you, Senator. I just want you to know that."

"Look, son, I appreciate your loyalty, but right now I want to be alone. Grant me that much?"

"Yes, sir." Tyler and Marlena left the room to find Hewitt coming down the hall with breakfast.

"I'll just leave this on his desk, Miss Lena," said Hewitt, reading their expressions. "Mr. Hamilton, I've left a filled washbasin and towels in the room down the hall. There's a couch in there as well, should you need to rest."

"Thank you, Hewitt, but I don't think any of us will be getting much rest for quite some time."

Jason Maxwell walked down the hall to his wife's room. In the last half hour a storm of emotions had rocked him. Desperation that it wasn't true. Grief that it might be, for it explained so much of his wife's behavior. Anger and shame at the thought of his own wife committing such a deed. Guilt at leaving her somehow unprotected, to be victimized so cruelly on that horrible night the Yankees stormed the port. More guilt and anger that his own political idealism had laid her open to this horrible exploitation, this public humiliation. He'd done it to her as surely as if he'd penned the words or held the knife.

Then came the jagged blade of betrayal. She'd kept it from him. She'd lied by omission. She'd not trusted him enough to keep her vows, not trusted the strength of his love no matter what had happened. She'd violated him as a husband. He tasted bile in his throat as his hand reached for the door latch.

He walked into the dark room and stood there. He heard the rustle of bedclothes and the sound of steady breathing. With a wrenching surge, his heart remembered the feeling of her close in the night. He walked slowly to the window and pulled back the drapes a foot or two, flooding the room with the sharp morning light.

She stirred.

"Claudia?" He was surprised at the calm in his voice. As if it came from someone else.

"Mmm . . . it's early . . . who . . . Jason?" She edged up in bed quickly as she came awake. She drew the covers closer to her neck. The impulse made Jason nearly wretch. His own wife, driven to fear.

"Claudia, you need to get up now. Right away."

"The children? Has something happened?" She swung her feet slowly toward the floor, eyeing him.

"They're fine, Claudia."

"Jason, what is going on?"

"We must talk." He handed her the dressing gown from the foot of the bed. She made sure their hands did not touch when she took it from him.

"Jason, you're frightening me. Tell me what is happening."

He watched his hand extend and give her the newspaper, as if it were disembodied, floating of its own free will.

Claudia opened the paper. She stared at the page and went white, making the most horrible, animal-like noise Jason had ever heard. Then she fell to her knees and vomited.

He wanted to go to her, to hold her head and calm her, but he couldn't. Not until he knew if it was true. Then, he hoped, the last shreds of this marriage might rekindle in compassion and thaw out the coldness that enveloped him right now. He knelt down, waiting until her wretches gave way to sobs.

Finally, he said quietly, "Is it true, Claudia?"

She turned on him, glaring. "What would it matter to you?!"

"I need to know. Did this happen?"

"Why?" she spat. "So you can consider holding another press conference?"

"Did that Yankee do what it says he did to you? Did that disgusting, vile excuse for a man do all that to you?"

"Yes." The word was a hiss. She pulled the corner of the sheet down off the bed and wiped her face.

"Bloody God, Claudia, how could you not tell me?"

"Look at you! You're Jason Maxwell! Bigger than life! How was I supposed to tell you that I would have given Galveston into the hands of the enemy? I'd have done it, too!" She melted into a whimpering cry. "He wanted to know where the blockade-running boats were. He knew I knew. But I was so scared. I was so terrified I was going to die, I couldn't even remember what you had told me."

Her eyes glossed over as she watched the scene play out again in her mind. "I'd have told him anything. But I couldn't remember where the boat was. He just stood there, scratching me with that disgusting, bloody knife, talking in my ear with that accent . . . that horrible, ghastly accent." She began twisting the sheet around her hands. "He said he was going to . . . to violate me. I thought I might be pregnant, Jason. I kept thinking I might give you a son and if this . . . this creature did anything to me, it might . . . I kept trying to remember what you had told me so he would just go away. Do you hear me? *I kept trying to remember so I could tell him!*"

Jason said nothing.

"But I couldn't. So I made something up. About a launch. I pulled a time and place out of thin air. But he knew I was lying. Then he cut my face." Her hand strayed to the scar. Jason's breath burned in his lungs. "He cut it slowly. Carefully. Like he was *carving*." She sucked in her breath as if she was going to be sick again.

"Then he told me he'd make sure everyone knew I'd told him when they sank the boats. 'We'll find them without you, anyway, but I'll tell everyone you told us where they were.' He told me he'd make sure the world

knew what I'd done for *the Yankee cause*." She spat the
last words out.

Her eyes turned to him again, liquid and hostile.
"And who would have believed me when that other
boat was sunk? An innocent little boat. No blockade-
runner, just people trying to get away. My made-up
story killed them, Jason. I made up a story out of fear,
and. they died just because they happened to be there.
How was I supposed to tell my husband, the Texas
hero, my pathetic version of the story? Everyone kept
saying how damned civilized the Yankees were being.
But they weren't civilized. Everyone was so horrified
when those people died. And I helped them die. How
could I live with what you'd think of me? And when it
turned out I wasn't pregnant . . ." Her voice fell off to
little more than a wail.

"You didn't kill those people. I'd have believed you,
Claudia. You are my wife."

"Fine standing that has these days, Jason!"

"I can't understand why you lied to me," he continued. "In heaven's name, Claudia, it explains so much. If
you'd only told me before, I would have—"

"You would have *what*, Jason? If my own feelings
weren't enough before, would some tragic story really
have swayed you?"

With a hollow blow Jason realized she was right.
Even if she had told him, even now, would he have
changed what he'd done? Probably not.

"I've hurt you," he said quietly.

"Yes. My God, Jason, yes you have."

There was a long, raw silence. He picked up the paper where she had dropped it. "Do you want him to
win, Claudia?"

"I don't care anymore."

"You betrayed no one. You gave away no military secrets. That scum of a man acted on information he knew was a lie and fired on a boat he knew wasn't a blockade-runner, just to save his worthless skin. It's *him* who's the traitor, Claudia, not you. Fate put those people in the line of fire, not you. You were trying to save your life." He was trying not to raise his voice. "What Stock is saying is a lie, Claudia. Do you want Arthur Stock to bring this family down with a *lie?*"

Her head fell back against the bed. "I want it all to go away," she moaned.

Jason's forehead fell to rest on his arm.

Then he felt it.

The tiny kindle he had hoped would somehow survive. He reached up and pulled the coverlet from the bed. He balled it up and mopped the floor while Claudia lay slumped against the bed.

"Claudia," he said quietly, "think of the girls. Don't they deserve to know this isn't the truth?"

She began to cry again. "It's no use."

He felt his back straighten. "You're wrong, Claudia. Don't let this destroy our family."

"And what have *you* done to protect this family, Jason?"

It was a long time before he answered. "Not enough."

Silence fell between them again. Finally Jason stood up. "Come downstairs, Claudia. Come down with me and we will start from there."

She rose slowly and pulled the dressing gown on, resisting help from Jason. While she brushed her hair, he watched her spine straighten into a semblance of her former self. He held the door for her and they walked quietly out onto the landing. Together. Not touching, but together. It was a start.

They reached the top of the stairs that led down to

the front hallway. There, in the light of the doorway, was Marlena. Hamilton was standing facing her. Close to her.

He heard Claudia suck in her breath. Then he saw Hamilton reach up and touch Marlena's cheek. He watched as the younger man ran his finger along her cheek, slowly following her jawline. It was an intimate touch. Tender. Shocked, he drew a breath to say something, but instead heard a savage wail from his wife.

She was staring horrified at Marlena. Her hand clawed at her own cheek, and in a snap Jason realized what was happening. Claudia wasn't seeing Lena and Hamilton; she was seeing herself and that soldier. Fear shot through him and he reached for Claudia, catching her arm.

"Don't you touch her!" she shrieked. "You filthy . . ." She flailed out of Jason's grasp, rushing toward the stairs. "Go away. Don't hurt her. *Go away!*"

She took two more steps and then something came over her. Her body shook and she made a choking, gurgling sound. Her arm reached for the railing, but she didn't make it. As Jason grabbed her by the shoulders, she wavered and one side of her body seemed to suddenly melt under his fingers.

"Claudia!" he cried. She sank eerily down as he struggled to hold her. She looked at him, frightened and confused, as thick, guttural sounds came instead of speech. "Claudia, what's wrong?!" Jason tried to hold her, for she seemed to be fading away from him. With a final, horrible sound, she sagged in his arms.

Jason fought for breath, terrified. She was still awake, conscious, but far away. He held her, but her head jerked unnaturally from side to side.

Jason heard Marlena rushing up the stairs. "Mother!

What's happened?" He held his wife's face. Her eyes rolled.

He heard a second set of heavier footsteps coming up the stairs. Hamilton. Jason tried to hold Claudia's gaze, but when she caught sight of Hamilton over Marlena's shoulder, her body went wild, in a gruesome kind of convulsion. Anguished, wordless sounds choked out of her throat. He held her tighter, fighting his own fear as well as her flailing. Claudia's hand flew out toward her daughter's face, catching her waistband and the watch fob instead. The fob broke under her frantic grasp, sending pearls dashing across the floor.

"For God's sake, Hamilton, get away! Go downstairs and send for a doctor!" He ignored Marlena beside him and put his face close to his wife's. "Claudia. Claudia! Stay with me. Look at me and try to breathe. Stay with me, Claudia."

⊰ Chapter Fourteen ⊱

Marlena rounded the corner of her father's desk for the twentieth time. "I should be up there."

Tyler's voice was weary. "The doctor's been sent for. Andrea said that your mother is resting quietly, that her trouble breathing has died down. There's nothing you can do, Lena."

She pushed her father's chair back under the desk. "I don't believe that."

Tyler caught her gaze. "I don't believe that what she needs right now is to see you. You saw what seeing . . . us . . . did to her. Don't you think it's best to keep a little distance right now?"

"No, I don't. She's my mother, Tyler." Marlena kept pacing, until Tyler grabbed her elbow.

"She's a woman who's been through hell. Her insides have been ripped out and spread on every doorstep in Austin." There was a sharp edge to Tyler's voice. They'd been up most of the night, and things were starting to fray.

Marlena shut her eyes. "I keep seeing that look on her face as she slumped down. Her eyes . . ."

"I know," Tyler said quietly. He pressed his fingertips against his own eyes, as if to push out the image.

The sound of her father's footsteps came from the hallway, and the study doors slid open.

Marlena started toward her father, only to be stopped

by a formidable glare and a single raised finger. "She's asleep. Andrea is sitting with her."

She watched Tyler rise from the corner of the desk, and forced in a deep breath. It was clear the senator was yielding the floor to no one.

"What the devil is going on?" he ground out.

Even though she'd spent the last hour trying to think what to say, Marlena was at a complete loss. "Daddy, Tyler and I . . . we . . ." The words just wouldn't come. The knife was already in his heart, and here she was affixing her hand to twist the blade.

No one moved. Then, without warning, her father leapt across the floor and thrust his fist squarely at Tyler's jaw. It sent Tyler lurching against the wall. Marlena gasped. With a rage that gave him strength well beyond his years, he grabbed Tyler by his lapels and shook him. "How *dare* you!" he bellowed into Tyler's face. He drew his arm back to strike him again, but Tyler blocked the blow.

"Daddy! Don't do this!"

Marlena gasped as he threw Tyler against the wall and walked away. He paced the floor like an angry lion, shouting, "I *made* you." He jabbed a furious finger at Tyler. "I pulled you out of that dusty law school and turned you into a first-class manager, and *this* is how you repay me? Taking advantage of my daughter?"

"No one took advantage of anyone, Father!" shouted Marlena. "This was not Tyler's doing!" When her father turned to her, she lowered her voice. "I am not some smitten schoolgirl. It happened. I chose to pursue it as much as Tyler did."

He stared at her. "Do you have any idea what you're doing?"

"Yes," Tyler broke in, coming over to her. "I do. And the cost of it. But, Senator, all the consequences in the world won't change the fact that . . . I love your daughter, sir. And I think you know that." Tyler took her hand in his.

"I love him, Daddy," she said calmly. "I won't apologize for it. Even if I am sorry for the trouble it causes."

Her father walked up close to Tyler. "I should fire you this minute. It would solve a lot of problems."

Tyler's grip on her hand tightened as he stood his ground. "I think we both know that's not true, sir."

"You've got unbelievable nerve, Hamilton."

"Yes, sir."

"I can't believe this." Her father's eyes narrowed.

Marlena gripped Tyler's hand in return. "I want your blessing, Daddy," she said, trying to keep the edge of defiance out of her voice.

He ignored her and stared at Tyler. "Behind my back, even. I swear to you, Hamilton, if you've done anything to compromise my daughter—"

"Daddy!"

"Well, damn it, Lena, I've got a right to know, and I haven't the patience or the inclination to be polite right now."

Just the same, she didn't care for her father's interrogation of Tyler's conduct, as if she were no party to anything that might have happened. "He's been a perfect gentleman, Father. You're being unreasonable."

"I'm damn entitled to be unreasonable, daughter." He had a point. He planted himself in front of her. "Lord, Lena, do you really love him? Hamilton? Are you really sure about this?"

It was an easy answer. "I am, Daddy. Quite, quite sure."

"God help us all." He walked over to his desk. "Lena, give me a moment alone with Mr. Hamilton."

"Daddy . . ."

His huge fist slammed down upon the desktop, rattling its contents. "Dear God Almighty, Marlena, if you don't—"

"All right!" She gave Tyler's hand a final squeeze before releasing it. Marlena pulled the sliding doors shut behind her and stood to the side in the hallway, listening.

"Hamilton," came her father's voice, "you went behind my back. I don't know what to think of the two of you, but you could have at least been honest with me before now. Lena claims she loves you. For that reason, and for that reason alone, I'll refrain from booting your sorry self back to Boston." Marlena tried to imagine Tyler's expression. "Sweet Jesus, Hamilton, I don't know what to do with this. I'm going back upstairs to Claudia. Dear God, did it occur to you what this would do to her?" He grunted. "I can't deal with this now. But until I do, I've got six words to say to you, and I want you to hear them loud and clear. Do I have your attention?"

"Yes, sir," came Tyler's voice.

There was a bit of a pause. "Keep your hands off my daughter!"

An hour later, after the doctor had arrived and declared Mrs. Maxwell fragile but stable, Tyler and Hewitt went to bring Deborah to the ranch. Marlena had pleaded to go along, but relented in favor of finally being permitted to sit with her mother.

"I'm glad somebody's come," said Mrs. Elrod when the men arrived at the boardinghouse. "I didn't know quite what to do when she ran out of the room at breakfast. I reckoned she'd send for somebody or something, but we haven't heard a peep out of her since. I was getting a mite worried." She jostled the enormous circle of keys at her waist while she eyed Tyler. He got the distinct impression Mrs. Elrod was none too fond of having Tyler Hamilton in her home, given the morning's press.

"It's been chaotic here all morning. With the fire and all."

"What fire?"

"Mr. Hamilton, how could *you* not have known?"

Tyler didn't care at all for the look in her eye. "Not known what, Mrs. Elrod?"

She stood with her pudgy hands on her hips. "Why, that the *Austin City News* presses burnt to the ground early this morning."

She eyed him again. "Just after the paper came out, they say."

Tyler hid his shock. "Mrs. Elrod, that's terrible news."

"Yes," she said, staring at him. "Isn't it?"

The other boarders in the parlor didn't even bother to hush their gossiping, crowding in the parlor door as Mrs. Elrod took the men upstairs to Miss Edgerton's room. Evidently the prospect of having him and Hewitt in her parlor was more gruesome than the impropriety of letting gentlemen upstairs.

"Miss Edgerton?" Mrs. Elrod rapped timidly at the door. "Miss Edgerton, Mr. Hamilton is here to see you. Are you all right in there, hon?"

The tumblers clicked open, and Tyler caught Mrs. Elrod's arm. "It's all right, Mrs. Elrod, we'll be fine. I'll call you if I need anything." Mrs. Elrod seemed glad of the chance to flee the scene. She bustled down the stairs without a backward glance.

The door opened very slowly. A hollow face resembling Deborah Edgerton's appeared. Her reddened eyes were cold and empty. The shades behind her were drawn, despite its being nearly noon.

Without greeting, she opened the door wider and let them enter the room. She returned to filling a carpetbag that lay open on the bed.

"Miss Edgerton, I don't . . . I haven't the words," stammered Tyler.

She looked so beaten.

"There's nothing to say, is there? What could there possibly be to say?" Her voice was thin and distant, yet she was violently stuffing clothes into the carpetbag. "I suppose the senator's told you it's true." Tyler nodded. Empty drawers lay gaping open throughout the room. She bristled when Tyler moved his hand out to stop her packing.

"Let Hewitt and me take you out of here," he said quietly. "The senator wants you to come stay at the ranch."

"No."

"Miss Edgerton, I don't think it's wise for you to stay here."

She struggled with the clasp until it snapped shut. "I have no intention of hiding under the great wings of the mighty Maxwell family anymore. I'm not one of them, and I'm weary of playing the poor relation."

Tyler took a step toward her. "You know that's not the case."

She turned on him, cold and sharp. "Beware, Mr. Hamilton. You're not one of them, either. And I'll thank you to leave me in peace."

Tyler backed off, sitting instead in a chair. "Where will you go?" he asked after a pause.

Miss Edgerton sat down on the edge of the bed. "I'm going to St. George's." Tyler wasn't really surprised that she had an answer, even if the local convent seemed a bit of an overreaction. "No one will bother me there. I don't want to be bothered for a very long time. Can you understand that, Mr. Hamilton?"

Tyler sighed. "Yes, I can." It seemed a horrible injustice that she'd become a target in this melee. She didn't deserve what had happened to her. She was just trying to carve a life out for herself.

Hewitt approached the bed. His formal demeanor melted into a fatherly voice as he gathered her bag. "Miss Edgerton, would you allow us to escort you? I'd consider it my duty to see you safely to St. George's. I'm sure the senator would have it no other way." There was tenderness and honor in his voice, which Tyler marveled at. Hewitt took the carpetbag in one hand, then held out his elbow to Miss Edgerton with the other. Tyler went about the room gathering the remaining boxes and bags. With a quiet formality of his own, he handed Deborah her parasol. She took it and resolutely stepped through the door. Tyler pulled it shut, and the trio started down the stairs.

The other boarders stood in the hallway, gawking. Deborah ignored them and calmly walked out the front door. When they reached the street, Hewitt opened the carriage door and gave Deborah a respectful bow of his head. Tyler held out his hand and helped her into the carriage. Before shutting the door, she reached into a pocket and pressed a small packet into Tyler's hand.

"Please take this. I don't want to see it ever again." Her voice quavered. She was hanging on to her composure by sheer strength of will.

"Of course." Tyler hoped his eyes spoke more comfort than his words. He shut the carriage door and slipped the package into his pocket.

"To St. George's, Hewitt," came Deborah's voice from inside the carriage.

"Most certainly, Miss Edgerton."

Tyler climbed up beside the dignified old man. "Hewitt?"

"Yes, Mr. Hamilton?"

"You were wonderful up there."

Hewitt started to say something in reply, but then simply nodded. "To St. George's, then."

"It's the brooch he gave her when he proposed." Marlena held up the small silver filigree pin. It was shaped like a peppermint, set with tiny red and white stones to create the candy's swirls. "I still can't believe it's true. How could she have kept it from me all these years? To go through that alone? Oh, I just ache for her, Tyler. Hasten's a monster." She handed Tyler the pin back. "Do you think he really felt anything for her?"

Tyler stared at the brooch. "As a matter of fact, I'm sure of it. He told me himself he gave the story about your mother to Stock in the hopes of getting him to drop his article about Deborah."

Marlena picked up a twig and tossed it into the flower bed. "Instead Stock ran both. I'm sorry he didn't burn in the fire. I hope he never prints another word the rest of his loathsome life. What kind of man does that? Destroys for pleasure."

Tyler put his foot on the wrought-iron garden bench where she was sitting. "And now he's destroyed. Don't you see? This is exactly what we're battling. It's been two decades since the war, and still people are inflicting horrors on each other. Men on both sides did horrible, inhuman things." He rewrapped the brooch and returned it to his pocket. "At some point one has to decide that such horrors simply can't drive one's actions anymore. Not that it wasn't—and isn't—important, but it can't stand in the way of reconciliation anymore."

Marlena put her hand on his knee. "I do believe that." She looked up at the drawn shades of her mother's bedroom window. "It's eating her alive. Lord, Tyler, do you think Mother can put it behind her ever? With all that's happened?"

"I couldn't say. She has a million reasons not to, I suppose." Tyler put his hand on top of hers. "She's a Maxwell, though, and I've learned never to underestimate the power of a Maxwell woman."

Marlena felt the heat of his hand atop hers. "Tyler, do you remember asking me if I could make the political argument for your being here?"

"I remember a rather nasty fight about it, as a matter of fact."

"I can. You should be here," Marlena said quietly, looking into his eyes. Affection poured over his features and he tightened his hand on hers.

"I would."

Marlena raised an eyebrow. "Would what?"

"During that same . . . *discussion,* you said a husband ought to put his wife first, above all else. You asked me if I would put you before everything. I would."

"I know." She felt her heart would crush under the weight of her love for him.

Tyler looked deeply, lovingly at her. He wrapped both of his hands around hers. "Marlena Winbourne Maxwell, will you marry me?"

Marlena smiled. "Excuse me, but aren't you supposed to be down on one knee when you ask that question? You're standing over me like some conquering knight." Suddenly her heart felt not crushed, but weightless.

Tyler cocked an eyebrow. "Lena, if your father should glance out the window and see me down on one knee before you, I do believe he'd run me through with the first available sharp object. I'm doing the best I can under trying circumstances."

"You've a point there."

"And?"

"Yes. A thousand yeses."

Tyler reached down and handed her a pebble from the path. "It only takes one, my love."

• • •

Tyler stared into his coffee cup the next morning. The new day had brought little change, except the welcome omission of an *Austin City News* edition. The senator spent his time in his wife's room, ignoring the political frenzy spinning around him. Tyler couldn't help thinking that was as it should be. For now, at least.

The kitchen door swung open and Hewitt came into "refill" Tyler's already full cup. Tyler was again amazed at the man's ability to express emotions in his conduct of everyday tasks. Somehow he filled a coffee cup with the same effect as a supportive hand on the shoulder.

"I've followed all your instructions, Mr. Hamilton. The property gates have all been locked and men stationed at each, with strict instructions to let no one in without your or the senator's approval. We've had a few reporters pestering the men with questions, but so far everything has been contained."

"It will only get more difficult, Hewitt."

"Regrettably, sir."

Tyler nodded and forced down more coffee, more for Hewitt's benefit than anything else.

Just then, a young man entered the room with the look of someone delivering unwelcome news. He cleared his throat in an unnecessary attempt to catch their attention.

"Yes, Ethan?" inquired Hewitt.

"Captain Hawthorne is here."

Tyler rose. "I thought I left strict instructions—"

"Captain Hawthorne," cut in Hewitt, not quite masking the concern in his voice, "is with the Austin sheriff's department, Mr. Hamilton."

Tyler turned to look at Hewitt.

"I'm sure Captain Hawthorne left the gatesman no choice but to let him in. Ethan, please show the captain to the front parlor and let him know that the senator will speak with him as soon as he is able."

Ethan turned paler. "He's not asking to speak to Senator Maxwell," he stammered. "He . . . he wants to speak with Mr. Hamilton, sir." Tyler's spine stiffened.

"Mr. Hamilton, it seems you have a guest. I'll have coffee brought to the front parlor at once."

Tyler walked down the hall in a whirlwind. He couldn't understand why Captain Hawthorne would need to speak with him before speaking with the senator. When he opened the parlor door, Tyler spied a stout, stiff-looking man in a semblance of military dress. He wore no recognizable uniform of any military branch, but a composite of military and western garb seemingly fashioned for his own office. The hat under his arm was an odd hybrid of cowboy hat and military cap. Several military-looking pins sat on his chest, next to a polished silver star. He definitely looked more the captain than the sheriff. He had a sharply pointed nose and a large mustache of thick silvery hair. These features, when paired with large black eyes, gave him the unmistakable look of a schnauzer dog. Even his voice had a bit of a bark to it.

"Hawthorne," he snapped, stiffly extending a hand.

"Tyler Hamilton. Good morning. How may I assist you, Captain?"

"Official business, my boy, so I'll come straight to the point: Mr. Hamilton, are you aware that the offices of the *Austin City News* burned in the hours just before dawn Saturday?"

"News of the fire did reach the ranch, Captain."

"The *Austin City News* didn't just burn, young man; it was set on fire—between three and six in the morning, by my estimate."

Tyler drew a slow breath, his mind's gears whirring. "I see. I hope there were no injuries?" With a chill,

Tyler remembered that he was with Lena in the stables between the hours of three and six A.M. *My God,* he thought, *could things get any worse?*

"No, the issue had been run and everyone got out in time. Look, Mr. Hamilton, the edition on the presses that night was quite unkind to you and your employer." Hawthorne twitched his nose and switched his hat to under his other arm. "Mr. Hamilton, can you tell me where you were between the hours of three and six A.M. Saturday morning?"

Tyler spoke slowly. "Captain Hawthorne, may I assume from your question that I am under formal investigation?"

"To put it bluntly, yes."

Tyler forced himself to take a long sip of coffee. "Let me assure you, Captain, that I intend to cooperate fully. But given the rather extreme circumstances of my situation, wouldn't you agree that it would be appropriate for me to retain a solicitor before this goes any further? I must ensure that the senator, his office, and his campaign are protected. I'm sure you understand."

"Well, that is your right. So long as you've nothing to hide, Hamilton."

"I've nothing to hide, Captain Hawthorne, but I wish to proceed carefully, in an effort to spare the senator any further distress." He returned the cup to its saucer. "Do you need to speak with the senator at this juncture, or may I relate these developments to him personally?" Tyler was speaking formally in an effort to stymie the captain.

"No, I've no need to speak with the senator this morning."

Magically, Hewitt appeared at the door to show the captain out. *How does he do that?* marveled Tyler. "Hewitt, would you please see Captain Hawthorne out?"

"Of course, Mr. Hamilton. This way, Captain."

Hawthorne snapped his boot heels. "Good day, Mr. Hamilton. I'll expect to be hearing from you."

"I assure you, you will. Good day, Captain Hawthorne."

Tyler listened to the captain's boot heels click down the hall. Only after he heard the front door close did he sink into a chair and exhale, letting his head fall into his hands.

⊰ Chapter Fifteen ⊱

"Everything is *not* under control, and don't take that tone with me, Hamilton," thundered Maxwell. "I'm up to my ears in problems, as it is. I've no patience for pleasantries now. Is that understood?"

Tyler was almost grateful to see the anger flare—it meant the senator hadn't given up all hope—at least not yet. *Ah, but he hasn't heard what you've still to tell him,* Tyler thought. "Understood, sir."

"All right, then. What's been done?"

Tyler clicked into his business self. "We've posted men at all the gates, with strict instructions to let no one enter without approval from either you or me." Marlena glared up from her coffee cup, forcing Tyler to add not-quite-factually, "Or Miss Maxwell."

"And who's come calling so far?"

"It's early enough that we haven't had to deal with that many inquiries yet, Senator."

"You can bet that will change. They'll be on us like flies on honey by sundown. As for Miss Edgerton— well, I hope they've got the decency to leave her alone."

"Dear God, I hope so," added Marlena. "I had hoped to go into Austin today, but as it is . . ."

"As it is, you're not to leave these grounds. Not you or your sisters. No one but the house staff is setting foot off this ranch again until we've got things more under control. Is that understood?" The senator's words were powerful, but his voice was still thin and lifeless. As a result, the words he spoke sounded more like curses under his breath than orders.

"As you wish, sir," responded Tyler.

Marlena handed her father a cup of coffee.

Tyler ventured, "We did have one visitor this morning."

Maxwell looked up.

Tyler inhaled and tightened his grip on the cup and saucer. "Captain Hawthorne was here just a while ago."

Marlena stopped in midpour of another cup.

"Hawthorne?" inquired Maxwell. "What business does Hawthorne have here? I'll not have him making a law-and-order show of Claudia's—"

"Senator, please, it wasn't—"

"I swear I'll bash his little military head in."

Marlena moved over to her father again.

"Senator, Captain Hawthorne was here, I regret to say, to see me."

"You? What in blazes does he want with you?"

"It seems the evidence suggests the fire at the *Austin City News* was arson."

Marlena edged down onto a chair. Maxwell paused. "Arson," the senator said slowly, "is a serious crime." He put down his coffee. "Hamilton, am I to understand that you are a target of this investigation? That you are suspected of having burned down the *Austin City News*?"

"Yes, sir. I'm afraid it would seem that I am." Tyler watched fear flash in Marlena's eyes.

"Sweet mother of God, how much more am I expected to endure?" growled the senator. There was a low note in his voice that sent a prickle of fear down Tyler's spine. He didn't expect it would be much longer before the senator's wrath would boil over, and he was certain it would be ugly when it did. As he watched the senator straighten, he recognized the signs of a man reaching for his last shreds of control. "What did Hawthorne want to know?"

"He asked me to confirm my whereabouts in the hours just before dawn yesterday."

"Oh," whispered Marlena.

The senator didn't seem to notice, but Tyler tried to send her a comforting look. It was useless.

"And what did you tell Captain Hawthorne?" asked the senator.

"I told him I felt it was appropriate for me to contact a solicitor at this point, before the investigation went any further."

"A good answer." Maxwell leaned toward Tyler. "For someone stalling for time. What would you tell me if *I* asked you where you were just before dawn on Saturday, Hamilton?"

He wouldn't lie to the senator. "I was here, sir." It wasn't exactly the whole truth.

"What do you mean?"

"I came straight here after seeing Stock, to warn you."

"Stop right there. *Stock?* You went to see Stock Friday night?" The senator wiped his brow. "How? Why? And has it occurred to you, young man, that there are now witnesses who can place you at the crime scene shortly before the crime? Sweet Jesus, Hamilton, when were you planning to tell me?" The senator's voice was rising toward a shout.

"I tried to stop him from running the issue."

"You tried to stop him from running the issue. Noble, but useless. What I still can't figure, Hamilton, is why Hasten told you the issue was running in the first place. Why were you talking to him? What aren't you telling me?" Maxwell's tone was accusatory.

Tyler took a deep breath. There was no saving Miss Edgerton now. The senator was going to have to know at least that much of it. Cautiously, Tyler recounted the tale of Miss Edgerton's relationship with Hasten, and the tavern meeting.

The senator listened, his face growing angrier by the minute. "I cannot believe this. What the hell is happening? Deborah with a *News* reporter? *That News* reporter? Lena, how much did you know about this?"

"I knew about Hasten. I only learned a week or so ago," she lied.

"Did it *occur* to either one of you to *tell me*?" boomed Maxwell, throwing his hands in the air.

"I had hoped to handle it, Senator," Tyler replied. Marlena just shook her head slightly.

"Goddamn it. Goddamn it all to hell. You listen, Hamilton, and you listen carefully. Go behind my back again and you're finished." Suddenly the senator's face went slightly pale as the pieces fell into place. "Oh, no. Sweet Jesus, Hamilton, exactly *where* here were you between three and six o'clock? And this had damn well better be the truth!"

"In the stable."

The senator spoke very slowly. "In my stable. And who can testify to this fact, Hamilton?"

"I can," said Marlena.

Maxwell rushed at Tyler. "You gave me your *word* she'd not been compromised, you—"

"Stop it!" Marlena yelled. "I'm tired of this! Daddy, I have not been compromised. And why do you keep asking *him* that, as if I'm not in the room?"

Maxwell turned on his daughter. "Not been compromised, have you? Even if you've done nothing—and by God, Hamilton, that had better be the case—what would you call having to publicly admit to this? Being alone in a stable—a blasted stable, Lena—all night with a man? Think about it!"

Marlena now turned on her father, her own temper getting the best of her. "All this—everything that has happened, the family in shreds—and you're concerned with how my honor might look to *society*? I'll tell you something, Father, I don't care how I look to society. I don't care if I never have another suitor again. I want to marry Tyler! I can't very well do that if he's in jail, now, can I?"

The fury in the room seemed to grind to a halt. *Oh, God,* thought Tyler, *now is not the time to get into this.* He sank back against the wall. There was no saving any of them now. The thorny tangle of issues thrust at them in the last forty-eight hours had just reached epic proportions. He was afraid to ask how it could get worse, for every time he asked the question, things did indeed find a way to deteriorate.

Maxwell turned to him. "Well? Is this true?!" He shouted the question rather than asked it.

"I love your daughter, sir. I do want to marry her." Marlena took a step toward him, but Maxwell put his hand between them.

"And at what point were you planning on telling *me*?"

"I hardly thought it appropriate to discuss it *now*." Tyler's own back was getting up.

"Appropriate? Son, we're miles past appropriate! Take a moment, you two, and think about what's going on upstairs. How do you expect me to react to something like this? Surely you don't expect me to hand you a cigar and welcome you to the family!"

"Why not?" Marlena broke in. "Why is this any different than what you've asked Mother to do?"

"It's a far sight different, Lena," countered the

senator. "Hamilton's employment was a professional decision."

"But you still ignored Mother's very personal objections. You asked *her* to ignore them as well."

"Employing the man and marrying him into the family are two different things!" The senator was getting angrier.

"Are they?" Marlena shot back. "You can't accept one and reject the other on the same grounds."

"I'm your father, damn it, yes, I can. Hamilton, you courted her behind my back. You've spent the night with her in my stable. I'd be angry at any man who did that, Boston or next door!"

The senator walked away from them, pacing the room. Tyler could see where Marlena inherited her habit of angry pacing. Sometimes she and her father were so much alike, it was uncanny.

"You're set on marrying him?" barked the senator, pointing at Marlena.

"Very much, Daddy."

Maxwell continued pacing. "You want to marry her?" The thick finger was now aimed at Tyler.

"I do, sir."

Still he circled. "She can't stand the sight of you," he said, throwing his hand to the ceiling, indicating Mrs. Maxwell's bedroom. No one had a reply to that.

Jason Maxwell planted himself in the middle of the room, hands on his hips. He stared up. "Is there anything else, Lord, that you'd like to heave at me before the week is out? I've two more daughters, you know. And a constituency that might be hungry to cut my throat. Men gunning for my downfall. Let's get it all out on the table now, for I'll be mighty angry if anything else comes calling tomorrow!"

Tyler felt an irrational prick of apprehension. It was

like the point in a wedding ceremony where the preacher asks if "anyone has just cause why these two should not marry?" No one truly expects a reply, but the air hangs still for a moment on the wild chance that one will come. Somehow it didn't seem impossible for God to open up the heavens and address Jason Maxwell.

"Get out of here, both of you, before I wring your damn-fool necks. Leave me alone while I figure out what to do with the whole lot of this godforsaken mess."

Tyler nodded his head and motioned Marlena to the door.

"So help me, God, Hamilton, don't you lay one hand—"

"For heaven's sake, Daddy, will you stop—" In the name of pure survival, Tyler shoved her out the door before she could finish.

An orchestra of crickets echoed out from among the hay bales. Marlena waited in the stable for Tyler. A late-night moon poured in through the window. Horses snorted and stomped in the stalls nearby. With all that had happened, she felt thirsty for his touch.

At last he stood in the doorway, his eyes glowing with affection and a peculiar amusement. "My God, but you're a loose cannon. You'll kill us all, Marlena Maxwell, but I don't care. Come here."

She needed no further enticement. Marlena rushed to him and poured her thirst into a flood of kisses. He tasted sweet and delicious and familiar. Intimate. She'd been with him all day without being close, and the un-touchable nearness of him had worked her into a frenzy. Tyler answered her demand with his own, his mouth eagerly seeking hers. Marlena knew their polite proximity had drawn his desire as taut as hers. She was wondering how much longer they could keep this duality up when Marlena noticed Tyler was keeping his hands behind his back. Was he hiding a gift?

"What have you there?" she teased, peeking around his side, for she was far too small to see over his shoulder. Her eyebrows shot up when she saw that Tyler's hands were haphazardly bound with the drapery cord from the guest room.

Tyler smiled wickedly. "Your father told me in no uncertain terms to keep my hands off you." He shrugged his shoulders. "I could see no other way."

Marlena's shock and amusement became the most potent arousal of all. She grinned and tugged at one of the knots. "Rather loose. You'd never do well as a sailor." She let her hands find their way lazily up his arms to stroke his shoulders.

Tyler bumped her away. "Well, it is rather difficult to do on oneself. Still, your father was most intimidating." Tyler launched into a poor imitation of the senator. "So help me, God, Hamilton . . ."

Marlena stepped back and surveyed him. "Imitations are not your talent. But you do have so many others. . . ." She folded her arms and unleashed a wicked smile of her own. "Tied up. Hmm. That would make you a prisoner, wouldn't it?"

"Pardon?" was all he could muster. Marlena very much enjoyed the effect she was having on him.

"You're standing here with your hands tied behind your back. You're a prisoner. *My* prisoner."

"I came here of my own free will." Tyler gulped. "I'm sure there's a treaty somewhere protecting my rights."

"Hmm. Doubtful," said Marlena, bringing her face inches from his. She ran her finger slowly along his jawline.

Tyler shivered. "You are not playing fair." His voice faltered slightly as Marlena kissed the hollow of his throat. He leaned against the wall and let out a low groan when Lena ran her fingers up his chest.

"I don't believe you're here for justice," she whispered into his ear as she nicked the edge with her teeth. She was surprising herself.

Her advantage was short-lived. In one quick move, Tyler stepped over her leg to pin her up against the wall with his chest. With his other foot he kicked the stable door shut. Within seconds every inch of him was pressing up against every inch of her. He stared at her hungrily. She had excited him and she knew it. He kissed her deeply, then moved down her throat and across her chest. She reveled in his power and the urgency driving his kisses. He was hungry for her, and she for him.

As they slid down the wall to a blanket on the hay, she felt him fumbling with the drapery cord. The fumbling soon gave way to an honest struggle. She heard Tyler curse under his breath. Amused, she tried to peek around his chest again. Tyler looked at her with a sheepish grin. "It would seem I'm a better sailor than we thought." He grunted as he pushed his arms about.

"Come, now, Tyler, you're not really stuck." She eased in to kiss him again.

"Well." He looked embarrassed, amused, and a touch intrigued at how Marlena might take advantage of the situation.

"Don't be ridiculous." She scrambled over him to have a go at the knots. Her hair and bosom swept over his chest as she did so, and she heard Tyler suck in his breath. He let it out in a gasp, however, as her elbow jabbed his side. She fumbled with the cord. "Good Lord, Tyler, I don't think I can loosen this."

Tyler's face was actually reddening. "This is nonsense." He grunted and struggled again. Meanwhile, Marlena sat back on her haunches, ardor overtaken with sheer amusement.

"Oh my, whatever shall we do?" she mused in her best belle drawl. "What on earth will Daddy say about this?"

"Let us hope he'd be pleased at the lengths I went to to keep my word. Come now, Lena, get these undone."

"Ah, but Mr. Hamilton, you weren't going to keep your word, now, were you?" She pressed her clasped hands to her lips. "I do have you at a disadvantage, don't I? This really isn't an opportunity I should let pass. Let's see, now, I shall need you to promise me your undying devotion. . . ."

"You have that. Undo the knots, Lena."

"I think a rather sizable amount of candy and flowers . . ."

"Candy from suitors has produced enough trouble as it is. Undo the knots, Lena."

"Well, yes, you are right about that one. Perhaps a shopping trip to Millington's. Then there's always jewelry."

"You can have anything you want. *Undo the knots, Lena.*"

She brought her face close to his. "Oh, but why, dearest?" she purred.

He raised his face to kiss her. "Because I can't ravage you with my hands tied behind my back," he said through gritted teeth. Tyler let his head fall back and squinted his eyes shut. *"For God's sake, Lena,"* he pleaded, *"undo the knots."*

Marlena broke into a rich laugh. "Well, all right, then. As long as I have your undying devotion." Tyler just grunted and rolled over, wiggling his fingers. She chuckled as she pulled and poked at the knotted cord. "Tyler?" she said, laughing harder.

"Yes?" Even Tyler was laughing now.

"I don't seem to be able to get these undone."

"Stop laughing and try harder."

His request had the opposite effect. Marlena was laughing so hard now, she could hardly speak. "No, really, Tyler. I can't undo these."

"Well, don't just sit there; go find a knife or something to cut the rope," urged Tyler through his own laughter.

"A knife. Cut them. Good heavens, why didn't I think of that sooner?" She laughed as she walked down the stalls into the tack room to look for something sharp, and returned with a small knife. "Now, hold still; I don't want to nick you."

"I'd feel better if you'd stop laughing before you came at me with a weapon."

"Hold still, you fool." With the aid of three or four cuts, Tyler pulled his hands free. They both fell into laughter again as Tyler rubbed his wrists. They were still laughing when he pulled her into his lap and held her close.

"I love your laugh," he whispered, kissing her forehead. "I haven't heard it much of late." Marlena sighed and snuggled closer to him. She closed her eyes and savored the feeling of being held by him. The passion of moments earlier was replaced with a deep, boundless affection.

He stroked her hair. "This will make quite a story for our children and grandchildren," Tyler mused.

"Once, of course, they're old enough to appreciate it," came a deep voice from the door.

Tyler and Marlena shot upright. Hewitt stood in the doorway, a bemused look on his face. Marlena groped for words, "Hewitt, we . . . I . . ."

"I had wondered why the senator asked me to personally check the stables at eleven-thirty." A hint of a smile crossed his face. "I'm sure he'll be relieved when I tell him I found nothing out of the ordinary. But I've reason to suspect he might search the house himself, so . . ."

Tyler's eyes were as wide as her own. "Of course," he stammered. He turned to Marlena after Hewitt disappeared.

Marlena could only raise her eyebrows in disbelief and amusement. "How . . . ?"

"I don't know," came Tyler's bewildered reply as he picked up the blanket. "I don't think I want to know."

Senator Maxwell spent the next morning at his wife's bedside. Just before lunch, Marlena took Tyler by the hand and pulled him into the study. Tyler couldn't guess what to expect. The options were far too many, and Maxwells were entirely too unpredictable.

Prepared as he was, even Tyler was astonished when the study door swung open to reveal a large board. *The* board. The one the senator always propped up in the study to map out campaign strategies. Tyler let out a soft whistle.

Marlena shot him a look. "We've a mountain of work ahead of us." She slid open her father's desk drawer and took out three sheets of blank paper. Filling a pen, she wrote one heading on each: ARSON, CAMPAIGN, and, with a bit of hesitation, SLANDER. She flapped them in the air for a moment to dry the ink and then tacked them to the board, forming three columns. "There it is. Now, let's see if there's a way out of this disaster."

"Not without a lot more coffee than that," Tyler quipped as Hewitt entered carrying a small coffee service.

"You're right. Hewitt, bring me an urn of coffee, and let's get on with it!"

"Indeed," said Hewitt, not quite hiding a smile from Marlena.

"Where do we start?" asked Tyler.

"Everywhere. Attack it all at once, until a plan shows itself."

"Fair enough. I can't see how we could do anything but improve, on all three fronts." Tyler poured two cups of coffee and handed one to Marlena.

For the better part of an hour, Tyler and Marlena began to test ideas, lay out problems, and look for strategies. It was a disheartening task. The only issue that became clearer was how awful everything looked.

Marlena sank into a chair and stared into the dark pool at the bottom of her coffee cup. Tyler was still staring intently at the board. "Tyler." He heard her sigh. "Now would be a good time to show some of that brilliant creativity you're famous for."

"I've just been thinking; maybe we've been looking at this in the wrong light. The arson, for example. Since my defense is, well"—he groped for the most delicate word—"complex at best, we might be better off focusing on solving the crime. We won't need to concern ourselves with publicly revealing my whereabouts if we can find the real criminal." Tyler picked up a blank card from the senator's desk. "I believe I have a good idea who set a torch to the *News*." He wrote a word on the paper and tacked it to the board in the middle of the "Arson" column.

"Gracious, you're right," gasped Marlena as she set her cup down.

Tyler reached out to wipe the dripping ink from the "n" in "Hasten."

"It makes sense. Hasten told me he pitched the story

about your mother in an attempt to stop the story he'd
broken about Miss Edgerton. When I met him at the
tavern, he thought he'd succeeded. Imagine his anger
to discover Stock merely ran both stories. And credited
him with neither—as your father so fortunately pointed
out to me. It was the ultimate insult. As a staff reporter,
I imagine Hasten would have had access to the
News offices as the paper was printed. It's highly likely
that he could have seen the edition coming out and
realized he'd been double-crossed. With his personality,
I don't think setting the building on fire to get back
at Stock would be too far-fetched for him. We already know he'd go to any lengths to get what he
wanted."

"If Hasten did it, he's far away by now."

"I'm not convinced. He's got an enormous ego.
He might just stay around to see how it all played out.
He has no reason to run. No one would suspect him,
because no one but he and Stock knew of his connec-
tion to the story. As a matter of fact, he might draw attention to himself if he left. At the moment, he's under
no more suspicion than any other News reporter who
was seen there that night. That's if he was seen there at
all. But if Hasten is still in Austin, how do we find
him?"

"Deborah," replied Marlena. "Samuel Hasten is in
love with Deborah. Look what he was willing to do to
spare her. Tyler, you know what an amazing judge of
character Deborah was. There *had* to be something real
between them, or she would have known it. It is just
possible that he's looking for her. To explain. It's a frail
string, but it's the only link we've got. Perhaps it's just
enough to draw him out of hiding."

"It is the thinnest string I've ever had to hang from.
But I suppose it is a chance we'll have to take. We've no
other option. How do we draw Hasten out?"

Marlena planted her chin on her palm and furrowed her brow. Tyler ran his fingers through his hair and walked over to the bookshelves. Neither one offered a solution for a disturbingly long time.

Without warning, Marlena jumped from her chair. "The brooch!"

"Of course!" Tyler replied.

At lunch they filled the senator in on their plan.

"The brooch, Daddy," explained Marlena, "is what Hasten gave Deborah when he proposed."

The senator glared at his daughter. "Proposed? That weasel *proposed* to Deborah?"

"Well, not exactly, sir," interjected Tyler, in an attempt to keep things calm. "It was more of a promissory gift. He had intended to propose when the situation was a bit more suitable."

"A cold day in hell. You knew about this, Hamilton?" Maxwell threw his hands up in the air. "Why in blazes am I the last to know everything around here lately? Is there anything *else*?"

"Well, there were the peppermints," said Marlena. Tyler's urge to gag her rekindled.

"What?"

"All those peppermints Deborah was eating. Hasten bought them for her. The brooch had red swirls on it, like a peppermint candy."

"She sat in my office eating confections bought by Samuel Hasten? That mindless minion of Arthur Stock's?"

Marlena nodded.

They just can't help themselves, Tyler thought. *They're like oil and water.* These two seemed intent on working each other into a lather. "Perhaps we ought to keep this in perspective, Senator," he offered, trying to keep the peace.

"Arthur Stock's paychecks bought candy eaten in my offices? By one of my own staff?" the senator bellowed.

"Candy, Daddy—it was only candy."

Maxwell jabbed a finger in his daughter's direction. "It was candy used to woo a member of my staff into her own undoing! Damn it, Frederick Edgerton was a loyal employee and a good friend. I gave my word to him that I'd take care of his girl. I didn't abandon her when things got sticky. I got her through a crisis, only to have it be plastered all over Austin? Not to mention what that snake has done to my own wife!" The senator lowered his voice to a fierce growl. "I want that miserable excuse for a man found. I'll wring his neck with my own hands just for being an underhanded jackal and slandering Claudia for a measly newspaper story. Hamilton, take anyone you need from the house or the stable, and get word to Hasten that we've got his blasted pin and you want to meet with him."

Maybe the oil and water aren't such a bad thing, thought Tyler, for the resulting lather had beckoned the return of Jason Maxwell's fighting spirit.

Marlena sat on her father's desk, leafing through a copy of Shakespeare's sonnets. She looked up to see Tyler coming into the study. "Did the message get sent to Hasten?"

"Loud and clear, I hope. We'll just have to wait for a reply." He motioned to the book. "Invoking the bard, are we?"

She let the book fall to her lap. "It's for Mother. Apoplectic strokes can have temporary effects or ones that last a lifetime. Dr. Roberts said that if we read to her, talk to her, perhaps she'll begin responding in some way. I don't understand all of it. It's eerie the way she just lies there, staring off, not really seeing anyone or anything. Dr. Roberts says he's confident she's not in pain, but no one can be sure how much she understands about what's happening around her. Maybe she takes it all in but just can't communicate. Perhaps she understands nothing at all."

"Shakespeare's sonnets?"

"They are favorites of hers. The doctor says things that inspire strong emotions are important. See, the corners of the pages are turned down for the ones she likes best." Marlena ran her fingers across the words, remembering. "Years ago I used to catch Daddy reading them to her on the front porch when I was supposed to be in bed."

"Somehow," quipped Tyler, "I fail to picture your father's drawl tumbling over 'thee' and 'thou' and 'forsooth.'"

Marlena laughed. "Oh, no, you're wrong. He was simply grand at it. Mother used to tell him his accent made the words sing."

Tyler plucked his glasses out of his breast pocket. "Do all the Maxwell women swoon when a man reads them Shakespeare?" He took the book from her and licked a finger to flip through the pages. "Have you a favorite, Lena?"

"I'm not at all sure that accent of yours will have the same effect, Tyler." On second thought, the prospect of having him recite love poems to her was rather enticing. "But you are most welcome to try," she added.

Tyler's eyes shot wide open. He snapped the book shut and stared at Marlena. "My God," he whispered.

"What? Tyler . . ."

Tyler threw the book down on the desk. He grabbed Marlena by both shoulders and gave her a huge kiss. "You're brilliant. You're astounding, that's what you are."

"Tyler, what are you talking about?"

"Exactly, my love, that's it exactly!"

Marlena was stumped. "I . . ."

Tyler pulled her to her feet. "Take this book, Marlena, and come with me. I do believe we may just have stumbled upon our miracle."

⇥ Chapter Sixteen ⇤

The drapes were parted to let a meager slice of sunshine light the room. Her mother lay propped up on a mountain of pillows, her silver-blond hair plaited into a thick braid that lay arranged on one shoulder.

Marlena walked over to Diana, who sat on the ever-present bedside chair doing needlework. "How is she, Di?"

"Same." Diana parked her needle in the edge of the cloth. "Her hand wiggles a bit now and then, but not much else."

Sarah came out from the corner, where she was wringing out a cloth in a basin of water. "She's able to take a bit of broth now and then, if you're careful about it. She ate more this morning than she did yesterday."

"That's good news," said Marlena, forcing optimism into her voice.

"I suppose," sighed Diana, unconvinced.

Marlena put her hand on her sister's shoulder. "Why don't you let me have a go at it for a while?"

Diana rose, packed up her needlework, and kissed her mother on the cheek. "Get better, Mama," she whispered.

Marlena studied her mother's face for some flicker of recognition. None came. She was grateful that the lack of awareness didn't seem to trouble Diana. The girl headed out the door, but Marlena heard her stop when she saw Tyler standing in the hallway. "What's *he* doing up here?"

Marlena shot a pleading look at Sarah, who took Diana downstairs.

Tyler stepped cautiously into the doorway. Marlena wasn't at all sure that this idea would work. It seemed just as likely to make things worse. But maybe, just maybe . . .

As if reading her thoughts, Tyler nodded silently and handed the book of sonnets to Marlena. She gripped the thin, worn volume and sat down next to the bed. Tyler stood behind her. She shut her eyes in a silent plea. *Please, please let this work. A little hope would go so far right now.*

Marlena took a deep, shaky breath and turned to the first dog-eared page. Quietly, she began to read.

> *Let those who are in favour with their stars*
> *Of public honor and proud titles boast,*
> *Whilst I, whom fortune of such triumph bars,*
> *Unlook'd for joy in that I honour most. . . .*

The sonnet went on about the frailty of fame and fortune. Marlena was struck at how the poignancy of the words applied to this moment. She continued with a lump in her throat.

> *The painful warrior famoused for fight,*
> *After a thousand victories once foil'd*
> *Is from the book of honour razed quite,*
> *And all the rest forgot for which he toiled:*
> > *Then happy I, that love and am beloved*
> > *Where I may not remove or be removed.*

Marlena looked up from the book, hoping for a sign of response in her mother's face. The eyes continued to stare off unseeing toward the window. Tyler's hands came to rest on Marlena's shoulders. She looked up at him, questioning.

He nodded, urging her to continue.

She turned to the next marked page, feeling Tyler's hands steady on her shoulders. She read through the sonnet.

> How would thy shadow's form from happy
>   show
> To the clear day with thy much clearer light,
> When to unseeing eyes thy shade shines so!
> How would, I say, mine eyes be blessed made
> By looking on thee in the living day . . .

Then in Marlena's ear, over her shoulder, she heard Tyler's voice, in a whisper, join with hers. He was slowly adding his voice to hers as she finished the sonnet.

> All days are night to see till I see thee,
> And nights bright days when dreams do show
>   thee me.

She closed her eyes, overcome by the intimacy of Tyler whispering such words beside her. All his longings to be with her in the light of public day seemed steeped in the words. Still her mother sat unmoving and distant.

Tyler knelt down on one knee beside her and put his hand atop hers as it turned to the next marked page. His whispered voice joined hers from the opening lines this time.

> Not marble, nor the guilded monuments
> Of princes, shall outlive this powerful rhyme;

But you shall shine more bright in these contents
Than unswept stone. . . .

They continued on in tandem, Tyler speaking louder
and more clearly with each sonnet. She felt his grasp
tighten on her hand and his arm circle around her. Yes,
he was inserting his voice into hers for her mother's
sake, but above all that floated the sound of him speaking these eloquent words of love to her. She fought the
choking emotion in her voice as they read on.

After his voice could be heard clearly apart from hers
for one or two poems, Marlena heard a low moan from
her mother. "Strong emotions," Dr. Roberts had said.
Of course. Tyler had seen that hate was as strong an
emotion as love. By intertwining the two, they had doubled the effect. She and Tyler stopped to stare at her
mother, who did not move but grew visibly agitated.
Tyler urged her to continue with a nod. Marlena read
on, Tyler lowering his voice a bit but still reciting with
her.

Again her mother stirred when Tyler's voice became
clearer. He kept his voice even with hers for a trifle
longer, and Marlena held her mother's hand. They went
on for an hour, riding wave after wave of the frail
woman's subtle responses, until at the last poem
Marlena felt her mother's hand move to tighten on hers.
Her mother was fighting her way to the surface.

It was a start. It was the little bit of hope she had
prayed for. Marlena rested her head on Tyler's shoulder,
wordless and grateful. She felt Tyler's head rest atop
hers and drop a gentle kiss. Silently, he rose and left the
room, leaving Marlena alone with her mother.

She clasped her mother's hand to her cheek. "He's
fighting for you, Mother. Come back. Find a way to let
him in. Please."

• • •

THE IMPOSSIBLE TEXAN 249

Marlena fingered the back of the chair where her mother would usually sit at breakfast. It sat as an empty reminder in the dining room, the hollow of her mother's weight still imprinted in the cushions. "I miss her, Daddy," she said quietly. "We used to fight like wasps, but now I miss her so much it's like an ax in my chest. She's going to get better. She grabbed my hand yesterday, I'm sure of it." Marlena had told her father about her mother's movements, but had not yet disclosed Tyler's role. She wanted to wait until they were sure what they were doing was making a difference.

"I know, sweetheart," came her father's hoarse reply. "I know."

Tyler rapped softly on the door as he entered the room. "Good morning, Senator. Miss Maxwell."

Marlena looked up. "Any news from Hasten?"

"Not yet. There's no doubt he knows I am looking for him. It may take him a day or two before he feels comfortable enough to answer an inquiry from me."

"We may not have a day or two," grumbled the senator. "Captain Hawthorne's not going to wait on you much longer."

"I've already made an appointment to see the captain this afternoon, Senator. I don't believe I could have put it off any longer and not damage my position. And pardon me for saying so, but I'm not sure how much longer you'll be able to hold off on a statement to the press. Hewitt told me one of the gatesmen coshed a reporter this afternoon for trying to sneak through the west fence."

"I've made enough mistakes with Claudia. I want to wait—if I can—and ask her what she wants to do before I go in front of the press." He ran his hand across his forehead. "She had better come back to us soon. We're running out of time. And we still haven't dealt with Deborah's situation."

"We can't just leave her there undefended," said Marlena.

"We can't deny the accusations, either," replied her father. "If she won't come to the ranch, there's not much we can do. Issuing a statement to the press would only send more reporters to hound her at St. George's."

Marlena shot her father a "we've got to do *something*" look.

"I'm doing all I can, child," he defended. "For God's sake, I got Alexander Sawyer to represent Hamilton. It's not as if people are rushing to come to our aid these days."

Marlena took a long, surprised look at her father. Representation by Alexander Sawyer, the city's finest solicitor, was no small favor, to be sure.

"I'm no fool, Senator," said Tyler, filling a coffee cup. "I know you twisted arms to get Sawyer. I'm still not so sure it wouldn't have been better for me to bring down our family solicitor from Boston. You shouldn't be calling in favors on my account right now."

"It would be a bad move to bring in someone from the outside, especially from Boston. We can't afford to offend anyone. And good Lord, Hamilton, if now isn't the time for cashing in our chips, I don't know when is. Have some breakfast. You look worn out."

"You asked Mr. Sawyer to represent—" Marlena cut the question short because something in her hesitated at saying "Tyler" in front of her father. Marlena was deeply pleased that her father had persuaded Sawyer to step in on Tyler's defense. She took it as a gesture of support, however indirect. "Thank you, Daddy."

Her father frowned. "Don't thank me. I've simply no desire to be associated with criminal activity. What is, is. We can't pretend it isn't there and hope it will go away. Speaking of which, Hamilton, you might as well drop the pretense of calling my daughter 'Miss

Maxwell' in my presence. Sounds silly. I know darn well you don't call her that when I'm not around." His tone was almost moping, as if he was beginning to grudgingly accept their relationship. It made Marlena smile broadly as she got up and kissed her father on his cheek.

"Why, Daddy, that's simply grand of you."

He shooed her away. "No, it's not. It just sounds ridiculous to be so formal when we're all under fire here. But I'll tell you one thing: I don't want to hear any 'dears' or 'sweethearts' or anything of the kind. I haven't decided what to do about the two of you yet."

"Yes, sir." Marlena noted that the senator still preferred that Tyler called him "sir." She curbed the impulse to let her father know she didn't need him to decide anything for her. Best not to pick that fight just yet. *One at a time,* she thought, remembering the stones Tyler continued to slip her at odd, affectionate moments.

Hewitt appeared at the doorway. "A young boy has just come to the door, sir. He claims to have a message for Mr. Hamilton."

Marlena, her father, and Tyler exchanged expectant glances. "Hasten?" whispered Lena.

"Let's hope so. I certainly hope it's not Hawthorne." Tyler followed Hewitt from the room.

Marlena closed her eyes and clutched her hands to her breast. *Oh, please, Lord. Please.*

Tyler returned, brandishing a slip of paper. "We've done it. I'm to meet him tomorrow night at the Silver Horse Tavern."

Marlena read the torn note:

Hamilton—
I want that brooch back.
Silver Horse tavern, 11pm.
                    —S. Hasten

"Oh, Tyler, we've done it!" She flung her arms around his shoulders. He stiffened and the senator let out a loud *hrrmph*.

Tyler smiled and took her hands. "Let's hope so. Marlena," he added with a sideways glance at her father, who was finding something else—anything else—to look at, "we're far from out of the woods yet."

"Quite right," the senator agreed. "We've no idea if Hasten's our man, or if you can get him to admit it. And even if you can, how are you going to get witnesses? Your word won't carry any weight."

"I've considered that," replied Tyler. "I'm just going to have to convince Captain Hawthorne to discreetly send someone from the sheriff's office to the tavern with me."

"And just how are you going to do that, Hamilton?"

"At the moment, sir, I have no idea. I was hoping we could come up with a plan."

"I hired *you* to come up with the plans, Hamilton."

Marlena could swear she heard a tiny hint of good-natured teasing in her father's voice.

Tyler had heard it, too. "I don't recall the class on tricking weasel reporters into confessing their criminal activities, sir. Perhaps I was ill that day."

Marlena watched her father actually smile. "It seems there's a lot you missed, Mr. Hamilton. Well, all right then, we'd best get to figuring this one out. Lena honey, you're going to need an urn of coffee for this, aren't you?"

Captain Hawthorne sat down at his desk. "Mr. Hamilton, do you understand the grave position you are in?"

"I do."

"And do you understand the most unusual nature of your request for a member of my squad to accompany you? To a meeting with Mr. Hasten, in the hope of drawing out a confession?"

"I am aware that my request is quite out of the ordinary, sir."

"Out of the ordinary is an understatement, Mr. Hamilton. Especially in light of your position. How do I know this is not a rather poorly devised attempt to deflect suspicion away from yourself?"

Tyler turned on all the charm he could muster. "Precisely because it is so poorly devised. I couldn't have dreamed up a more outlandish story if I had tried. Were I trying to divert suspicion, surely I would have bothered to fashion a more credible tale."

Captain Hawthorne turned his attention to the solicitor. "Alex, are you really convinced of this man's innocence?"

"I'll admit he seems too bright a lad to come up with a story this ridiculous. I'd say it's worth investigating."

The captain sat in thought. Sawyer cleared his throat. "The senator and I would consider it a *personal favor* if you'd at least send a man out. I don't see how you've anything to lose."

"I dislike granting favors, Alex." Hawthorne rose again and strode to the window. "I've not been dissuaded, Mr. Hamilton. I'm convinced you are protecting someone. You are grasping at some very small straws to keep from revealing where you were Saturday morning." Tyler said nothing. "You do realize, I hope, that you may go down with your noble ship, young man." Again Tyler said nothing. There was a long, uncomfortable silence. Finally, the captain spoke. "Very well, then, Mr. Hamilton, I will grant your request—on one and only one condition. If no confession is forthcoming from Hasten, you will tell me where you were during those hours, and with whom. If you do not, I'll have no choice but to consider formal charges against you. Do we understand each other?"

Tyler breathed an audible sigh of relief. "Indeed we

do, sir." He rose and offered his hand to the captain.
"Thank you, sir."

"Don't thank me, Hamilton. It's you who may hang
yourself tonight. Be here at ten-thirty and I'll have a
man follow you to the Silver Horse. You'd better pray
this turns out in your favor, young man." Hawthorne
nodded. "That press was an awful blow."

"I agree," commented Alex Sawyer, shaking the captain's hand. "But if I know Jason, we'd best not count
him out of the running yet."

"We shall see," was all the captain would offer.

• • •

> Let me not to the marriage of true minds
> Admit impediments. Love is not love
> Which alters when it alteration finds,
> Or bends with the remover to remove;
> O, no, it is an ever-fixed mark,
> That looks on tempests and is never shaken. . . .

Tyler's voice was equal with Marlena's now. The ritual
of sitting together reading to Mrs. Maxwell had
become a sort of vow to him. It became a declaration of
love to Marlena in the exquisite words of a poet. But it
had to be more. It had to be a balm, to take words Mrs.
Maxwell loved and wrap them in an accent she once
hated.

He had been here most of the evening. Mrs. Maxwell
had stopped growing agitated at the sound of his voice
blending with Marlena's. He had come to realize that
he was here as much for himself as for Marlena or her
mother. Now it was time. He turned the page. They
started the poem together:

> Some glory in their birth, some in their skill,
> Some in their wealth, some in their body's
>   force . . .

Tyler looked into Marlena's eyes and held up a quieting finger. She wrapped her hand around his and slowly let her voice drop until Tyler continued on alone:

> *Thy love is better than high birth to me,*
> *Richer than wealth, prouder than garments' cost,*
> *Of more delight than hawks or horses be;*
> *And having thee, of all men's pride I boast;*
> > *Wretched in this alone, that thou mayst take*
> > *All this away and me most wretched make.*

As Tyler and Marlena watched, Mrs. Maxwell's body stiffened and her breath came quick and shallow. Marlena took her mother's hand and stroked it until the response subsided. Tyler turned the page and began another poem, in a softer voice.

They went on, cycling through Mrs. Maxwell's ebbing and peaking responses, until her body no longer stiffened at the sound of his voice. Tyler was hoarse and weary, Marlena exhausted, but they continued on. Marlena laid her head in Tyler's lap as he continued reading. After two more poems, Tyler could speak clearly in Mrs. Maxwell's presence without disturbing her.

Then, in a moment that seemed to stop time, he saw Mrs. Maxwell's head turn from the window toward him. Her eyes were closed, but she had turned toward him, not away. Her face bore the expression of one sleeping, not the eerie mindlessness of the day before. He recited the poem's final couplet and closed his eyes in silent thanks. He stroked Marlena's hair.

"Hamilton," came a tight voice behind him. Tyler turned his head to see the shaken figure of Jason Maxwell standing in the doorway. He evidently had been there for some time. His face was flushed with emotion, vulnerable and transparent in a way Tyler had never seen.

"Sir?" he said quietly.

"What are you doing?"

Emotion suddenly choked in Tyler's throat. "Fighting for your wife, sir." For all his speechmaking, right now he couldn't find the words to tell the senator what this had come to mean to him. "I thought . . . well, I hoped my accent might bring out a response in her. Coupled with the poems she loves . . . I thought it might bring her back." They weren't the right words. He didn't know how to make the senator understand.

"It's working," whispered Marlena.

"How long have you been reading to her?" Maxwell walked toward them.

"Days. I thought if I could somehow . . . replace the memory for her. Give her something good to associate with the accent. She might . . . wake up." He stopped. The words just weren't coming. Finally, he looked at the senator and said, "I just want her to come back for you, sir." *Dear God, let him see it. Let him understand how much this family means to me.*

They stood for a while in silence.

"Hamilton?"

"Yes, sir?"

"Marry her."

A sensation for which Tyler had no name washed through him. It wasn't relief; it wasn't victory or gratitude; it was the pure, quiet beat of life falling into place.

Marlena lifted her head. "Daddy?"

Maxwell walked over to them as they both rose from the chairs. Without a word, he took the volume from Tyler's hand. He placed Marlena's hand in Tyler's and kissed his daughter tenderly on the cheek. The gesture might have seemed pompous or contrived, but it didn't. It was simple and heartfelt.

"You have my blessing, Lena honey. Marry the man."

"Oh, Daddy." Marlena's voice was thick with tears.

The senator looked at Tyler. "I want the next voice she hears to be mine."

Tyler simply nodded. Marlena kissed her father. They left the room so that Jason Maxwell could make the words sing for his wife one more time.

❧ Chapter Seventeen ❧

"I ought to cosh you over the table right now," came a voice from over his shoulder. Tyler looked up to see Samuel Hasten sporting a sizable bruise on his jaw. "You have a hard fist for a Northern boy, Hamilton."

Tyler forced a smile. "I'd punch you again if I thought it would knock morals into that scrupleless brain of yours, Hasten." He motioned for Hasten to sit down. Hasten remained standing. "For God's sake, Hasten, sit down. The last thing I need is you drawing attention to my sitting here. I am not exactly a public hero these days, thanks to you and your upstanding employer."

Hasten sat down. He drained the brandy Tyler had set on the table in two swallows. "Good brandy. *Former* employer. I am no longer with the *Austin City News*."

"Stock let you go after all you did for him? After the story you brought him? After the number of papers I'm sure your information sold all over this city? Stock's more of a snake than even I gave him credit for." Tyler lifted his own brandy. "At least the ship on which I am sinking has my name on it." He downed his brandy and ordered another round.

Hasten grumbled, "I left. No one fired me." Tyler knew he had hit a nerve.

Tyler feigned wooziness. He wanted Hasten to think

he'd been drinking a bit. "Well, I suppose that's smart. Surely with your name behind such an earth-shattering story, you will be able to get a position with any paper you choose."

"Hamilton, I'm in no mood to sit here and chat with you all night. Give me the brooch and be done with it."

"Humor me, Mr. Hasten. All I have left is the pleasure of watching my own good name go up in smoke. The least you can do is keep me from drinking alone." Tyler refilled the snifters. "You owe me that much."

"Sweet Jesus, Hamilton, you talk too much." Hasten took another long swig.

Tyler looked at him. "Come to think of it, you're in a bad spot, too. You just broke the story of the year, but your name's not on it; the woman you were trying to save has been ruined anyway; and you've no job, no lady. My, it's difficult to know who's in a worse position—you or me. We'd both better have another drink."

The mention of Deborah had the desired effect. "I'm well aware of my position. Now just give me the brooch."

Tyler looked at Hasten with wide eyes. "You're not going to let him get away with this, are you? I can't imagine you are going to simply stand by and let him double-cross you like that. You're a despicable man, but *even you* deserve vengeance." Tyler hoisted his snifter at Hasten, who grumbled but took a healthy swig.

"Stock will get what's coming to him."

"If I know you, he will." Tyler held the brandy up to the light. "Actually, I suppose he already has."

Hasten's eyes narrowed. "What do you mean?"

Tyler smiled. "You don't think it was coincidence that the *News* building burned within hours of that issue, do you?" He leaned back in his chair. "Someone had to make that man pay for what he had done." Tyler took a drink. "Arthur Stock is a jackal and his paper deserved to burn in hell. It was a grand gesture."

Hasten looked angry and puzzled. "What are you saying, Hamilton?"

Tyler leaned in and spoke softly. "I just thought you would appreciate knowing I gave Arthur Stock the justice he so richly deserved."

Hasten's face grew red. "You lie."

"Of course not. It was a pleasure to send that newspaper up in smoke. I would do it again."

"You didn't do it the first time, you swine."

"Oh, you underestimate me, Mr. Hasten. Even blue blood can boil."

"Goddamn it, Hamilton, you didn't burn down the *News* and you know it."

"I most certainly did."

"No, you little weasel, you did not. I did!"

"You what?"

"I set fire to the *Austin City News*. I burned down that paper and I'm only sorry Stock didn't burn with it."

"I knew that."

"What?"

"I suspected all along that you set fire to the *News*. I just wanted to hear you say it. I wanted the pleasure of knowing you were as unconscionable as I had imagined. You're vicious, Samuel Hasten."

"I think highly of you, too, Hamilton. Now that the confessions are done with, hand over the brooch and I'll bid you good night."

Tyler looked up to see the man standing behind Hasten with handcuffs in his hands. "Oh, no, Mr. Hasten, I'm afraid confessions are just beginning. May I present Sergeant Goodman?"

"You little . . ." Hasten ducked to the side and

rushed at the officer, making a dash for the door. He knocked Goodman low, sending him over into a neighboring table. Tyler leapt out of his chair and flew after Hasten. With a last jump he tackled him just as he stepped out the door. The pair fell, sprawling, into the street.

Tyler winced as Hasten's fist found his ribs. Cursing, Tyler set a punch squarely on Hasten's jaw. Hasten landed a sharp blow to Tyler's forehead. Tyler returned with a blow to Hasten's side. Tyler was pulling back for a second swing when Sergeant Goodman caught his hand. "I'll be taking it from here, Mr. Hamilton." At the mention of his name, the gathered crowd began to buzz with conversation.

"Indeed, Sergeant," said Tyler, looking around and dusting himself off. "Perhaps it would be best if we leave immediately."

"That hurts a great deal, you know." Tyler winced as Marlena put a cold cloth to his brow. The sun coming through the kitchen window was painful enough. He didn't need her prodding his swollen eye further.

"It looks it. Tyler, you look as if you've been in a barroom brawl." She wet the cloth again, then wrung it out.

"Lena, I *was* in a barroom brawl." Marlena's raised eyebrow was annoying. "Well, perhaps 'brawl' is a bit of an overstatement. But it was most definitely a fight. A fair number of punches were thrown."

"Most of which were at you, from the looks of it. Hold still." Marlena brought the cloth to his face again.

"Hasten's far worse, don't worry." Tyler swatted away her hand. "Get away from me with that. It just makes it worse. Senator, call her off." Tyler threw a pleading look toward Maxwell.

"Hamilton, you ought to know by now Lena pays

blasted little heed to what I tell her." He set a cup of coffee down in front of Tyler. "I've been trying to tell her you don't just haul off and get married on a moment's notice, but she won't listen to me on that point, either."

"Pardon me?" Tyler was wide awake now, coffee or no coffee.

"Marlena wants to get married tomorrow. I don't seem to be able to talk her out of it."

Tyler squinted at Marlena. "Don't I have a say in this?"

She narrowed her eyes and came at him with the cloth again. "Are you objecting?"

He snatched the cloth from her hand. "I don't know—yet. But it won't help to threaten me with your brand of nursing." Marlena shot him a look. "For God's sake, I at least need a chance at recovering. I've been up all night being brave and all."

"Indeed," said Marlena. "That's why I gave you till tomorrow."

Tyler let his head fall to his hands. "I am ruined." He peered from between his bruised knuckles. "Every man should be so happy."

"It's settled, then," announced Marlena.

"No," said Tyler, still not lifting his head, "it's not. I'll wed you the day after, and not a moment before."

"Tyler . . ."

"Marlena Winbourne Maxwell," declared Tyler, using her full name in Jason Maxwell style, "I've labored long and hard to win you as my wife. I've given of life, limb, and mind in the name of this family and Texas. I will not—I repeat, will not—wed you on the quick and sly. We shall be married on . . ." He had to take a moment to think what day it was and what day would be two days hence. "Wednesday, with all the ceremony we can muster. But there is one thing."

"My God," remarked the senator with a wide grin, "I do believe Lena *has* met her match."

"And that is," continued Tyler, running a tongue over his split lip, "that I'd much rather marry you with the consent of your mother. Even if I have to debate *her* to get it."

"Claudia's of the same mind, Hamilton," the senator replied with an even wider grin. "But you'd better clean yourself up before you go upstairs and ask her."

"Sir?" Amazed, Tyler stood.

"Mrs. Maxwell came back to us about four this morning, Hamilton. You're not the only one who's been up all night."

Tyler grasped the senator's hand. "That's wonderful, Senator."

Marlena came to Tyler's side. "She knows what you did, Tyler. She remembers hearing your voice."

"And what she didn't remember, I told her." After a moment, the senator added quietly, "It's a fine thing you've done here, Hamilton. I'm indebted to you."

"My pleasure," replied Tyler, but it was hardly sufficient. He grasped Marlena's hand and felt his heart lurch in his chest. There was an emotional silence in the room for a moment.

"Well," Maxwell broke in gruffly, "you'd best go find a clean shirt and get up there. These Maxwell women don't take kindly to being put off."

Tyler fumbled his way wearily upstairs to where Hewitt stood waiting with a basin, towel, and clean shirt. Once restored, Tyler shook Hewitt's hand warmly before heading down the hallway to Mrs. Maxwell's room.

She was lying on a couch, propped up with pillows but still pale. She had on a dressing gown and her hair was pinned up in a simple bun. Maxwell stood behind

her; Marlena sat on a footstool in front of the couch.
Mrs. Maxwell looked drained, but with considerable
effort she turned her head slowly toward Tyler when he
entered the room. He knelt down on one knee in front
of her, next to Marlena.

Mrs. Maxwell's mouth worked to form a word.
While she had regained her consciousness and her composure, it became clear that her speech and movement
had been significantly damaged. Shutting her eyes for a
moment in effort, she said, "Ask."

Tyler took Marlena's hand. With a deep breath and
the solemnity due the moment, he said, "Senator and
Mrs. Maxwell, I should like your consent to marry
Marlena."

A crooked semblance of a smile emerged on Mrs.
Maxwell's weary face. "Earned," she said.

Marlena sighed and put both her hands in Tyler's.
Tyler stood and pulled her up beside him. "Thank you.
Thank you both. I assure you, you'll not regret it."

The senator patted his wife's shoulder. "I can only
hope to say the same of you, Hamilton."

Tyler enjoyed the sleep of the redeemed until well after lunch. When he did waken, he felt as if the senator's
herd of longhorns had trampled over him. He had an
assortment of bruises to prove it as well. The ache in his
ribs, however, was nothing compared to the set of fire-
works going off in his chest. He found a need to remind
himself things had truly worked out. Well, almost
everything had worked out, and he held an unsinkable
optimism for the problems that remained. He buttoned
his vest gingerly over the bruises and headed downstairs.

Coming into the front foyer, Tyler saw the figure of
Senator Maxwell on the porch. He walked out to stand
next to the man, and together they looked out over the

sprawling pastures, surveying the landscape in companionable silence.

The senator gave a long draw on his cigar and sighed. "I've done some considerable thinking, Hamilton, about what's really at stake here."

Tyler felt no need to reply. He nodded his head slightly but kept quiet. The massive blankets of flowers gave a grand beauty to the hills. The world seemed in sharper focus this day.

"I've asked Claudia if she wishes me to pull from the campaign." After a moment, he added, "I've never in my entire life asked her such a thing." He flicked his cigar ash off the end of the porch and walked around to the other corner. Tyler followed. Maxwell put a foot up on the porch rail and puffed. "She said no."

Tyler leaned against a column. "She's an astounding woman, Senator."

"She is at that." Again there was silence. "She asked for my word, though," he said after a moment, "that this be my final term."

"I see." Tyler pulled his vest straight. "Well, I suppose that leaves us with only one option."

The senator turned to Tyler. "Being . . . ?"

"We'd damn well better win, hadn't we, Senator?"

⊰ Chapter Eighteen ⊱

Marlena stood at the top of the landing, trying to remember how to breathe. Her corset stays seemed intent on crushing her. She adjusted her bustle a fourth time. The lace was pulling on her hair and prickling her shoulders.

Her father tugged once at the yellow rose in the lapel of his morning coat. "I have to say, Lena honey, I've been wondering about this day for a long time. Thinking what on earth it was going to feel like when we finally got here. And now that we're here, it doesn't feel anything like I expected."

"I surely didn't expect to feel sick. I swear I'm going to fall." Marlena clung tighter to her father's arm.

"Nonsense, child. It's all that blasted coffee you had this morning. And there isn't a bride in the world who isn't jittery. I reckon I'd be scared if you were calm. But I imagine this will help." He pulled a stone from his pocket. "Hamilton said to give this to you just before the ceremony. It doesn't make a lick of sense to me, but he told me you'd know what it was for." He put it in her palm.

Marlena gazed at the pebble, feeling its warmth from her father's hand radiate through the lace of her glove. The nervousness left her, replaced by a blissful expectation. She undid the button of her right glove and slid the stone onto her palm. "He was right. I'm ready."

"You look beautiful, honey. I wish the whole world were here to see you."

"I wish Deborah were here, that's what I wish."

He gave her a sad look. "I know. Give her time. She cares about you; she just can't show it now."

Marlena sighed. "I suppose I have everybody I need right here. The rest of the world can wait."

A broad smile came across her father's face. "I do believe you're right, darlin'. What do you say we get on with it?" And with that, he escorted her down the stairs and into the front parlor.

Marlena surveyed the room as they stood in the entranceway. Andrea and Diana preceded her inside, and stood off to her left. Her mother sat regally in a chair just next to them, a bouquet of yellow roses adorning her lap. She looked more herself than Marlena had seen her in months. The afternoon sun cast the room in a spectacular wash of gold.

There, at the room's far end, stood Tyler. His blue eyes sparkled as he gazed at her in expectation. The crisp white of his shirt gave the line of his jaw an even greater power. *Stunning.* The words of her first meeting with him echoed in her chest. He was far and away the most handsome man she had ever seen. He looked at her as if there were not another soul on the planet. She could swear there was no ground beneath her feet as she moved forward to stand next to him.

"Who gives this woman to be married?" asked Judge Grayson, looking at the senator with a wide smile.

"I do." The tightness in her father's voice brought a Texas-size lump to Marlena's throat. When he kissed her on the cheek and put her hand in Tyler's, a pair of tears slid down her face. "Good luck, honey," he whispered.

"Luck has nothing to do with it, Daddy," she whispered back, choking on the last word.

She spent the ceremony in the vast blueness of Tyler's eyes. She barely heard the service, until the question that mattered most was posed to her, and she heard herself say, "I do." When she heard Tyler's voice say the same, it chimed out like bells through her fingertips. She watched as he tenderly slid the gold band onto her left hand. With a shiver she thought of the pleasures he'd promised her once it got there. And when he lifted the lace and kissed her, she felt she would melt in the sheer joy of it all.

Then the room was filled with laughter and cheers and handshakes. Kisses and embraces flooded one over the other as the tiny band of guests gave their good wishes. Glasses clinked and mounds of food appeared under the command of a near-smitten Hewitt. Happiness such as the Maxwell household had not seen in far too long a time swelled throughout the room.

Tyler looked at his wife. *His wife.* The words hung on his lips like the very best of wines. He caught her eye and felt an unbridled love for her surge through him. He drank deeply of the champagne, still locking his eyes to hers. He had waited a long time to make her his. The heat rose in his body and he shuddered. The evening shadows couldn't come quickly enough.

When finally the celebration died down, he watched Marlena as she excused herself to go upstairs. With a wicked smile he wondered what she'd say when she found her bedroom filled with three bottles of champagne and four boxes of chocolates—no mints. Hewitt had raised an eyebrow at the supplies, but Tyler didn't care what anyone thought about his peculiar request. Tonight was his and Marlena's, and nothing would get in the way of its being beyond wonderful. He was growing nearly irrational with the expectation of it, and excused himself at the earliest opportunity.

Irrational shifted to stunned when he opened the

door of Marlena's bedroom. She stood at the open window, waiting. Waiting for him. Waiting for what they'd craved together for such a very long time. A jolt of pure, sharp need burst through him at the sight of her.

An impossibly sheer satin gown rippled around her body in the warm breeze. The moonlight played across the shimmering fabric, splashing light in marvelously suggestive curves. Her hair—that hair of hers that drove him mad with want—tumbled down loose and inviting over her shoulders. Its beckoning, glossy blackness set off the porcelain glow of her skin. Ripples of lace from her robe foamed up just barely across her bosom to meet at a cascade of tiny buttons down the front of her gown. *One at a time.* The thought teased, filling his mind with the delightful prospect of undoing them. Slowly, if he could manage it.

"You've been busy," she purred, inclining her head to the bottles and boxes on the table.

"You ought to know a Hamilton always makes good on his word," replied Tyler, finding it necessary to remind himself how to walk and breathe. The concentration required to open the first bottle of champagne was astounding. With considerable effort, he poured two glasses, then crossed the room to where she stood framed in the moonlight. She took a deep, sighing breath, drawing Tyler's gaze to the perfect, creamy curves rising above the lace. She looked exquisitely soft and smooth.

He handed her a champagne flute, delighting at how her wedding band clinked against the glass. Tyler brought her hand to his lips and kissed her ring finger. Her skin smelled of an appealing combination of flowers and spice. He let his lips linger there, listening to the way her breath quickened when he did.

Tyler marveled at his satisfaction in kindling her desire. She was such a pleasure to ignite, offering such a

potent promise of heat. Tyler had always known Lena
was capable of great passion. Tonight he would luxuri-
ate in it. As she moved her fingers against his cheek, he
wondered how he was ever going to keep his desire
from overtaking him. But he would. He would slit his
own throat before he'd rush this night.

Tyler set down his champagne glass, no longer need-
ing it. Instead, he dipped a finger into her glass, then
pressed his wet finger to her lips. She licked it playfully,
and when she sucked just the smallest bit, he felt the air
around him sizzle. His wife would be no shy lover. With
a shudder, he slid his finger to her cheek and leaned in
for a long, slow kiss. Champagne bubbles mixed with
the thick taste of chocolate and he laughed softly
against her mouth. "You've been into the chocolate, I
see."

He felt the breath of her own subtle laughter play
across his cheek. Her free hand roamed its way through
his hair as she brushed up against him, satin gliding
over his chest. "You didn't expect me to just sit there
and stare at them, did you?"

"Oh, no, not at all," replied Tyler, allowing his hand
to run across the smooth curve of her hip, now pressing
against his. *Dear God*, she was impossibly soft. The
heat of her skin seeped through the sheer fabric. "In
fact," he continued, "I have considerable plans for
those chocolates."

"Really?" Tyler adored the flush that spread across
her chest. He pulled her hand from his hair and clasped
it, leading her to the chocolate boxes. The satin flowed
against her as she walked, hinting at the stunning figure
beneath. Tyler pulled her close as he stood next to the
four stacked chocolate boxes. With a smile he noticed
that no less than six confections were already gone. He
dropped her hand and picked up a candy, letting his
other hand roam up her side. Her eyelids fluttered and a

shiver rippled across her skin. The flute tipped danger-
ously in her hand, the champagne spilling a bit. It took
concentration to find his voice again. "The first box is
for me."

"I object," teased Lena, reaching for the box.

"For me to *feed* you," continued Tyler, pulling his
hand up to intercept hers. He laced their fingers together.

"I don't think I object anymore," she said with a velvety sigh. Her eyes slid closed as Tyler fed her the con-
fection. She savored it, a view Tyler enjoyed even more
than he'd imagined he would. "No," she moaned behind a mouthful of chocolate, "I'm quite sure I don't
mind."

"I knew you'd consent," murmured Tyler. He let his
hand stray down her neck as she swallowed, then down
across her curves to linger amid the lace. He fed her another chocolate. As she enjoyed this one, Tyler cupped
her breast through the thin fabric, running his thumb
across the perfect peak now rising beneath the satin.
His hunger doubled, and he caressed her with both
hands, watching the way her shoulders and spine
arched in response. "My God, you are beautiful," he
whispered.

"I thought you said I was wicked." She cooed, nearly
dropping the glass as she let her head fall back.

"Ah, that's the beauty of it, Mrs. Hamilton." Tyler
relieved her of the champagne flute. By God, he wanted
those hands free to roam. "Lucky is the man who can
call his wife both." And she was—in extremes.

"Oh, my, I like the sound of that." Her hands met his
and then stroked up his arms.

"Wickedly beautiful?"

"Well, yes, but I'm especially fond of the"—she
caught her breath as Tyler's thumbs made tiny circles
again—"the Mrs. Hamilton part."

"As the Mr. Hamilton in question, I'm quite inclined to agree." He slid his hands up to the clasp of her robe and then under the edge. Moving his body against hers, he edged the creamy fabric down. The ripples of lace fell away to leave the smooth sheath of her nightgown and that maddening cascade of buttons. The delicious angles of her neck and shoulders lay bare now, hiding under only a pair of tiny, silky straps that made him ache beyond reason.

Marlena felt the room spin. Tyler's touch—the hunger in his hands—entranced her. She knew his touch, but tonight it held a promise of more. His caresses spoke of unconstrained ardor. The thought of it left her breathless. Marlena felt her body spring to life under the heat of his palm. With her eyes closed, she could feel his body yearn for more of her. His hunger was so palpable, it had a scent she could breathe in. The craving to be with him—to be finally, completely with him—consumed her, and Marlena found her own hands exploring his body in matched eagerness. Anxiety may have bubbled under the surface sometime before, but it now yielded easily to the ferocious longing Tyler stirred in her.

The potent pleasures of husband and wife. The gift of a perfect, permanent intimacy. All this lay wide open to them now.

Marlena allowed the slow curl of desire to spread unchecked throughout her body, and welcomed the arousal. She yearned to feel his lips where his hands were, his skin where his lips had been. The delicious glow spread out over every place he touched, every inch of skin.

"Would you like another piece of chocolate?" he said huskily against her shoulder as his hands slid down into the small of her back. The low timbre of his voice rippled down across her bosom. His question hinted of far more than candy.

"Mmm" was all she could muster.

"I had a feeling you'd say that." He put one last chocolate in her mouth, licking his fingers in a way that made her knees buckle. With a wicked smile he swept her up into his arms and extinguished the room's single lamp. The moonlight splashed in through the open window as he laid her down on the bed.

Tyler eased alongside her, coming up on one elbow. With his hand he started at her temple and stroked his way languidly down her face. His blue eyes danced as his fingers traced the edge of her ear, sending shivers down her spine. Lena let her eyes close as he trailed his hand across her shoulder. A soft moan escaped her when the hand slid down to trace the outline of her breast. She arched into him, eager.

Tyler made a satisfied sound from deep in his throat. "I happen to know you're quite fond of sweets."

"I am." She sighed as his hand continued to roam. "I'm very . . ." Her voice left off into a gasp when she felt his warm, hungry lips come at her through the fabric. She felt his teeth under the smooth, wet satin, and thought she would explode.

"Coffee, too," he said in a husky growl as his mouth sought more of her. Marlena could feel the tension in his thighs and the shudder in his hips. The mechanics of speech eluded her under the onslaught.

"Coffee . . ." she managed to echo, her fists grasping at the blanket. A rich moan escaped her lips. In a moment she would rip the buttons off herself. Wicked. Wonderful.

"There are things, Lena," murmured Tyler as he finally began to pull at her gown's top button, "that far

exceed such meager pleasures." Her skin went wild at
the touch of his lips and fingers. He worked his way
down the gown, one excruciating button at a time. She
pressed her chest and hips against him in instinctive
waves, craving the friction. "Such shallow delights of
food and drink," he was saying, "pale in comparison to
a marriage bed."

At the last of the buttons Tyler spread the gown
open. Marlena felt the cool wash of the evening air over
her exposed skin. Her head swayed under the massive
sensations. She opened her eyes to see Tyler staring at
her. Marlena reached up and tunneled her fingers
through his hair. His eyes misted over at her touch, and
she watched his control dissolve.

He brought his body down upon her with a ravenous
passion, his lips and tongue and teeth devouring every
inch of her. His mouth poured a thousand sensations
over her breasts and neck until she could barely
breathe. Suddenly frantic to taste his skin, Marlena
pulled at his shirt collar, lavishing his neck with deep,
beseeching kisses. Breathing heavily, Tyler leaned to the
side and tugged at his shirt. The moonlight played
across the planes of his chest and the curves of his muscles as he worked to rid himself of the stiff shirtsleeves.

Marlena now knew the ache he felt looking at her.
She nearly lunged at him in her eagerness when the shirt
came free. Pushing him over onto his back, she let her
own hands light fire to his skin. Marlena watched his
muscles ripple when she ran her fingernail across his
chest. She reveled in the way his chest heaved under her
lips, the way his eyes fell shut under her tongue, and the
way he groaned when she dared to use her teeth. It was
intoxicating to fuel his arousal, to please this husband
of hers.

With a deep and fierce kiss, Tyler rolled her onto her
back. He pulled himself up and urgently slid the last of

her gown from her body. Inside the fiery passion of his expression was an intimacy and reverence that took her breath away.

"As your husband . . ." he whispered, caressing her.

"My husband . . ." she breathed. There was no embarrassment as she reached for the fastening of his trousers, only a searching for the intimacy she'd seen in his face. He shed the last of his garments and she took a moment to behold his body. *Yes,* she thought, *"behold" is the word for it.* It was her turn to know the feeling she'd seen in his eyes.

"As your husband," he repeated in a low, velvety tone as he succumbed to the wandering of her hands, "I've the privilege . . ." He leaned down and slowly, deliberately draped his body over hers. To feel the spark of skin upon skin, to soak in the contact of the hard and soft places, the curves where they fit together, was bliss. Tyler never finished the sentence. There was no need to.

Marlena drowned in it all. Warm, urgent hands followed curves. Sighs revealed places of delight and arousal. Marlena gave him the deepest parts of herself, meant solely for their lives together. She gasped as Tyler's hand ran up her thigh. Then his hands were everywhere, all at once, awakening new and wonderful places. And then they were in only one place, one astounding, blissful place that seeped out rich and thick through the rest of her body. Tyler's hands and his lips and the soft callings of his words wound together around her. Until . . . until, in a glorious gift of a moment, the sensations careened together in light and heat and absolute joy.

When she had caught her breath, wide-eyed and glowing, Tyler watched Lena's hands come up to caress his face. The wonder in her eyes struck him more deeply than he could describe. To please this woman, his wife, his love, was a near-sacred thing. She was his to know forever as his own. His body and soul would find its home always in her. Now, this night, this moment, this union he needed more than breath or life, would be his. Theirs. Her eyes open and knowing, Lena pulled him down. Tyler's body reeled with the nearness of his release. With agonizing efforts at tenderness, he eased into her.

"Dear God, finally," he groaned. It was an unpoetic, raw blurt of infinite waiting. But she smiled. It was the same for her. *Oh, dear God, finally.* He squinted his eyes shut, shaking with the force of his need but determined not to hurt her. He moved slowly. She gave a short gasp and then a wondrous exhale of receiving, of cleaving, of being one flesh at last. A gentle rhythm pulled him into her, gathering force as her body responded to him. She clung to him, her breaths deepening with his. He wrapped his arms around her shoulders, pulling her closer, breathing her name into her neck as the cadence built. Finally he could control himself no longer, and he gave himself over to it. The inexplicable, holy moment of man and woman crashed over him and he cried deep in his throat as she arched under him. "My wife. My love," he said over and over as he fell into her embrace. *One flesh. At last. At last.*

A wondrous silence, broken only by ragged breaths, poured between them. Surely it was no accident that this was the force from which life sprang. It was life itself. Rich, glowing, potent. Immutable. Precious.

When their breath returned, Marlena ran a finger across his glistening cheek. "My," she sighed. Tyler felt a surge of delight and satisfaction.

" 'My' indeed." He grinned. "And to think we've three more boxes of chocolates to go."

Marlena's face held its own delight. He felt her fingers trace languidly down his spine. "Not to mention the two more bottles." Her hand slid along his thigh. "I fear it may be a long night, Tyler."

"It can't be long enough," he growled, wrapping his arms around her. "Not in a decade of nights."

The thin wail of a hawk sounded in Tyler's dream. It was followed by a soft, melodic humming, a small rustling noise, and then a slight moan. As he began to wake, he felt the bedding shift. Then came another rustling noise, followed by a second moaning sound— more satisfied than the first. Lazily, he opened one eye to find Marlena beside him, lying up on her elbows, beside him, picking through the last box of chocolates. She licked her lips and smiled at him with sparkling eyes.

"Uh oval mnmones are uh est," she offered behind a considerable mouthful. He watched her swallow as a ripple of tousled hair fell across her face. "I might share if you ask very nicely." She poked through the paper wrappers to find another. "But you'd have to be quite convincing." She held one up to him for inspection in the traces of dawn light before popping it into her mouth. Tyler watched her toes wriggle out from underneath the sheet that lay languidly draped across her body. "Ere's only a ew eft . . ."

"Really?" groaned Tyler, coming up onto his elbow to watch her devour the confections.

Marlena smacked her lips. "Really. But they're getting rather soft. I think they're melting."

Tyler chuckled. "Save me one."

She bit into another one. "Well, then, you'd better hurry; there's only one left and it's—"

"Mine!" Tyler pounced on her, grabbing the box and sending the little pleated papers flying everywhere. Marlena yelped as he flipped her onto her back, pinning her arms with one hand while he nabbed the remaining chocolate out of the box. With an overstated possessive grunt, he tossed the box over his shoulder and let the chocolate fall into the delicate hollow between her ribs.

"Tyler!" Marlena squirmed under his hands, a delightful sensation. "You're impossible." He cocked an eyebrow. "Tyler, it's melting." Laughter trickled into her voice. "It's melting, and it tickles."

Tyler was watching it melt. Intently.

Marlena stopped squirming and the laughter softened into something like a sigh. The motion sent a tiny trickle of brown toward her navel. He felt her thighs contract against his.

"Well," Marlena said in a hinting tone, "are you just going to lie there staring and let it melt?"

"Only at first," murmured Tyler, eyes on the sliding square now angling toward one hip. "I'll improvise from there."

❧ Chapter Nineteen ❧

"You're serious." Marlena set down the book she was holding.

"As a matter of fact, I am, honey."

Marlena saw the gleam of fire in her father's eyes. It meant he was now immovable on the subject.

"What did Mama say to this?"

He retrieved a pen from his desk drawer. "It was her idea." He looked up, his expression pleased that he had shocked her.

Marlena planted her hands on the desk. "Come now, Daddy, surely you don't expect me to believe Mama *asked* you to call a press conference. Pigs'd have wings first."

"Then you'd best start flying after your pork chop, Lena honey. Now, are you going to force me to make the press list all by myself, or are you going to get that newlywed brain of yours out of the clouds and help me?"

"Must I defend my wife's intellect to her own father?" came Tyler's voice as he slid open the pocket doors. "Good afternoon, Senator."

"Afternoon, Tyler." He threw his hands up in agitation. "Hell, I can't get my mouth around that yet. You're Hamilton. Familiarity, my backside."

Tyler smiled. "No rush, sir, 'Hamilton' will do just fine." He planted a brief kiss on Marlena's cheek. "Hello to you, too."

Marlena willed away a blush. It felt naked to have their affections out in the open now. Every glance at Tyler flooded her mind with the exquisite things he did to her body. How wonderful they were together. How she couldn't wait to be alone with him. Such wanton thoughts in polite company? Surely the near-constant desire showed all over her face, for she could see it in Tyler's eyes every time he looked at her.

After a long moment Marlena's thoughts were interrupted by her father. "Perhaps I ought to chalk you two up as hopeless and do this myself."

"Hmm?" she murmured, half-hearing.

A sheet of paper suddenly appeared across her face. She turned to see her father furiously waving the paper between her and Tyler. "Snap out of it, you two, or I'll have to call this press conference off for lack of staff!"

The remark effectively got Tyler's attention. Marlena watched him blink at the senator. "This *what,* sir?"

"You heard me, Hamilton, a press conference."

"Are you serious?"

Marlena shot her father a "See? I'm not the only one!" look, pleased at Tyler's identical reaction. "That's exactly what I said," she remarked smugly.

"Why is it no one can believe your mother asked me to hold a press conference?"

Tyler balked. "*Mrs. Maxwell* asked for a press conference?"

Her father glared at Tyler. "Is that *so* impossible to believe, Hamilton?"

"Well, I'd have to call it unlikely." Tyler backpedaled when the senator's glare failed to soften. "But certainly not unwelcome," he added.

"Well then," said her father gruffly, "I'm calling it for Friday morning, right here at the ranch. On our front steps, to be exact. I want it known far and wide that the Maxwells aren't out of the fight, not by a long shot."

Tyler pulled up a chair. "I'm not going to have to de-bate Marlena again to prepare for this, am I?"

"For God's sake, no, Hamilton. Looks like you two have been at each other enough as it is."

Marlena huffed at her father.

Tyler beamed and took her hand.

Within three hours the board was back up and filled, the telegraphs were ready, and the Maxwell campaign declared itself back in full swing. When the senator was upstairs with his wife just before dinner, however, a boy knocked on the study door, bearing a message for Marlena. Tyler watched her face change as she opened the envelope.

"It's from Deborah," she said softly. Tyler realized what a loss of friendship Miss Edgerton's self-imposed exile had meant for his wife. He watched how tenderly her hands held the paper. Marlena looked up and caught his eye. "She wants us to come see her tomor-row." Emotion ran thick in her voice.

"Of course," he said quietly. Tyler would have driven the carriage that moment if Marlena had asked.

"And Tyler, she asks you to bring the brooch."

He was surprised. "She told me she never wanted to see it again."

"Well, yes, as a matter of fact she mentions that, but asks me to remind you that every woman reserves the right to change her mind."

Tyler laughed. "The astounding Miss Edgerton. It's fortunate I haven't had time to dispose of the piece yet. I can't say I'm happy about the request, though. I hope this doesn't mean she's changed her mind about Samuel Hasten."

"That's just the thing, Tyler," said Marlena. "She says she wants us to take her to see him."

"To see Hasten? In jail?" Tyler leaned over Marlena's

shoulder to read the message. "Dear God, Lena, do you think that's wise?"

"I *think*," countered Marlena with a furrowed brow, "that Deborah deserves our support no matter what action she chooses to take."

"Of course we'll go." Tyler moved to the window seat and patted the cushion for Marlena to come and sit next to him.

"I still can't believe she kept such an enormous secret to herself all that time." Marlena sighed as she sat down. Tyler leaned her back against his chest and wrapped his arms around her. He was still dizzy with the freedom to touch her like this in broad daylight.

He brought her a little closer. "Miss Edgerton is an amazing woman. I was just thinking this afternoon as we were assembling the board . . . she was so dependable, so unflappable, I fear we all took her quite for granted. Quite forgot her entitlement to a private life and personal feelings."

"Until Hasten."

"Damn Hasten," Tyler swore softly. "She deserved so much better. Surely not a rat like him."

"I know. I almost feel guilty for being so happy when everything's so awful for her. Taking her—even there—is the least we can do." Marlena fingered the gold band on her left hand. Tyler smiled. His own ring still felt new and delightfully unfamiliar on his finger. "Do you think she really won't come back to the office?" she asked.

Tyler brought her band to his lips and kissed it. "I do. Miss Edgerton deserves a fresh start. I wouldn't deny her that after all she's been through. But I do admit it's a shame to finish the campaign without her. As it was a shame to get married without her."

"I wish she had been there, Tyler. I understand why she couldn't come—I don't know that I could have, had

I been in her place. All the same, I wanted her to be there," Marlena sighed.

With a sudden surge, Tyler rose from the seat and pulled her up beside him. "Mrs. Hamilton?" He grinned, enjoying her new title.

"Yes, *Mr.* Hamilton?" He loved that his smile could still seem to pull the ground out from under her feet.

He extended an elbow. "Come take a walk with me."

Tyler led her out the doors and across the pasture, to the grove of trees atop the hill. Once there, he reached into his coat pocket for a small blue velvet packet. "I've something for you."

Marlena took the velvet pouch from his hand. "Why, Tyler."

"I actually arranged for it the day after it broke, but haven't found the right moment to present it to you. Now seems as good as any."

He watched her reach inside the pouch. Her fingers knew the object even before she pulled it out, and the look on her face was worth the world. She held up her grandfather's watch, newly strung back onto its fob of freshwater pearls, only now gold beads set with green stones alternated on the chain with the pearls. The final link before the watch was a small polished pebble set in gold.

"Oh, Tyler. It's beautiful." She fingered the stone. "And a pebble, too. It's just wonderful."

"I hope you don't mind that I had the watch inscribed. I'll admit that part was an afterthought, after the wedding." Tyler turned the watch over so Marlena could read the inscription:

Yours for all time,
Tyler

"I am, you know." His hands stole around her waist. "I don't intend to settle for anything less permanent.

Forever is the very least I'll require." Marlena slipped
the watch and fob into place and spread her hands
across Tyler's chest. Now it was she who could pull the
ground out from under his feet. He responded by languidly running his lips down her neck.

"Can I interest you in something more immediate?"
he growled into her neck, his hands making their way
slowly up from her waist in a most convincing manner.

"What have you in mind?"

Tyler lifted her in his arms and deposited her against
a tree. He pinned her there with his hips while his hands
undid her hairpins.

"I have a very . . . pressing . . . issue that requires
your immediate attention." He had to admit the issue
was pressing rather hard at the moment.

"Here? In the open?"

Tyler's eyes gleamed. "At first."

Marlena raised an eyebrow. "At first?"

"Then I've a theory I must expound upon in greater
privacy. But I'll need to lay the groundwork for this issue very carefully."

"Tyler! Anyone could see us!"

"Yes," he murmured as he kissed the base of her
throat. "Anyone could see us now, in broad daylight.
Isn't it wonderful?"

"You're being highly improper." He continued his
kisses and sent his fingers roaming through her hair until she added breathlessly, "Every woman should be so
happy."

"Not to worry, love. I'll retire to someplace more dis-
creet when I'm sure I have your complete attention."

Marlena's head fell back, her concentration completely destroyed. Tyler let out a soft, silky laugh and
proceeded to state his case ever so clearly.

⇥ Chapter Twenty ⇤

Deborah followed the sergeant down the short hallway, past a cluster of empty cells. Her breath tightened as they reached the last closed door on the left. She suddenly regretted her decision to ask Tyler and Lena to stay behind in the sheriff's office. This suddenly seemed too hard to do alone.

Her courage returned as a pathetic-looking silhouette came into view. A limp figure of a man, facing away from the door, his back slumped against the wall. Even the set of his shoulders sickened her. A fresh wave of anger at being so deceived surged through her body. She was glad. It was what she needed. She could do it now.

"Hasten," coughed the sergeant. "You've a visitor."

Deborah watched his head aimlessly turn in the direction of the door. When he caught sight of his visitor, it registered through his entire body. She felt her fingers tighten on the brooch in her pocket until its edges cut into her palm. The boyish grin was gone. Instead, his face held the bland expression of beyond caring.

"Well," he said, dragging his body around to face her. "Cain't say as I expected this." His voice was bitter and distant.

"Samuel." She watched an echo of pain flicker across his face at the sound of his name. With a stab she remembered how he loved to hear her say it. Or so he'd said.

His head fell back against the wall. "Why are you here?" he asked thinly. In an odd show of respect, the guard shuffled a few feet away from them, offering what privacy he could.

Any affection she had left twisted itself into pity. Her grip loosened on the brooch. "Because I would not let you win. I'm going to stand here and tell you I will not be taken down. I won't let you have that power. You don't deserve it."

She pulled the brooch from her pocket. It weighed a hundred pounds in her palm. With an exhale she tossed it through the bars, onto the dirt of the cell floor. He made a small noise as he reached his foot out and dragged it closer to him with his shoe.

"You know, Deborah"—she had to shut her eyes for just a moment when he said her name, but it was gone as quickly as it came—"I care for you. I tried not to, but it just seemed to happen anyway. Like I couldn't stop it. Though I doubt you believe that just now."

She swallowed. "I believe you think you care for me," she replied slowly, "but I don't believe you even know how." There was a long silence. Deborah felt the weight falling off her chest. She stared through the bars of Hasten's narrow cell window. "I suppose I even have to thank you, in a way. You've thrust me out from under the Maxwells' wings." She felt her shoulders pull back. "I'm leaving. I intend to make a life of my own. Somewhere else. Away. I don't imagine I'd have done that if it hadn't been for your cruelty." It amazed her how easily she could say it.

Samuel picked at his shirt with grimy fingers. "Life's mean that way, ain't it?"

"No," said Deborah, her breath coming easier now. "Life's not mean. People are. And even then, only just some." After a long silence she said, "Good-bye, Samuel Hasten. I don't care what happens to you anymore."

At that he turned and looked at her. She wanted to turn away, but his face held her gaze. His eyes bore a shade of sorrow and regret, as if he really did care, in some twisted way. Deborah drew a sharp breath, feeling as if her chest were splitting open. In that moment, she knew the raw pieces of a life were waiting in there somewhere.

It was over now. She could leave.

The walk down the hallway felt as if she were coming up onshore, pressing out of the undertow onto solid ground. When Marlena extended a silent hand, she took it. They walked out into the sunlight.

The three were silent for a moment, then Tyler said softly, "Why don't I take the two of you back to St. George's? There's something I need to tend to in town. I'll pick you up when I'm done, Marlena."

Deborah was suddenly exhausted. "Fine," she replied simply.

Tyler took her hand in both of his. He looked at her with what she knew to be genuine affection. Yes, she could still see it, still recognize it. "Courage, Miss Edgerton."

She nodded.

When Tyler returned for Marlena he was carrying a parcel, but wouldn't discuss its contents. He would say only that there was someone who deserved to see it first. Marlena pressed no further, but simply laid her head on Tyler's shoulder and held his hand for the long ride home.

"I went to see Richard," Tyler offered eventually.

Marlena didn't respond, but lifted her head to look at him. She waited for him to continue.

"I didn't know what to expect. I wasn't even sure he'd receive me. He did, though. I walked into his parlor, and there he was, standing, smoking his pipe. He walked over to me and said, 'I ought to shoot you.' I just stood there. Then he broke into that damn friendly smile of his and said, 'But I can't drum up the nerve. I'm too fond of you. And of her. So I'll just have to perfect my graceful loser attitude.' "

Marlena returned her head to Tyler's shoulder. "Poor, perfect Richard." She sighed.

Tyler's arm slipped around Marlena's shoulders and brought her closer. She felt him rest his chin on the top of her head. "Damn fine man," he said into her hair.

Tyler still had not explained the package, but they continued on in silence for the rest of the ride. Marlena was spent from seeing Deborah, and grateful no one had bothered them on the streets in Austin. She was eager to get back to the ranch. The public could very well wait until tomorrow's press conference.

At the ranch, Tyler quietly took Marlena's hand and led her from room to room until they found her parents. It was nearly dusk, and they were seated in the speckled shade of the arbor on the far side of the porch. Marlena thought her mother was looking better each day, returning slowly to her former self. She still spoke with effort and moved haltingly, but her dignity was steadily reasserting itself.

Tyler let go of Marlena's hand and sat on the steps beside the foot of Claudia's chair. Marlena sat down on the wicker settee next to her father. She wondered at Tyler's quiet disposition and oddly formal attitude. His manner told her the package was for her mother, but she couldn't guess what it was.

"I've something for you, Mrs. Maxwell." He pulled the wrapper off the parcel to reveal a tattered leather book. "This is his journal, ma'am. Sergeant Logan's. The man from Galveston. Captain Hawthorne's men retrieved it from Hasten's rooms."

Marlena watched her mother reach for the book. Her fingers broke away some of the flecks of old leather when she clutched it. She held it for a moment, staring, then with a lumbering effort, she flung it into the dirt at the base of the steps. "Burn it, Jason."

"Claudia?"

"Burn it. Right now."

Without another word, Marlena watched her father find matches and set fire to the book. She walked over and put her hand on Tyler's shoulder as the four of them watched the fragments of pages crumble into gray ash and dissolve in the wind.

Tyler turned to her mother again. He pulled an envelope from his coat pocket and held it up before her. "This is a copy of his death certificate. He was shot for desertion at the Louisiana border. He's dead."

A grim, hard look settled on her mother's features. She reached out and squeezed the paper in one frail fist, grabbing Tyler's hand with the other. She shook them both.

"*We* are not," she declared.

The Double X lawn hosted semicircles of chairs in front of the porch steps. The sharp air of the coming autumn blew steadily through the trees that cast arching shadows on the scene. Marlena stared at the set stage. There were no packets, no door list, and no battalion of house staff. It suited.

She heard the door swing open behind her, followed by the familiar cadence of Tyler's footsteps. His hand slipped into hers as they stood on the porch. "They ought to be here soon." Marlena ran the fingers of her free hand along the fob and flipped the watch open. She caught Tyler's broad smile as she snapped it shut again.

"My, but that watch suits you fine, Lena," he said. "More than fine."

"Indeed." She fingered the pearls and beads. "It does at that."

A holler from the gatehouse and a cloud of dust signaled the first carriage coming up the drive. Marlena squeezed Tyler's hand and turned toward the house.

"They're here, Daddy. The first one's coming up the drive now."

Her father straightened up from where his wife was adjusting his tie. She thought they looked regal together. Again. Together her parents were stronger than the sum of their parts. *Which is,* she thought, bringing Tyler's hand up to her lips, *as it should be.*

"All right, Lena honey, go be charming and settle 'em all in. Your mother and I will be out directly. Hamilton, you're with me. I can't have you getting my daughter all gooey-eyed in front of the press just yet."

Marlena laughed and kissed her father on the cheek. "Good luck, Daddy."

"Luck has nothing to do with it, Lena honey."

Twenty minutes later, the snap of Marlena's watch cover set the press conference in motion. This time Marlena didn't watch from the back of the parlor, but stood on the porch next to her father, mother, and husband. Her sisters flanked the other side. The Maxwell family was out in full force.

"Gentlemen," the senator began, "I'll pull no punches as to why you're here. Get out your pens, boys, and take this down: I will not back away from this race. No dirt-digging reporter will destroy the life of any member of my staff. No lie-slinging paper will slander my wife in an effort to take this family down. This is far—I repeat, *far*—from over." He continued on, restating his campaign platform and his intention to pull Texas into its future by the bootstraps if need be. He then motioned to Tyler, who stepped forward.

Tyler spoke commandingly. "We will not sidestep any

issue. The information regarding Miss Edgerton is, in fact, true. But no useful purpose is served by having her suffer the travesty of its being pasted on a front page. It was an ugly, underhanded tactic that will not be permitted to succeed. This family continues to stand behind Deborah Edgerton, to defend her character, and to support whatever direction she may choose from here. The base exploit of an immoral opportunist will not be allowed to deny her a future."

Now Marlena stepped into the center. "Nor will the egotistical lies of a vile man be allowed to taint my mother's honor. She was attacked, threatened, and wounded by a Union sergeant named David Logan, whose contemptible conduct is only worsened by the lies he spread. Fearing for her own life and the life of the child she believed she was carrying, my mother created a story she hoped would divert Logan. Instead, he wounded her for the sheer pleasure of it and twisted the information to his own gain. She gave him a fictitious time for a boat launch. She betrayed no one. Revealed no military secrets. It was an act of God and Logan's ambition that placed an innocent craft in the water at that time. Logan's unit fired on and destroyed that civilian boat in an effort to save credibility."

Marlena placed a hand on her mother's shoulder. Her father took Claudia's other hand and the two of them helped her slowly to her feet. Marlena watched her mother draw herself up straight and proud. She drew a breath and declared as loudly as her body would allow, "This family shall not fall to a lie."

For an achingly long minute, silence hung in the air. Then one single clap rang out from the back row. Another followed, then another, until applause pealed out over the lawn.

"Now, gentlemen," cut in the senator, "I'll stand here till next Tuesday answering any questions you may

have, and till every last one of your curiosities are satisfied. But I'll ask your indulgence to let my wife go inside." With a gleam in his eye and a wink at Marlena,
he added, "Mr. and Mrs. Hamilton will be happy to
take your questions until I return."

As a distraction, it was worth its weight in gold. A
tidal wave of questions swelled up at Tyler and
Marlena. They stood there, hand in hand, responding
to a spectrum of inquiries that ran from shocked to con-
gratulatory to downright nosy.

Finally, at one small break in the frenzy, Marlena
leaned in to Tyler. "Did you know he was going to do
that?" she hissed.

"As a matter of fact," replied Tyler, igniting that
dashing smile for both his wife and the press, "it was
my idea. Rather an effective distraction, don't you
think?"

"Tyler Hamilton, we need to talk."

"Certainly, but not now. We've a campaign to run.
Next question, please!"

⊰ Chapter Twenty-one ⊱

"There. Right there. Ahh. Harder. Oh dear God, Tyler, I think my feet were ready to fall off even before Christmas."

Tyler pressed his fingers into the exquisite flesh of his wife's left foot. My, but she did have stunning ankles. His gaze traveled up the rest of her leg with distinct satisfaction. "Any better?" He planted a kiss on the top of her foot.

"Not by much. Whose idea was that door-to-door campaigning, anyway? Austin's far too big a town for such tactics. Ow, careful, that one hurts." Marlena groped across the couch arm for her coffee cup on the side table.

"Yours, my love. And a damn fine tactic it was. With only a four percent margin of victory, I'd wager it was those endless weeks of personal visits that put your father over the top. I wouldn't be so quick to complain if I were you."

Marlena let her head fall back. "My toes fail to appreciate a four percent margin of victory. Especially when followed by so many parties." She drained her coffee cup. "And then all those holiday invitations. Dear God, it's a wonder I have any feet left at all."

Tyler smiled. "Nonsense. Besides, I never doubted victory for a moment."

Marlena cocked one eye above the cup rim. "Liar."

Tyler pinched a toe. "All right, there were a few moments where I gave in to small waves of doubt."

"Propaganda. Pure propaganda." She poked at his chin with her big toe as she put down the cup. The view along the curve of her leg made Tyler's head spin.

"Very well, then. I was frightened to death at times." He ran his hand up her leg, enjoying her reaction. "Really quite terrified." He tugged on her ankles until he pulled her legs across his lap. Then he leaned down toward her until they were beside each other on the couch. "Satisfied?"

"Not nearly." She reached up and ran her hand across his cheek. The playful look in her eyes sent tingles through his stomach.

"My God," he said softly as he reached for a hairpin. "It was wonderful to see the legislature in session today. We did it. The people granted Senator Jason Maxwell his final term in office."

She smiled. "It is wonderful, isn't it? You should be proud of yourself, Tyler."

"I am," he admitted. "But I've a confession to make."

"Hmm?" Her hands were playing havoc with his shirt buttons, not to mention his composure.

"We could have lost and I'd have still been among the happiest men alive." He kissed her forehead while the last pin fell to the carpet. "We've not had nearly enough time alone since the election."

"Oh, I think we've found considerable time—and some rather intriguing opportunities—to keep you the happiest man alive."

Tyler's hands wandered. "Care to see how much happier you can make me?"

A languid, wicked look danced across Marlena's face. "Mmm. Quite a tempting offer. But, really, you've no idea what you're in for."

"Oh," purred Tyler, "but I think I do. And I'll admit to some very high expectations."

He watched her think for a moment, deciding something. "Well, then, I've no choice. High expectations are not to go unmet. Not on a day like today. All right, Mr. Hamilton, pay attention; I've a very important question to ask you."

"Trust me, Lena," Tyler said, immersing his face in the dizzying cascade of dark hair. "You have my complete attention." He felt her hands wind their way along the back of his neck and sighed at the pleasure of it.

"Is one allowed a fourth?"

"A fourth what?" he murmured into her ear.

"A fourth. You know, IV, roman numerals and such."

Tyler went still. "IV roman numerals and such for what?" he said slowly. He pulled back to find the most extraordinary expression on his wife's face.

"Well," she replied, trailing her finger down his cheek to his chin. "You are Tyler Hamilton the third. Is one allowed a Tyler Hamilton the fourth or must one come up with something completely new? I've never paid attention to such things."

Tyler's mouth fell open.

"It's going to be a rather pertinent question soon enough. We ought to know the protocol."

Tyler took her face in his hands. He thought his chest would explode. She nodded, beaming. He kissed her gently, tenderly. "My God," he whispered, still reeling. "Really?"

"Really. As sure as one can be about such things."

Suddenly he was touching her everywhere. "My God. My God. Are you . . . is it . . . do you . . . how are you?"

"Among the happiest women alive." She ran her hands up along his back. "Care to see how much happier you can make me? Odds are against your besting that, you know. As I said, I've high expectations on a day like today."

"Oh, how you forget, my dear wife," said Tyler huskily as he swept her into his arms, "overwhelming odds are my specialty."